THE LAST LEAF
OF HARLEM

THE LAST LEAF
OF HARLEM

SELECTED AND NEWLY DISCOVERED

FICTION BY THE AUTHOR

OF *The Wedding*

DOROTHY WEST

Edited by

LIONEL C. BASCOM

St. Martin's Press
New York

THE LAST LEAF OF HARLEM. Copyright © 2008 by Lionel C. Bascom. All rights reserved. Printed in the United States of America. No part of this book may be used or reproduced in any manner whatsoever without written permission except in the case of brief quotations embodied in critical articles or reviews. For information, address St. Martin's Press, 175 Fifth Avenue, New York, N.Y. 10010.

www.stmartins.com

"The Typewriter," "The Five Dollar Bill," "Jack in the Pot," and "The Richer, The Poorer" are from *The Richer, The Poorer* copyright © 1995 by Dorothy West. Used by permission of Doubleday, a division of Random House, Inc.

All other stories included in *The Last Leaf of Harlem* are used by permission of the Estate of Dorothy West and the Dorothy West Scholarship Fund of Martha's Vineyard Regional High School.

Library of Congress Cataloging-in-Publication Data

West, Dorothy, 1907–1998.
    The last leaf of Harlem: selected and newly discovered fiction by the author of *The Wedding* / edited by Lionel C. Bascom.—1st ed.
        p.   cm.
    Includes bibliographical references and index.
    ISBN-13: 978-0-312-26148-1
    ISBN-10: 0-312-26148-9
    I. Bascom, Lionel C.   II. Title.

PS3545.E82794A6   2007
813'.54—dc22   2007032503

First Edition: February 2008

10 9 8 7 6 5 4 3 2 1

Contents

Acknowledgments   IX

The Last Leaf: An Introduction   XIII

ONE

Early Fiction

Hannah Byde   3

The Typewriter   15

Prologue to a Life   27

Cook   42

The Five Dollar Bill   60

TWO

The WPA Years

My Baby . . .   71

Ghosts   82

Pluto   89

Amateur Night in Harlem: "That's Why Darkies Were Born"   94

CONTENTS

Temple of Grace   102

Cocktail Party   111

THREE

Pulp Fiction

Jack in the Pot   123

Papa's Place   142

Bessie   149

Mother Love   156

The Puppy   163

A Boy in the House   169

The Cottagers and Mrs. Carmody   175

Skippy   180

A Matter of Money   185

Wives and Women   191

The Letters   196

Made for Each Other   201

Homecoming   206

Summer Setting   211

The Lean and the Plenty   217

Babe   222

The Richer, The Poorer   228

Interlude   234

The Long Wait   239

The Birthday Party   245

Mrs. Creel   250

CONTENTS

The Stairs   256

Bent Twig   262

A Tale of Christmas and Love   267

Chronology   275

Selected Bibliography   279

Acknowledgments

My interest in finding and resurrecting the forgotten or lost work of important authors like Dorothy West, Ralph Ellison, and a Harlem writer named Vivian Morris began in the 1980s. I learned the value of retrieving misbegotten stories, essays, or novels of an earlier time in 1982 with the discovery and publication of *Our Nig*. This nineteenth-century novel was rescued as part of the Black History Fiction Project at Yale College by Henry Louis "Skip" Gates. The discovery of this 1859 manuscript and subsequent publication of *Our Nig; Or, Sketches from the Life of a Free Black* by Gates was a landmark event. Gates declared *Our Nig* to be the first published novel written by an African-American. This proclamation, made in the pages of scholarly journals as well as the pages of *The New York Times, The New Yorker,* and other popular publications where Skip appeared regularly, illustrated for me the importance of rescuing work like the stories in this collection.

Compiling *The Last Leaf of Harlem* would not have been possible without the generous help and scholarship of many people, including Dr. Pearlie-Mae Peters at Rider University, the staff at the Schlesinger Library at Radcliffe College, and others who all helped me cobble together a list of stories and the dates each may have been printed in various publications over a period that spanned more than seventy years. I am especially indebted to the staff at the many libraries where I sought help repeatedly. Those institutions include the Beinecke Rare Book and Manuscript Library, the Library of Congress, the Ruth Haas Library, and the Schomburg and central branches of the New York Public Library. The Beinecke staff helped resurrect the details of a rather intimate relationship between West and poet Langston Hughes, as well as decipher and authenticate at least two pseudonyms used by West but not universally recognized. I particularly would like to thank my friend Joan Reitz at Haas and Western Connecticut State University. Joan helped me on many projects. This time she helped me find and sort through the many databases currently available for this kind of work.

I was also helped by librarians at news morgue at the *New York Daily News* and the New York Public Library. Working with them, I quickly realized just how much fiction had been lost in newspaper archives in the last century, when short stories and poetry were common in most newspaper but were not indexed.

I also would like to thank writer and editor Eileen Dorsey, who rescued this project in an eleventh-hour request to edit late copy. Eileen was busy at the time writing in a new genre.

I will always be indebted to the staff of the Probate Court on Martha's Vineyard in Edgartown, Massachusetts, for keeping me abreast of developments as the estate of Ms. West wended its way through an endless process I otherwise would not have been able to follow.

Finally, to my daughter, Molli, I'd like to say it did not go unnoticed that you grew into a productive young woman while your father was giving birth to this book. You did it without much help from me, and you've done a fine job coming of age. I will be sending you off to Boston University at about the same time I am sending off this tribute to my literary grandmother, Dorothy. As you start your adult life in that city, please know that the spirits of your paternal great-grandfather, your great-grandfather, and my literary grandmother are there, too. Boston served them both well. You will be in good hands, too, Molli.

This book is dedicated to you, Molli, and the hope that you have four good years at Boston University.

The Last Leaf: An Introduction

In the acclaimed autobiography of playwright Lillian Hellman, readers of *Pentimento* were treated to an uneven but realistic journey through the life of a twentieth-century writer that was sometimes fulfilling, usually exhausting, and occasionally cataclysmic. This choice to chronicle life as you see it as a writer has always been a risky business for a woman whether she has the fortitude, means, or stamina to sustain herself.

Taking her cue from another literary fixture of an earlier time, Dorothy West always staked out a room of her own where she could go to think and to write. This need to go off by herself to write is a recurring theme for West, who launched a career as a writer of short fiction as a teenager in her native Boston, a writing life that lasted for more than seven decades. It was an adventure for its creator, who was both an enigma of and a significant contributor to the landscape of twentieth-century American literature.

Dorothy West died in the summer of 1998 at the age of ninety-one. This collection is a literary rendering of her short fiction, compiled just before her death in an attempt to shed new light on the obscure and sometimes shadowy writing life of a literary figure. Throughout her life, West was a curiosity. She was an only child but was surrounded by close and distant relatives taken in by her family. She never married but used pseudonyms like Jane Isaac. This name was used on her story "Cook," which appears in this collection, but "Cook" was first published in *Challenge,* a magazine financed and published by West.

Dorothy West lived the life of a writer, carving out her fiction from the days and nights of her own life. Her writing life began with long, intimate pieces about family in Boston, where she was born on June 2, 1907. She was the only child of Isaac Christopher West, a freed slave who became a successful businessman who sold produce. Her mother was Rachel Pease Benson, one of twenty-two children.

Her career was bookmarked by many essays about life in Boston and Harlem, as well as living on Martha's Vineyard. Most of her work paints an idyllic portrait of life as Dorothy West saw it. But her work was informed, too, by the racism and poverty that she also saw and experienced as a black woman writer in America. Contrary to the image of her as the soft-spoken voice of old-fashioned ways and the gentle mores of the black middle class, Dorothy West was often a social critic. She wrote short stories with the moral twists, human drama, and tragedy that mark all literature. Like her Russian mentor, Fyodor Dostoevsky, West aspired to create and re-create portraits of the human dilemma. In different ways and to different degrees, she succeeded but her work is rarely credited for having this kind of edge.

Dorothy West was largely a short story writer, but she wrote two novels that both chronicled and satirized black middle class and life on Martha's Vineyard, where she lived for most of her life. The stories, sketches, and remembrances in this volume were found over a period of years in widely scattered archives at colleges, universities, and newspaper morgues that I visited in Boston, New York, and Washington, D.C. Her publishing credits began with the long short stories she published in Boston in the first two decades of the twentieth century. Her career came to a close at the end of the century with the writing of brief sketches that she published in the *Vineyard Gazette,* the newspaper that published her work for more than fifty years. One of the persistent criticisms her life and work as a writer is the idea that she was not prolific, that her work was spotty, and that her career was marred by long, dark periods of inactivity. This notion is perhaps the greatest fiction.

Dorothy West was never totally silent, despite claims that she went long periods without writing. All writers experience slow periods. Their work is ignored, is no longer popular, or is just impossible to sell or publish. The writing life of Dorothy West was apparently no easier than Hellman's, and like every writer who tries to make a living writing, her life was often interrupted by bouts of financial, political, and personal woes, according to people who were close to her. A Connecticut lawyer who represented heirs of her estate, for example, told me once that West worked many odd jobs during her life, including a stint as a cashier at a restaurant on the Vineyard. We generally view the lives of creative artists in retrospect, seeing them almost exclusively on the high perches where we've placed their lives next to their greatest works. But this tendancy robs us of the rare opportunity to witness their climb to greatness, and it skews our view of both the art and its creator.

This book is not intended to double as a critique of West or her work. I am not a literary critic. I am a journalist, a self-styled literary anthropologist who tells stories by adding new flesh to the old bones of literary biography.

The bulk of Dorothy West's fiction was first published in newspapers, a long tradition in publishing. Her first story may have been published as early as 1915. Her first stories appeared in the now defunct *Boston Post,* and her last stories were published posthumously in the *Vineyard Gazette* and the *New York Daily News* in the late 1990s. The path her work took from creation to publication did not always follow a straight or narrow line. "My Baby," a story she wrote in the late 1930s while a writer for the federal Work Progress Administration's New York Writer's Project, was not published until the year 2000 after I discovered it in an archive at the Library of Congress. I sent it to *Connecticut Review,* where it was first published more than fifty years after West had written it. Subsequently, it republished in *America's Best Short Stories,* 2001, edited by Barbara Kingsolver. These kinds of gaps between creation and publication go a long way toward explaining the true nature of a writer's life, not its fictions.

As you will see, this collection contains a wide range of her short fiction, most of it written for daily newspapers. This fact alone does not render the work inferior, although some have argued that West was "a second-rate journalist." As a writer and journalist, I have discovered that some of the best American fiction and prose of world literature could be found in the pages of newspapers. In fact, it is a much-maligned literary genre that most literary critics have ignored.

Much of the great literature of modern times was first published in newspapers like *The Times* of London, *The New York Times,* and the *New York Daily News.* In fact, the *Daily News* and *The Times* ran regular sections containing short fiction until late into the twentieth century. This fact places Dorothy West at the same literary table as Charles Dickens, Stephen Crane, Ernest Hemingway, and many others. This also means that West may also have been among the last surviving members of a very large group of notable writers who all launched literary careers by first publishing their fiction in newspapers. Her work could also be placed in the same canon with thousands of unknowns who together created a widely popular genre of literature called pulp fiction. The plots in pulp fiction are usually anchored in the daily lives of relatively ordinary people, much like the plots of opera and the most popular Shakespearean dramas. The stories in this collection have been culled from this generally ignored genre.

No work is created in a vacuum, so the circumstances under which this work was created (for money, influenced by prevailing political winds, etc.) are factors that need consideration, too. Although much of this work appeared in newspapers, it is not journalism. It is pulp fiction intended for the working-class readers who paid nickels or a dime to be entertained by their daily newspapers. The stories were not meant to be literature, no more than the pulp fiction of Dickens, Crane, or Hemingway was considered literary at the time it first appeared in print. Dorothy West belongs to this literary club. Her membership in it began with the fiction she sold and published in short story contests sponsored by the *Boston Post* during or shortly after World War I. Back then, it was still common to see fiction and poetry in the same columns where crime and society news were staples of the news business.

This fact will disappoint some and may tend to taint her work and career in some eyes. This is inevitable.

There are more surprises imbedded in the content of these stories. Most of the characters she created for newspaper readers in the 1940s and in later decades were white. This fact, when juxtaposed with the idea that black writers have always been forbidden to write about white characters, hurls West into the center of a long-standing controversy. In American literary circles, it has never been accepted that black authors could write freely and accurately about white communities or characters. West was called the chronicler of the black middle class, but she also created characters who were presumed to be white.

Who gave Dorothy West permission to step out of her assigned role as a black woman writer? Certainly not the same folks who gave William Faulkner, George Gershwin, DuBose Heyward, William Brashler, and Joel Chandler permission to write about black folks and other cultures not their own. Faulkner certainly knew and could write well about Southern blacks. Gershwin and Heyward successfully captured the character of Gullah culture in *Porgy and Bess*. Brashler, a Chicago writer, was often criticized in the 1970s for trampling on the territory black writers saw as their own in his book *The Bingo Long Traveling All-Stars & Motor Kings,* his novel about the Negro baseball leagues. Chandler, the Southern journalist from Atlanta, was the nineteenth-century chronicler of black folktales in the Uncle Remus stories. Dorothy West joins these folks in this sensitive subgenre, but she stands on the other side of the color line.

She made no apologies for this, so I make none for her in this collection, either. None is necessary. This fact merely illustrates a more important idea, the fact that Dorothy West was an innovator at a time when America was a segregated nation where blacks and whites did not intermingle anywhere in public and rarely in literary circles. Her experiences in Harlem in the 1920s and later in Russia and Europe are exceptions worth noting.

Dorothy West wrote most of her pulp fiction between 1940 and the 1960s. Her stories were syndicated in some of the largest circulation newspapers in America, including the *New York Daily News* when the newspaper had a daily circulation of more than two million readers.

The work in this collection spans decades, years that were noticeably glossed over in some of the literary criticism I have read about West. Those same years and many more of her accomplishments are correctly noted in a general library reference work called *Contemporary Authors*. In it, I found a hint about the real legacy of Dorothy West, buried in between the lines of a small blurb about her career. "Critics and aficionados hope to read more of her creations, many of which remain unpublished," it read. The sheer number of stories she wrote refutes the widely held claim that the years between her two novels, 1948 and 1995, were silent. Dorothy West was rarely idle as a writer during her long life.

Dorothy West was no fool. A graduate of the prestigious Latin Girls School in Boston, West grew up in black Boston. She grew into a black woman who knew the sting of racism in America even though her work didn't always reflect a direct awareness of it.

She wrote protest literature against racism, sexism, and all of the other social ills that befell America after World I and during the economic depression and World War II, which followed in the 1940s. Dorothy West was a social critic, but protest literature written by blacks in the early part of her century and in the succeeding decades did not sell when West was trying to establish herself as a writer. She was the daughter of a former slave. She had to know the realities and the consequences of being black in America during her lifetime. But she was no fool when it came to knowing what would sell and what would not. Protest literature would fail an aspiring black woman trying to sell short stories to white publishers.

The themes West chose to write about generally focused on social or moral issues. This does not mean she never wrote about race, but she was a pragmatist who used satire, subtle shadings, and outright subterfuge to deliver narratives that tackled difficult issues like racial prejudices or the oppression of women in America. Neither of these subjects was an area publishers were willing to pay a black woman or a woman of any color to explore. Yet, Dorothy West started a writing career in the early 1920s and sustained it for the next seventy years. This sometimes took courage and a great deal of cunning. Dorothy West had both.

Whether tending to the needs of the many relatives who drifted in and out of her life as a girl in Boston or working as a welfare investigator in Harlem, she was a writer first. When she joined a federal work project in the late 1930s or when she worked as a restaurant cashier, Dorothy West was still a writer in the act of gathering material for her next book or story.

Her fiction generally mirrored her surroundings, and her stories are filled with the black and white people who were involved in her life. Hers was a life that seemed to always coexist with her stories, sometimes making it difficult for an outsider like me to distinguish facts about her life from the fictions in it. Such is the life of a writer's writer. Dorothy West lived and worked inside of her muse, not side by side with it. The two were enmeshed into a kind of literary soup. This was a contemplation that she began early in her life as a teenager that later made the fact and fictions of her life inseparable.

As a self-styled literary anthropologist, I first became acquainted with Dorothy West through a happy accident. In researching another collection of stories I was doing about the Harlem Renaissance, I knew that West was a legendary black writer from that time. The Harlem Renaissance began in the mid-1920s when an unprecedented number of literary figures gathered in this all-black section of Manhattan and began to publish a wide assortment of novels, short stories, and essays. It was during my research in the early 1990s that I first found and began to admire her odd, old-fashioned writing style. My interest in her work was later heightened when I found several unpublished stories she had written in the Manuscript Division at the Library of Congress in Washington, D.C. It was mingled in among the works of others, including such well-known writers as Ralph Ellison, author of *Invisible Man,* and Zora Neale Hurston, author of *Their Eyes Were Watching God.*

The first story that impressed me is "Pluto," a nonfiction title taken from the dog character in the Walt Disney cartoon Mickey Mouse. In this first-person narrative, West is disturbed one morning while she is writing in her Harlem apartment by an unexpected knock on her door. What follows is precise, chilling social commentary about hunger and poverty during the Depression years in America and her own indifference to it. The piece is both subtle and piercing. It was so carefully crafted that it teeters on that precarious border where fact often meets fiction and the two collide in your mind.

"Pluto" was written in the late 1930s when West worked as a twenty-dollars-a-week writer for the Work Progress Administration's Federal Writer's Project. It had never been published when I found it in the late 1990s. I immediately wondered why.

To my amazement, there were at least a half dozen other stories by West in the same archive. The Work Progress Administration was a make-work federal project more commonly known as the WPA that was abruptly disbanded around 1940. When it closed down, thousands of manuscripts were shelved and forgotten for decades. These stories were part of a larger cache of narratives from the Federal Writer's Project. The stories had been edited and earmarked for publication, but most never made it into print. This is a dramatic example of the vagaries of publishing all creative disciplines must endure.

Other work by West had been published throughout her career, but much of it was equally obscured but for different reasons. Many of the stories she wrote were buried in old archives that had never been indexed. Other work had been carefully indexed but was hard to find because it was buried deep inside the literary collections of other writers like Langston Hughes and James Weldon Johnson in library collections at Yale, Boston University, and Harlem's Schomburg Center for Research in Black Culture. This is how I found pieces of her work in libraries up and down the Atlantic coast, each with a similar story.

In these hushed surroundings, I found manuscripts, old newspapers clippings, and pieces she wrote that were published under at least two different pen names. This work was certainly prized by the librarians who helped me locate the manuscripts I was collecting. But the ideas, sketches, and stories by the aging woman whose literary life I was stitching together had been obscured by years of this kind of neglect, time, and an array of unusual circumstances.

Ironically, Dorothy West was enjoying a renaissance of her own about the same time. Her name and reputation were being resurrected in wider literary circles, and important literary scholars and popular critics were again feting her life and her work. *Time* magazine, for example, said she was enjoying a second round of well-deserved fame with the publication of her second novel, *The Wedding,* in 1995. Jacqueline Kennedy Onassis, then an editor for Doubleday books, had discovered West living on Martha's Vineyard, where West still wrote for the *Vineyard Gazette.* Onassis's decision to publish the first novel West had written in almost fifty years was cause for some celebration. Her first novel, *The Living Is Easy* (1948), had already been republished by The Feminist Press in 1982 and was still in print.

This renewed attention meant that Dorothy West had lived long enough to become a literary enigma in her own time. She was famous and obscure at the same time.

Although she always saw herself as more of a short story writer than a novelist, she was most famous for the two novels. The five decades in between the years 1948 and 1995 are the years critics said Dorothy West appeared to have stopped writing. This was fiction. Dorothy West was prolific.

The career they were celebrating near the end of her life began when she started to win short story contests sponsored by the *Boston Post.* She was also a regular contributor to *Saturday Evening Quill,* a small Boston literary magazine that published the stories of local writers.

Her career broadened around 1924 when she won a literary prize for "The Typewriter." *Opportunity,* the New York–based magazine started by the National Urban League, had chosen the story and invited West to New York to pick up her cash prize. When she arrived, she joined a loosely formed network of Negro writers in Harlem who collectively became known as the Harlem Renaissance writers.

A decade later, West joined the New York Writer's Project of the WPA. In the 1930s, she founded a literary magazine called *Challenge.* It was later renamed *New Challenge,* and she coedited it with writer Richard Wright, who came to New York from the South by way of Chicago. In the limited circles of black Boston and in Harlem, Dorothy West had become famous by the end of the 1930s.

By the start of the next decade, her work caught the attention of literary agent George T. Bye, a high-powered figure in New York. Bye represented First Lady Eleanor Roosevelt, Rebecca West, Katherine Anne Porter, and many other important writers of the period. In a lucrative deal, he negotiated for West to write regularly for the *New York Daily News.* She began a long-term relationship with the *News* to write short stories for the Blue Ribbon Fiction section of the paper. Laid out in the comic strip section, Blue Ribbon Fiction stories often ran on a page anchored by the popular *Terry and the Pirates* comic strip. For the next twenty years, between 1940 and the early 1960s, this is where the name Dorothy West appeared on more than forty short stories.

The first story depicted the life of a black couple in a Harlem tenement during the lean years of the Depression. It was called "Jack in the Pot." "They liked 'Jack in the Pot,' the one and only black story [of mine] they printed. I wrote it for a contest [at a magazine]. The magazine forwarded it to them for their Blue Ribbon Fiction," West said in an interview in 1978 for the Black Women Oral History Project at Radcliffe College. "I had to cut it. I learned a great deal at the *News*. I learned to cut," West said.

"All my friends were so contemptuous that I was writing for the *News*," she said. "It was keeping me eating. I got four hundred dollars." She said friends attributed the high fee she was paid to the fact that she had Bye as her literary agent.

"George Bye had me in his stable. He had Eleanor Roosevelt and a lot of famous people. I got him through Fannie Hurst. Zora Neale Hurston introduced me to Fannie Hurst," West said.

Ironically, while West was represented by an agent whose clients were famous, her fame and her work began to slip into obscurity even though she was now producing stories being read by millions of daily newspaper readers. After "Jack in the Pot" appeared, the stories she wrote over the next twenty years were distributed to numerous other newspapers throughout the world by the News Syndicate, Inc., making Dorothy West one of the most widely read black writers in America at the time. But since her characters weren't black, and she wasn't identified as a black writer, either, few people knew this about her.

This situation is ironic for several reasons. At a time when her fame and notoriety should have soared because of this relationship with Bye and the *News,* it plummeted instead. She fell from the view of critics, who either did not know she was now a regular contributor to the *News* or the fact that West, a black writer regularly writing stories with an all-white cast, had become a taboo subject for them. What is most probable is that they did not know her story. In either case, her career as a short story writer fell prey to rumors that she had retired. This claim remained a fixture in the literary biographies about her throughout the rest of her life. So while West was writing for a syndicate that distributed her fiction to newspapers throughout the world, this time became one of obscurity for West.

The *News* was distributed on newsstands throughout the many white, working-class neighborhoods of New York City. Many readers were white immigrant women whose lives were far removed from the realities that most often confronted black Americans. In order to be published here, West seemed to have no choice but to invent white characters with whom her readers could relate. This begins a significant chapter in West's literary career. Dorothy West became what author Robert A. Bone called an assimilationist.

She wasn't alone. West was developing as a writer in the late 1920s when she met Zora Neale Hurston, Ralph Ellison, Richard Wright, Frank Yerby, and other fledgling artists in Harlem. In the early days of the Renaissance, these writers enjoyed being published in the mostly black, little magazines that sprang up solely to publish their work. In the years between 1920 and the late 1930s, the fiction of Harlem writers like West appeared in *The Crisis,* the NAACP magazine; *Opportunity,* the Urban League magazine; and *Challenge,* later *New Challenge.*

About the same time, Hurston, Hughes, and others were published in *Fire!!,* a single-issue literary magazine its founders said "was intended to burn up a lot of the old, dead, conventional Negro ideas of the past." The political writings of other Harlem writers found an outlet in a socialist magazine called *The Messenger,* founded and edited by A. Philip Randolph and Chandler Owen.

The plight of black life in America was regularly laid bare in these magazines. But by the 1940s, almost all of them except *The Crisis* had folded, leaving black writers like West with almost no place to publish their stories.

"A good index to the general temper of the period is the lack of any center of gravity for a specifically Negro art," Bone says in his book *The Negro Novel in America.* "There are no little magazines in the forties and fifties to perform the function of *Fire!!* and Harlem during the Renaissance, or of *Challenge* and *New Challenge* during the Depression." So there was no cohesive movement in contemporary black literature, Bone said, which led writers like West, Yerby, and even the acerbic Hurston to become what he called assimilationist writers.

"On the whole," Bone said in examining the period, "the young writers have preferred to seek nonracial outlets for their work. In doing so, these writers were abandoning the assertively racial fiction pioneered by Wright in novels like *Native Son.*"

Assimilationists turned to commercial fiction, which meant abandoning racial themes and, in most cases, black characters and all-black communities altogether. In the years between 1945 and the early 1950s, some thirty-three novels by black authors were published. Thirteen, or more than a third of these, had predominantly or all white characters.

Among the most notable writers of this genre were Frank Yerby, Zora Neale Hurston, and Ann Petry.

Yerby, who had published stories in *Challenge,* too, had also worked with West and Ellison on the staff of the New York Writer's Project of the WPA. According to Bone, Yerby had been a race-conscious Southerner during his early years in New York, too. By the mid-1940s, he was still writing protest stories, but by the early 1950s, Yerby had moved to Spain and began to write wildly popular romantic potboilers that featured mostly white plots and white characters. Others followed this path as well.

Chester Himes wrote *Cast the First Stone* in 1952. Willard Motley wrote *Knock on Any Door* in 1947 and *We Fished All Night* in 1951. All are novels with raceless characters. In 1948, Hurston wrote *Seraph on the Suwanee,* a novel set in the rural South. In it, Hurston's familiar black characters, communities, and themes have been abandoned for a whiter literary landscape. A year earlier, Connecticut-born writer Ann Petry, known for her protest Harlem novel, *The Street,* published *Country Place.* This story of dying values is set in New England, presumably patterned after Petry's mostly white hometown of Old Saybrook, Connecticut. All of these writers became assimilationists and continued striving to break into the arena of mainstream publishing.

Dorothy West joined this group when she began writing for the *News.* She said the *News* did not want stories about black characters, and this stipulation was made implicit in her agreement with the News's editors, who agreed to publish her stories if she complied. Rather than showing us people with unusual character, who also happened to be black, West repeatedly delivered stories with ironic twists aimed at the hearts and minds of readers who were mostly working-class whites. These characters sometimes lack the magnetic substances. These stories were syndicated by the News Syndicate, Inc. and were read by tens of millions of newspaper readers throughout the country and possibly the world. This made West one of the most widely read writers from the Harlem Renaissance, not just the youngest member of the elite group. Unfortunately, this work was never indexed, so it disappeared from public view days after it was published with little or no way to retrieve it weeks, months, or years later.

Other works by West also disappeared because they were written under her pen names. She used at least two, Mary Christopher and Jane Isaac. A third name, Mildred Wirt, has been attributed to West, but she denied ever having used it. Mildred Wirt is the name of a real writer who was born about the same time as the real Dorothy West. Wirt was one of the many writers for the famous *Nancy Drew* mystery series. A source who knew Wirt told me that the real Wirt once used the name Dorothy West as *her* pseudonym for a children's book she wrote that was entitled *Dot and Dash*.

Shortly before she died in August 1998, West told an interviewer for *The New York Times Book Review* that she was the last leaf on a now famous tree of black authors from Harlem. Of course, West was talking about her place among the black intellectuals of the Harlem Renaissance. This lasting image of Dorothy West as just the literary kid sister to Ralph Ellison, Richard Wright, and Claude McKay does not reflect her unusual vigor as a productive writer.

Dorothy West probably was the youngest writer identified with the Harlem Renaissance, but she was probably also the most widely published author of the period, too, a credit she has never been given in life or in death. Paying this tribute to her now in no way diminishes the notable achievements of important writers like Ellison, Hurston, and the others from her days in Harlem. It just reflects her role more accurately.

When the Renaissance years ended in the early 1930s, West stayed in New York for a few years. She founded *Challenge*, traveled to Russia to make a film, and traveled in a road show of

Porgy and Bess as an actress. When a relative fell ill on Martha's Vineyard in 1940, Dorothy West left New York and never returned.

In the succeeding years, she would write just two novels, many years apart, a fact for which she would be chided throughout her life. Without access to the pundits who had been charmed by her early work and presence in New York, the name Dorothy West faded from public view. West did seem like a fallen literary figure of the Harlem Renaissance. Her creative flame appeared to flicker briefly in the 1920s, then go out. This tragic story about the premature end of a promising literary career just seemed to be true. As romantic as these notions are, they were not true. When she died, these same images appeared in the many obituaries and eulogies published about her. They failed in almost every way to document the rich literary legacy Dorothy West actually left behind for us to ponder.

I came by this conclusion only gradually as I found more and more of her work. The fact that this work existed and I was finding it wasn't the nature of my true discovery. I knew that various scholars in different locations and disciplines knew about these obscure stories and that some had read many of them.

A librarian at Harlem's Schomburg Center for Research in Black Culture clarified the significance of what I was really seeing—the obscured work of a writer. The work of Dorothy West had never been thoroughly indexed, making a comprehensive collection of it difficult, if not impossible, to compile, she said.

After a thorough search at the Library of Congress and other libraries, this omission became the center of my real discovery. I zeroed in even closer on the stories, which had been published by the *News,* and have compiled them for the first time into this collection. This is what makes this collection significant. Librarians at the *News* did the hard work of helping me find the probable dates of nearly twenty of these stories. It took them months. Dr. Pearlie Peters, a professor in the English Department at Rider University in New Jersey, offered me a list of nearly twenty other stories she had located from sources in Boston. Together, we had located and found more than forty stories.

For all of the reasons I have discovered, Dorothy West became invisible after she left New York, an almost terminal condition that her Harlem contemporary, Ralph Ellison, first identified and explored repeatedly during his lifetime and in his novel *Invisible Man.* Ironically, the era that made both West and Ellison famous seemed to suffer the same fate. Harlem itself became an invisible no-man's-land after 1929 when worsening economic conditions dried up the loose life that had brought white tourists uptown to Harlem in droves. That's when standard history books say the Harlem Renaissance abruptly ended, despite the fact that West, Ellison, and Zora Neale Hurston all published landmark novels years later.

Like the unnamed character in Ralph Ellison's novel, Dorothy West had gone underground and remained there until Dr. Henry Louis "Skip" Gates from Harvard and Jackie Onassis found her again living on Martha's Vineyard. But as West told an interviewer for *Ms.* magazine in 1995, just because "I had left New York . . . didn't mean I had stopped writing."

In a tribute following her death, the *Vineyard Gazette* reprinted some of the columns she had written for that newspaper. In one of them, West tells the story of how she began writing at the age of seven:

> "When I was little, I asked my mother if I could go to my room."
> "'Yes,' my mother said, 'but why do you want to go to your room?'"
> "'To think,' I told her."
> "I went to my mother again later. This time, I asked if I could go to my room and lock the door."
> "'Yes,' my mother said, 'but why do you want to lock the door?'"
> "'Because I want to write,'" I told her.

Over the next century, that room was in a fashionable section of Boston, a tenement building on 110th Street in Harlem, and later in her life, she wrote from the two-bedroom cottage her father had built for family retreats in a wooded section on Martha's Vineyard. The last room Dorothy West lived in was in a hospital in her native Boston, where she died.

ONE

Early Fiction

Hannah Byde

One comes upon Hannah in her usual attitude of bitter resignation, gazing listlessly out of the window of her small, conventionally cheaply furnished parlor. Hannah, a gentle woman crushed by environment, looking dully down the stretch of drab tomorrows littered with the ruins of shattered dreams.

She had got to the point, in these last few weeks, when the touch of her husband's hand on hers, the inevitable proximity in a four-room flat, the very sound of his breathing, swept a sudden wave of nausea through her body, sickened her, soul and body and mind.

There were moments—frightful even to her—when she pictured her husband's dead body, and herself, in hypocritical black, weeping by his bier, or she saw her own repellent corpse swirling in a turgid pool and laughed a little madly at the image.

But there were times, too—when she took up her unfinished sack for the Joneses' new baby—when a fierce, strange pain would rack her. Her breath coming in little gasps, she would sink to the floor, clutching at the tiny garment. Somehow, soothed, she would be a little girl again with plaited hair, a little eager, visioning girl—"Mama, don't cry!" she'd say. "Some day I'll be rich an' ev'rything. You'll see, Mama!"—instead of a spiritless woman of thirty who, having neither the courage nor strength to struggle out of the mire of mediocrity, had married at twenty, George Byde simply because the enticing honeymoon to Niagara would mark the first break in the uneventful circle of her life.

Holiday crowds hurrying in the street. . . . Bits of gay banter floating up to her. . . . George noisily reading his paper. . . . Wreaths in the shop window across the street. . . . A proud black family in a new red car. . . . George uttering intermittent, expressive little grunts. . . . A blind beggar finding a lost dollar bill. . . . A bullying policeman running in a drunk. . . . George, in reflective mood, beating a pencil against his teeth—

With a sharp intake of breath she turned on him fiercely, her voice trembling with stifled rage, angry tears filming her eyes.

"For God's sake, stop! You'll drive me mad!"

He dropped his paper. His mouth fell open. He got to his feet, a great, coarse, not unkindly, startled giant. "Hannah, I ain't— What under the sun's the matter with you?"

She struggled for composure. "It's nothing. I'm sorry. Sorry, George." But her eyes filled with pain.

He started toward her and stopped as he saw her stiffen. He said quietly, "Hannah, you ain't well. You ain't never bin like this."

She was suddenly forced into the open. "No," she said clearly. "I'm not well. I'm sick—sick to death of you, and your flat, and your cheap little friends. Oh," she said, her voice choked with passion, "I'd like to throw myself out of this window. Anything— anything to get away! I hate you!"

She swayed like some yellow flower in the wind, and for a moment, there was the dreadful silence of partial revelation.

He fumbled, "No, no, hon. You're jes' nervous. I know you women. Jes' you set down. I'll go see if Doc's home."

She gave a deep sigh. Habitual apathy dulled her tone. "Please don't bother. I'm all right. It's nerves, I guess. Sometimes the emptiness of my life frightens me."

A slow anger crept over him. His lips seemed to thicken. "Look here, Hannah. I'm tiahed of your foolishness. There's limits to what a man will stand. Guess I give you ev'rything anybody else's got. You never have nothing much to do here. Y'got a phonygraph—and all them new records. Y'got a piano. I give you money las' week to buy a new dress. And yisterday y'got new shoes. I ain't no millionaire, Hannah. Ain't no man livin' c'n do better'n his best."

She made a restless, weary little gesture. She began to loathe him. She felt an almost insane desire to hurt him deeply, cruelly. She was like a taunting mother goading her child to tears.

"Of course I appreciate your sacrifice." Her voice shook a little with hysteria. "You're being perfectly splendid. You feed me. You clothe me. You've bought me a player piano which I loathe—flaunting emblem of middle-class existence—Oh, don't go to the trouble of trying to understand that—And a stupid victrola stocked with the dreadful noises of your incomparable Mamie Waters. Oh, I'm a happy, contented woman! 'There never is anything to do here.'" She mocked in a shrill, choked voice. "Why, what in God's name is there to do in a dark, badly furnished, four-room flat? Oh, if I weren't such a cowardly fool, I'd find a way out of all this!"

The look of a dangerous, savage beast dominated his face. He stood, in this moment, revealed. Every vestige of civilization had fled. One saw then the flatness of his close-cropped head, the thick, bull-like shortness of his neck, the heavy nose spreading now in a fierce gust of uncontrollable anger, the beads of perspiration that had sprung out on his upper lip, one wondered then how the gentle woman Hannah could have married him. She shut her eyes against his brutal coarseness, his unredeemed ignorance—here no occasional, illiterate appreciation of the beautiful—his lack of spiritual needs, his bodily wants.

And yet one sees them daily, these sensitive spiritless Negro women caught fast in the tentacles of awful despair. Almost, it seems, as if they shut their eyes and make a blind plunge, inevitably to be sucked down, down into the depths of dreadful existence.

He started toward her, and she watched his approach with controlled interest. She had long ago ceased to fear his anger and had learned to whip him out of a mood with a flick of her scathing tongue. And now she waited unmoving for the miracle of his heavy hand to end her weary life.

His eyes were black with rage. "By God you drive me mad! If I was any less of a man I'd beat you till you ran blood. I must have been crazy to marry you. You— you—!

There was a sharp rapping at the door, drowning his crazy words. Hannah smiled faintly, almost compassionately.

"The psychological moment. What a pity. George."

She crossed the floor, staggering for an instant with a sudden, sharp pain. She opened the door and unconsciously caught her lip in vexation as she admitted her visitor.

"Do come in," she said, almost dryly,

Tillie entered. Tillie, the very recent, very pretty, very silly wife of Doctor Hill, a newly wed, popular girl finding matrimony just a big cramping.

She entered boldly, anticipating and ignoring the palliative annoyance in the stern set of Hannah's face. She even shrugged a little, a kind of wriggling that her friends undoubtedly called "cute." She spoke in the unmistakable tone of the middle-class Negro.

"Hello, you! And big boy George! I heard you all walking about downstairs, so I came on up. I bin sittin' by myself all evenin'. Even the gas went out. Here it's New Year's Eve, I'm all dolled up, got an invite to a swell shebang sittin' pretty on my dresser—and my sweet daddy walks out on a case! Say, wouldn't that make you leave your happy home?"

George enjoyed it. He grinned sympathetically. Here was a congenial, jazz-loving soul, and, child-like, he promptly shelved his present grievance. He wanted to show off. He wanted, a little pathetically, to blot out the hovering bitterness of Hannah in the gay camaraderie of Tillie.

He said eagerly, "Got some new records, Tillie."

She was instantly delighted. "Yeh? Run 'em 'round the green."

She settled herself in a comfortable chair and crossed her slim legs. Hannah went to the window in customary isolation.

George made a vain search of the cabinet. "Where're them records, Hannah?" he asked.

"On the table edge," she murmured fretfully.

He struggled to his feet and shuffled over to the table. "Lord," he grumbled, "you ain't undone 'em yet?"

"I've been too tired," she answered wearily.

He and Tillie exchanged mocking glances. He sighed expressively, and Tillie snickered audibly. But their malicious little shafts fell short of the unheeding woman who was beating a sharp, impatient tattoo on the windowpane.

George swore softly.

"Whassa matter?" asked Tillie. "Knot?"

He jerked at it furiously. "This devilish string."

"Will do," she asserted companionably. "Got a knife?"

"Yep." He fished in his pocket, produced it. "Here we go." The razor-sharp knife split the twine. "All set." He flung the knife, still open, on the table.

The raucous notes of a jazz singer filled the room. The awful blare of a frenzied colored orchestra, the woman's strident voice swelling, a great deal of "high brown baby" and "low down papa" to offend sensitive ears, and Tillie saying admiringly, "Ain't that the monkey's itch?"

From below came the faint sound of someone clumping, a heavy man stomping snow from his boots. Tillie sprang up, fluttered toward George.

"Jim, I'll bet. Back. You come down with me, G. B., and maybe you c'n coax him to come on up. I got a bottle of somethin' good. We'll watch the new year in and drink its health."

George obediently followed after. "Not so worse. And there oughta be plenty o' stuff in our icebox. Scare up a little somethin', Hannah. We'll be right back."

As the door banged noisily, Hannah, with a dreadful rush of suppressed sobs, swiftly crossed the carpeted floor, cut short the fearful din of the record, and stood, for a trembling moment, with her hands pressed against her eyes.

Presently her sobs quieted, and she moaned a little, whimpering, too, like a fretful child. She began to walk restlessly up and down, whispering crazily to herself. Sometimes she beat her doubled fists against her head, and ugly words befouled her twisted lips. Sometimes she fell upon her knees; face buried in her outflung arms, and cried, aloud to God.

Once, in her mad, sick circle of the room, she staggered against the table, and the hand that went out to steady her closed on a bit of sharp steel. For a moment she stood quite still. Then she opened her eyes, blinking them free of tears. She stared fixedly at the knife in her hand. She noted it for the first time: initialed, heavy, black, four blades, the open one broken off at the point. She ran her fingers along its edge. A drop of blood spurted and dripped from the tip of her finger. It fascinated her. She began to think: this is the tide of my life ebbing out. And suddenly she wanted to see it run swiftly. She wanted terribly to be drained dry of life. She wanted to feel the outgoing tide of existence.

She flung back her head. Her voice rang out in a strange, wild cry of freedom.

But in the instant when she would have freed her soul, darkness swirled down upon her. Wave upon wave of impenetrable blackness in a mad surge. The knife fell away. Her groping hands were like bits of aimless driftwood. She could not fight her way through to consciousness. She plunged deeply into the terrible vastness that roared about her ears.

And almost in awful mockery the bells burst into sound, ushering out the old, heralding the new: for Hannah, only a long, gray twelve months of pain-filled, soul-starved days.

As the last, loud note died away, Tillie burst into the room, followed by George and her husband, voluble in noisy badinage. Instantly she saw the prostrate figure of Hannah and uttered a piercing shriek of terror.

"Oh, my God! Jim!" she cried, and cowered fearfully, against the wall, peering through the lattice of her fingers.

George, too, stood quite still, a half-empty bottle clutched in his hand, his eyes bulging grotesquely, his mouth falling open, and his lips ashen. Instinctively although the knife lay hidden in the folds of her dress, he felt that she was dead. Her every prophetic, fevered word leaped to his suddenly sharpened brain. He wanted to run away and hide. It wasn't fair of Hannah to be lying there mockingly dead. His mind raced ahead to the dreadful details of inquest and burial, and a great resentment welled in his heart. He began to hate the woman he thought lay dead.

Doctor Hill, puffing a little, bent expertly over Hannah. His eye caught the gleam of steel. Surreptitiously he pocketed the knife and sighed. He was a kindly, fat, little bald man with an exhaustless fund of sympathy. Immediately he had understood. That was the way with morbid, self-centered women like Hannah.

He raised himself. "Poor girl, she's fainted. Help me with her, you all."

When they had laid her on the couch, the gay, frayed, red couch with the ugly rent in the center Hannah's nerve-tipped fingers had torn, Jim sent them into the kitchen.

"I want to talk to her alone. She'll come around in a minute."

He stood above her, looking down at her with incurious pity. The great black circles under her eyes enhanced the sad dark beauty of her face. He knew suddenly, with a tinge of pain, how different would have been her life, how wide the avenues of achievement, how eager the acclaiming crowd, how soft her bed of ease, had this gloriously golden woman been born white. But there was little bitterness in his thoughts. He did not resignedly accept the black man's unequal struggle, but he philosophically foresaw the eventual crashing down of all unjust barriers.

Hannah stirred, moaned a little, opened her eyes, and in a quick flash of realization stifled a cry with her hand fiercely pressed to her lips. Doctor Hill bent over her, and suddenly she began to laugh, ending it dreadfully in a sob.

"Hello, Jim," she said, "I'm not dead, am I? I wanted so badly to die."

Weakly she tried to rise, but he forced her down with a gentle hand. "Lie quiet, Hannah," he said.

Obediently she lay back on the cushion, and he sat beside her, letting her hot hand grip his own. She smiled a wistful, tragic, little smile.

"I had planned it all so nicely, Jim. George was to stumble upon my dead body—his own knife buried in my throat—and grovel beside me in fear and self-reproach. And Tillie, of course, would begin extolling my virtues, while you—Now it's all spoilt!"

He released her hand and patted it gently. He got to his feet. "You must never do this again, Hannah."

She shook her head like a willful child. "I shan't promise."

His near-sighted, kindly eyes bored into hers. "There is a reason why you must, my dear."

For a long moment she stared questioningly at him, and the words of refutation that leaped to her lips died of despairing certainty at the answer in his eyes.

She rose, swaying, and steadied herself by her feverish grip on his arms. "No," she wailed, "no! No! No!!"

He put an arm about her. "Steady, dear."

She jerked herself free, and flung herself on the couch, burying her stricken face in her hands.

"Jim, I can't! I can't! Don't you see how it is with me?"

He told her seriously, "You must be very careful, Hannah."

Her eyes were tearless, wild. "But, Jim, you know—You've watched me. Jim! I hate my husband. I can't breathe when he's near. He—stifles me. I can't go through with it. I can't! Oh, why couldn't I have died?"

He took both her hands in his and sat beside her, waiting until his quiet presence should soothe her. Finally she gave a great, quivering sigh and was still.

"Listen, Hannah," he began, "you are nervous and distraught. After all, a natural state for a woman of your temperament. But you do not want to die. You want to live. Because you must, my dear. There is a life within you demanding birth. If you seek your life again, your child dies, too. I am quite sure you could not be a murderer.

"You must listen very closely and remember all I say. For with this new year—a new beginning, Hannah—you must see things clearly and rationally, and build your strength against your hour of delivery."

Slowly she raised her eyes to his. She shook her head dumbly. "There's no way out. My hands are tied. Life itself has beaten me."

"Hannah?"

"No. I understand, Jim. I see."

"Right," he said, rising cheerfully. "Just you think it all over." He crossed to the door and called, "George! Tillie! You all can come in now."

They entered timorously, and Doctor Hill smiled reassuringly at them. He took his wife's hand and led her to the outer door.

"Out with you and me, my dear. We'll drink the health of the new year downstairs. Mrs. Byde has something very important to say to Mr. Byde. Night, G. B. Be very gentle with Hannah."

George shut the door behind them and went to Hannah. He stood before her, embarrassed, mumbling inaudibly.

"There's going to be a child," she said dully.

She paled before the instant gleam in his eyes.

"You're—glad?'

There was a swell of passion in his voice. "Hannah!" He caught her up in his arms.

"Don't," she cried, her hands a shield against him, "you're— stifling me."

He pressed his mouth to hers and awkwardly released her.

She brushed her hands across her lips, "You've been drinking. I can't bear it."

He was humble. "Just to steady myself. In the kitchen. Me and Tillie."

She was suddenly almost sorry for him. "It's all right, George. It doesn't matter. It's—nothing."

Timidly he put his hand on her shoulder. "You're shivering. Lemme get you a shawl."

"No." She fought against hysteria. "I'm all right, George. It's only that I'm tired. . . . tired." She went unsteadily to her bedroom door, and her groping hand closed on the knob. "You—you'll sleep on the couch tonight? I—I just want to be alone. Good night, George. I shall be all right. Good night."

He stood alone, at a loss, his hands going out to the closed door in clumsy sympathy. He thought: I'll play a piece while she's gettin' undressed. A little jazz'll do her good.

He crossed to the phonograph, his shoes squeaking fearfully.

There was something pathetic in his awkward attempt to walk lightly. He started the record where Hannah had cut it short, grinning delightedly as it began to whir.

The jazz notes burst on the air, filled the narrow room, crowded out.

And the woman behind the closed door flung herself across the bed and laughed and laughed and laughed.

The Typewriter

It occurred to him, as he eased past the bulging knees of an Irish wash lady and forced an apologetic passage down the aisle of the crowded car, that more than anything in all the world, he wanted not to go home. He began to wish passionately that he had never been born, that he had never been married, that he had never been the means of life's coming into the world. He knew quite suddenly that he hated his flat and his family and his friends. And most of all, the incessant thing that would "clatter clatter" until every nerve screamed aloud, and the words of the evening paper danced crazily before him, and the insane desire to crush and kill set his fingers twitching.

He shuffled down the street, an abject little man of fifty-odd years, in an ageless overcoat that flapped in the wind. He was cold, and he hated the North, and particularly Boston, and saw suddenly a barefoot pickaninny sitting on a fence in the hot, Southern sun with a piece of steaming corn bread and a piece of fried salt pork in either grimy hand.

He was tired, and he wanted his supper, but he didn't want the beans, and frankfurters, and light bread that Net would undoubtedly have. That Net had had every Monday night since that regrettable moment fifteen years before when he had told her—innocently—that such a supper tasted "right nice. Kinda change from what we always has."

He mounted the four brick steps leading to his door and pulled at the bell, but there was no answering ring. It was broken again, and in a mental flash he saw himself with a multitude of tools and a box of matches shivering in the vestibule after supper. He began to pound lustily on the door and wondered vaguely if his hand would bleed if he smashed the glass. He hated the sight of blood. It sickened him.

Someone was running down the stairs. Daisy probably. Millie would be at that infernal thing, pounding, pounding. . . . He entered. The chill of the house swept him. His child was wrapped in a coat. She whispered solemnly, "Poppa, Miz Hicks an' Miz Berry's awful mad. They gointa move if they can't get more heat. The furnace's birnt out all day. Mama couldn't fix it." He said hurriedly, "I'll go right down. I'll go right down." He hoped Mrs. Hicks wouldn't pull open her door and glare at him. She was large and domineering, and her husband was a bully. If her husband ever struck him, it would kill him. He hated life, but he didn't want to die. He was afraid of God, and in his wildest flights of fancy couldn't imagine himself an angel. He went softly down the stairs.

He began to shake the furnace fiercely. And he shook into it every wrong, mumbling softly under his breath. He began to think back over his uneventful years, and it came to him as rather a shock that he had never sworn in all his life. He wondered uneasily if he dared say "damn." It was taken for granted that a man swore when he tended a stubborn furnace. And his strongest interjection was "Great balls of fire!"

The cellar began to warm, and he took off his inadequate overcoat that was streaked with dirt. Well, Net would have to clean that. He'd be damned—! It frightened him and thrilled him. He wanted suddenly to rush upstairs and tell Mrs. Hicks if she didn't like the way he was running things, she could get out. But he heaped another shovel full of coal on the fire and sighed. He would never be able to get away from himself and the routine of years.

He thought of that eager Negro lad of seventeen who had come North to seek his fortune. He had walked jauntily down Boylston Street, and even his own kind had laughed at the incongruity of him. But he had thrown up his head and promised himself: "You'll have an office here someday. With plate-glass windows and a real mahogany desk." But, though he didn't know it then, he was not the progressive type. And he became successively, in the years, bellboy, porter, waiter, cook, and finally janitor in a downtown office building.

He had married Net when he was thirty-three and a waiter. He had married her partly because—though he might not have admitted it—there was no one to eat the expensive delicacies the generous cook gave him every night to bring home. And partly because he dared hope there might be a son to fulfill his dreams. But Millie had come, and after her twin girls who had died within two weeks, then Daisy, and it was tacitly understood that Net was done with child-bearing.

Life, though flowing monotonously, had flowed peacefully enough until that sucker of sanity became a sitting-room fixture.

Intuitively, at the very first, he had felt its undesirability. He had suggested hesitatingly that they couldn't afford it. Three dollars: food and fuel. Times were hard, and the twenty dollars apiece, the respective husbands of Miz Hicks and Miz Berry irregularly paid, was only five dollars more than the thirty-five a month he paid his own Hebraic landlord. And the Lord knew his salary was little enough. At which point Net spoke her piece, her voice rising shrill. "God knows I never complain 'bout nothin'. Ain't no other woman got less than me. I bin wearin' this same dress here five years an' I'll wear it another five. But I don't want nothin'. I ain't never wanted nothin'. An' when I does as', it's only for my children. You're a poor sort of father if you can't give that child jes' three dollars a month to rent that typewriter. Ain't 'nother girl in school ain't got one. An' most of 'ems bought an' paid for. You know yourself how Millie is. She wouldn't as' me for it till she had to. An' I ain't going to disappoint her. She's goin' to get that typewriter Saturday, mark my words."

On a Monday then it had been installed. And in the months that followed, night after night he listened to the murderous "tack, tack, tack" that was like a vampire slowly drinking his blood. If only he could escape. Bar a door against the sound of it. But tied hand and foot by the economic fact that "Lord knows we can't afford to have fires burnin' an' lights lit all over the flat. You'all gotta set in one room. An' when y'get tired settin' y'c'n go to bed. Gas bill was somep'n scandalous last month."

He heaped a final shovelful of coal on the fire and watched the first blue flames. Then, his overcoat under his arm, he mounted the cellar stairs. Mrs. Hicks was standing in her kitchen door, arms akimbo. "It's warmin'," she volunteered.

"Yeh," he was conscious of his grime-streaked face and hands, "it's warmin'. I'm sorry 'bout all day."

She folded her arms across her ample bosom. "Tending a furnace ain't a woman's work. I don't blame your wife none 'tall."

Unsuspecting, he was grateful. "Yeh, it's pretty hard for a woman. I always look after it 'fore I goes to work, but some days it jes ac's up."

"Y'oughta have a janitor, that's what y'ought," she flung at him. "The same cullud man that tends them apartments would be willin'. Mr. Taylor has him. It takes a man to run a furnace, and when the man's away all day—"

"I know," he interrupted, embarrassed and hurt, I know. Tha's right, Miz Hicks, tha's right. But I ain't in a position to make no improvements. Times is hard."

She surveyed him critically. "Your wife called down 'bout three times while you was in the cellar. I reckon she wants you for supper."

"Thanks," he mumbled and escaped up the back stairs.

He hung up his overcoat in the closet, told himself, a little lamely, that it wouldn't take him more'n a minute to clean it up himself after supper. After all Net was tired and prob'bly worried what Miz Hicks and all. And he hated men who made slaves of their womenfolk. Good old Net.

He tidied up in the bathroom, washing his face and hands carefully and cleanly so as to leave no—or very little—stain on the roller towel. It was hard enough for Net, God knew.

He entered the kitchen. The last spirals of steam were rising from his supper. One thing about Net she served a full plate. He smiled appreciatively at her unresponsive back, bent over the kitchen sink. There was no one could bake beans just like Net's. And no one who could find a market with frankfurters quite so fat.

He sank down at his place. "Evenin', hon."

He saw her back stiffen. "If your supper's cold, 'tain't my fault. I called and called."

He said hastily, "It's fine, Net, fine. Piping."

She was the usual tired housewife. "Y'oughta et your supper 'fore you fooled with that furnace. I ain't bothered 'bout them niggers. I got all my dishes washed 'cept yours. An' I hate to mess up my kitchen after I once get it straightened up."

He was humble. "I'll give that old furnace an extra lookin' after in the mornin'. It'll las' all day tomorrow, hon."

"An' on top of that," she continued, unheeding him and giving a final wrench to her dish towel, "that confounded bell don't ring. An'—"

"I'll fix it after supper," he interposed hastily.

She hung up her dish towel and came to stand before him looming large and yellow. "An that old Mix Berry, she claimed she was expectin' comp'ny. An' she knows they must'a come an' gone while she was in her kitchen an' couldn't be at her winder to watch for 'em. Old liar," she brushed back a lock of naturally straight hair. "She wasn't expectin' nobody."

"Well, you know how some folks are—"

"Fools! Half the world," was her vehement answer. "I'm going in the front room an' set down a spell. I bin on my feet all day. Leave them dishes on the table. God knows I'm tired, but I'll come back an' wash 'em." But they both knew, of course, that he, very clumsily would.

At precisely quarter past nine when he, strained at last to the breaking point, uttering an inhuman, strangled cry, flung down his paper, clutched at his throat and sprang to his feet, Millie's surprised young voice, shocking him to normalcy, heralded the first of that series of great moments that every humble little middle-class man eventually experiences.

"What's the matter, Poppa? You sick? I wanted you to help me."

He drew out his handkerchief and wiped his hot hands. "I declare I must'a fallen asleep an' had a nightmare. No, I ain't sick. What you want, hon?"

"Dictate me a letter, Poppa. I c'n do sixty words a minute—you know, like a business letter. You know, like those men in your building dictate to their stenographers. Don't you hear 'em sometimes?"

"Oh sure, I know, hon. Poppa'll help you. Sure. I hear that Mr. Browning—sure."

Net rose. "Guess I'll put this child to bed. Come on now, Daisy, without no fuss. Then I'll run up to Pa's. He ain't bin well all week."

When the door closed behind them, he crossed to his daughter, arranged himself, and coughed importantly.

"Well, Millie—"

"Oh, Poppa, is that what you'd call your stenographer?" she teased. "And anyway, pretend I'm really one—and you're really my boss, and this letter's real important."

A light crept into his dull eyes. Vigor through his thin blood. In a brief moment the weight of years fell from him like a cloak. Tired, bent, little old man that he was, he smiled, straightened, tapped impressively against his teeth with a toil-strained finger, and became that enviable emblem of American life: a businessman.

"You be Miz Hicks, huh, honey? Course we can't both use the same name. I'll be J. Lucius Jones. J. Lucius. All them real big doin' men use their middle names. Jus' kinda looks big doin', doncha think, hon? Looks like money, huh? J. Lucius." He uttered a sound that was like the proud cluck of a strutting hen. "J. Lucius." It rolled like oil from his tongue.

His daughter twisted impatiently. "Now, Poppa—I mean Mr. Jones, sir—please begin. I am ready for dictation, sir."

He was in that office on Boylston Street, looking with visioning eyes through its plate-glass windows, tapping with impatient fingers on its real mahogany desk.

"Ah—Beaker Brothers, Park Square Building, Boston, Mass. Ah—Gentlemen: In reply to yours at the seventh instant I would state—"

Every night thereafter in the weeks that followed, with Daisy packed off to bed, and Net "gone up to Pa's" or nodding inobtrusively in her corner, there was the chameleon change of a Court Street janitor to J. Lucius Jones, dealer in stocks and bonds. He would stand, posturing importantly, flicking imaginary dust from his coat lapel, or, his hands locked behind his back, he would stride up and down, earnestly and seriously debating the advisability of buying copper with the market in such a fluctuating state. Once a week, too, he stopped in at Jerry's, and after a preliminary purchase of cheap cigars, bought the latest trade papers, mumbling an embarrassed explanation: "I got a little money. Think I'll invest it in reliable stock."

The letters Millie typed and subsequently discarded, he rummaged for later, and under cover of writing to his brother in the South, laboriously with a great many fancy flourishes, signed each neatly typed sheet with the exalted J. Lucius Jones.

Later, when he mustered the courage, he suggested tentatively to Millie that it might be fun—just fun, of course!—to answer his letters. One might—he laughed a good deal louder and longer than necessary—he'd be J. Lucius Jones, and the next night—here he swallowed hard and looked a little frightened—Rockefeller or Vanderbilt or Morgan—just for fun, y'understand! Millie gave consent. It mattered little to her one way or the other. It was practice, and that was what she needed. Very soon now she'd be in the hundred class. Then maybe she could get a job!

He was growing very careful of his English. Occasionally—and it must be admitted, ashamedly—he made surreptitious ventures into the dictionary. He had to, of course. J. Lucius Jones would never say "Y'got to" when he meant, "It is expedient." And, old brain though he was, he learned quickly and easily, juggling words with amazing facility.

Eventually he bought stamps and envelopes—long, important-looking envelopes—and stammered apologetically to Millie, "Honey, Poppa thought it'd help you if you learned to type envelopes, too. Reckon you you'll have to do that, too, when y'get a job. Poor old man," he swallowed painfully, "he came 'round selling these envelopes. You know how 'tis. So I had to buy 'em." Which was satisfactory to Millie. If she saw through her father, she gave no sign. After all, it was practice, and Mr. Hennessey had said that—though not in just those words.

He had got in the habit of carrying those self-addressed envelopes in his inner pocket where they bulged impressively. And occasionally he would take them out—in the car usually—and smile upon them. This one might be from J. P. Morgan. This one from Henry Ford. And a million-dollar deal involved in each. That narrow, little spinster, who upon his sitting down, had drawn herself away from his contact, was shunning J. Lucius Jones!

Once, led by some sudden, strange impulse, as an outgoing car rumbled up out of the subway, he got out a letter, darted a quick, shamed glance about him, dropped it in an adjacent box, and swung aboard the car, feeling, dazedly, as if he had committed a crime. And the next night he sat in the sitting room quite on edge until Net said suddenly, "Look here, a real important letter come today for you, Pa. Here 'tis. What you s'pose it says," and he reached out a hand that trembled. He made brief explanation. "Advertisement, hon. Thas'al."

They came quite frequently after that, and despite the fact that he knew them by heart, he read them slowly and carefully, rustling the sheet, and making inaudible, intelligent comments. He was, in these moments, pathetically earnest.

Monday, as he went about his janitor's duties, he composed in his mind the final letter from J. P. Morgan that would consummate a big business deal. For days now letters had passed between them. J. P. had been at first quite frankly uninterested. He had written tersely and briefly. He wrote glowingly of the advantages of a pact between them. Daringly he argued in terms of billions. And at last J. P. had written his next letter would be decisive. Which next letter, this Monday, as he trailed about the office building, was writing itself on his brain.

That night Millie opened the door for him. Her plain face was transformed. "Poppa—Poppa, I got a job! Twelve dollars a week to start with! Isn't that *swell!*"

He was genuinely pleased. "Honey, I'm glad. Right glad," and went up the stairs unsuspecting.

He ate his supper hastily, went down into the cellar to see about his fire, returned and carefully tidied up, informing his reflection in the bathroom mirror. "Well, J. Lucius, you c'n expect that final letter any day now."

He entered the sitting room. The phonograph was playing. Daisy was singing lustily. Strange. Net was talking animatedly to Millie, busy with needle and thread over a neat, little frock. His wild glance darted to the table. The pretty, little centerpiece, the bowl and wax flowers all neatly arranged: the typewriter gone from its accustomed place. It seemed an hour before he could speak. He felt himself trembling. Went hot and cold.

"Millie—your typewriter's—gone!"

She made a deft little in and out movement with her needle. "It's the eighth, you know. When the man came today for the money, I sent it back. I won't need it no more now! The money's on the mantelpiece, Poppa."

"Yeh," he muttered. "All right."

He sank down in his chair, fumbled for the paper, found it. Net said, "Your poppa wants to read. Stop your noise, Daisy."

She obediently stopped both her noise and the phonograph, took up her book, and became absorbed. Millie went on with her sewing in placid anticipation of the morrow. Net immediately began to nod, gave a curious snort, slept.

Silence. That crowded in on him, engulfed him. It blurred his vision, dulled his brain. Vast, white, impenetrable. . . . His ears strained for the old, familiar sound. And silence beat upon them. . . . The words of the evening paper jumbled together. He read: J. P. Morgan goes—

It burst upon him. Blinded him. His hands groped for the bulge beneath his coat. Why this—this was the end! The end of those great moments—the end of everything! Bewildering pain tore through him. He clutched at his heart and felt, almost, the jagged edges drive into his hand. A lethargy swept down upon him. He could not move, nor utter sound. He could not pray, nor curse.

Against the wall of that silence, J. Lucius Jones crashed and died.

Prologue to a Life

In 1896, Luke Kane had met and married Lily Bemis. He had been very much in love with her. And she had literally fallen at his feet, stumbling over his bicycle, lying flat before the back door, and sprawling before him, her full skirts bellowing about her, and quite all of the calves of her legs showing.

Luke, in an instant, was out of the kitchen, and had gathered the hired girl in his arms, and was cursing his bicycle and soothing her in the same breath.

She was small and soft. Though her face was hidden against his breast, he saw that her arms were golden, and her dark hair wavy and long.

"Is that your old bicycle?" Lily asked tearfully. "You're fixin' to kill somebody."

"Ain't I the biggest fool!" he agreed.

She got herself out of his arms and, sitting down on the steps, she tried to do things with her clothes and hair.

But he was staring into her eyes.

"How long you been working for Miz Trainor?"

"I've seen you before," she told him. "Lots."

"Yeh? Don't you speak to nobody?"

"Gentlemen to whom I been introduced. Oh, yes."

"I'm somebody 'round these parts," he boasted. "Ever heard of Manda Kane?"

"Sure. We get our fancy cakes from her when we're having parties and things."

"I'm her son," he informed her, proudly. "I been up here delivering. My name's Luke."

"Yeh?" Her eyes were bright with interest. "Mine's Lily Bemis."

"Come from the South?"

"Born there. Yes. But I came up with the Mitchells when they came. That's been five years. But then old Mrs. Mitchell died, and the two girls got married. I never cared much for old Mister Mitchell, so I came on to Springfield. 'Cause Mamie Cole went on to Boston and said I could take her place here. I knew Miz Trainor was good and all, and didn't have no small children. So I sorta thought I'd try it. Gee, I'm young and everything. If I don't like it here, I can travel on."

He plumped down beside her.

"Listen," he said softly, "I hope you'll like it here."

Her eyes were two slits and dangerous.

"Why—Luke?"

" 'Cause then," he said huskily, "you'll stay. And I can be likin' you."

She bent to him suddenly. "You're the funniest coon. Your eyes are blue as blue."

"Yeh. It's funny, black as I am," he said modestly.

She put two slim yellow fingers against his cheek. "You're not black at all. You're just dark brown. I think you're a beautiful color."

His eyes that were like a deep sea glowed with gratitude. "I sorta like yours the best."

"Oh, me, I'm not much!" she said carelessly. "What makes you think I'm pretty?"

"I dunno. You're so little and soft and sweet. And you ain't so shy."

She was instantly on her feet. "If you think I'm bold, sitting out here with you, when we never been introduced—"

"Looka here!" He was on his feet, too. "Women's the funniest things. I'm liking you 'cause you're not like everyone else, and you're bristling! I can have any girl in this little old town of Springfield I want. But I'm not making up to any 'cause I ain't found none that suited me. My mother's orful particular. We got a name in this town. You're the first girl I'm liking, and you cutting up!"

But she was inside of the screen door now, and he saw her hook it. She came very close to it, but she was careful not to press her nose against it.

"Listen, Mr. Kane, I like you, too. I want to meet you proper. What would folks say if they knew we met like this? Me with two buttons off my shirtwaist and my hair net torn? But tomorrow's prayer meeting night, and I'm going. I'm an A.M.E. If that's your church, too, you come on over. I'll get Miz Hill to get Reverend Hill to introduce us proper."

He gulped. "Can I bring you home after?"

She considered it. "Maybe I'll let you be keeping my company," she promised.

There followed a whirlwind month of courtship. Lily had a hundred moods. They were a hundred magnets drawing Luke.

She did not love him. Deep within her was an abiding ambition to see her race perpetuated. Though she felt that her talents were of a high order, she knew she would escape greatness through her lack of early training. And she had the mother instinct. Thus she would rather bear a clever child. In her supreme egoism she believed the male seed would only generate it. She would not conceive of its becoming blood of her child's blood, and flesh of her child's flesh. Men were chiefly important as providers. She would have married any healthy man with prospects. . . .

Late in the summer, Lily and Luke were married. Lily didn't want a church wedding. They were married in Reverend Hill's front parlor. Miz Hill and Manda Kane stood up with them. Ma Manda was tearful. She was losing her only son to a low-voiced yellow woman. She knew the inescapable bond of soft skin and hair.

Lily, standing quietly by Luke's side, felt a vast contentment. She respected the man she was marrying. She faced the future calmly. She only wanted their passion to be strong enough to yield a smart and sturdy son.

Later that day they were on a train that was bound, by the back door route, for Boston. They sat in the coach with their little belongings piled all about them. Luke made sheep's eyes at Lily and felt very proud. He was wondering whether it was obvious that they had just been married. He rather wanted the phlegmatic passengers to admire his golden bride.

He drew her round dark head onto his shoulder, and caught his hand in the tendrils of her hair.

"Guess I'm the happiest man in the world, the proudest."

"Ho, you're not proud of me!"

"You are the moon and the stars, Lily, and the bright sun."

She twisted her head and looked deep into his kind eyes.

"Luke, do you love me as much as that?"

"You watch me," he told her. "I'll bring you the world on a silver platter. Lily, I'll make you a queen."

She rubbed her little hand up and down his arm.

"How much money we got now, Luke?"

"Enough," he boasted, "to live like millionaires for maybe a week in Boston."

"Luke," she said earnestly, "we're not going back. Ever."

He was pleased. "Our honeymoon will last wherever we are."

She was almost impatient. "It ain't that!"

"What in the name of God—"

"Let's eat," she said, and dug about for Ma Manda's hamper.

She put the linen napkins on her lap and laid out the sandwiches, licking her fingers when the mayonnaise or jam or butter had oozed through.

"Chicken," she announced, "and ham, and I reckon this is po'k, Luke!"

He balanced the coffee on his knee. "There's cups somewheres, Lily."

Presently, they were hungrily eating, Luke almost wolfishly.

"We've caught our train," said Lily, with a little nervous laugh. He was making her rather ill.

He took a great gulp of coffee.

"Always was a fast eater. Father before me was."

Her hand tightened over his. "You could die," she said with real concern, "of indigestion."

He ducked his head suddenly and kissed her wrist.

"But, I'll make you your million before I do."

Thus she let him go back to his eating, and she gave him an almost indulgent smile.

Once in the vast South Station they stood for a moment, bewildered. They both felt newly married and foolishly young. Lily had a sudden sense of panic. Suppose Ma Manda never forgave them. Suppose Luke died or deserted her. Suppose she was never able to bear a child.

And then she saw Mamie Cole coming toward them. She flew into her arms.

"The blushing bride and groom!" cried Mamie, and offered her cheek to Luke.

"Well, it's nice to see you," said Luke, rather shyly after kissing her.

"I'm only off for an hour," she explained, "so we better get up to the flat. I got you three real nice rooms, Lily, in front."

"Three—?" echoed Luke. His voice fell in disappointment. "I kinda thought—a hotel—"

"Luke!" Lily caught his arm fast. Her brown eyes were dark with pleading. "Luke, it's not a hotel room I want. It's a home."

He asked in bewilderment: "Here—in Boston?"

"Listen, we're not going back. We're laying our cornerstone here. There's far and away more business in Boston than in Springfield. Just you see. I want my husband. Luke, I want my home. I want my—son. Back home we'd have to live with your mother. She's got big house. And, Luke, I can't get along with no women. I almost hate women. They're not honest. They're weaklings. They care about cheap things. God knows you're going to find it hard to live with me—and *you* love me. I don't want nothing but my man and my son. That's me, Luke."

He had the most terrible longing to take her in his arms.

"Your man and your son? Lily, my girl, you've got your man. By God, you'll have your son. . . ."

In 1898 Lily gave birth to twins.

They were boys, with Lily's soft yellow skin and fine brown eyes and all about them the look of her, somehow. Jamie and John. They were completely sons of Lily. To her they were gods.

Luke had been getting on in a fair sort of way before the twins were born. He had opened a tiny lunch stand in the South End. Lily had been helping with the cooking. After a barely perceptible start, business had picked up nicely. Luke could cook almost as well as his mother. And Lily, growing prettier and plumper every day, and rapidly learning badinage, was an obvious attraction.

She worked until the week before the twins were born. Then Ma Manda, in panicky self-reproach, hurried on to Boston, saw to it that a proper girl was hired, packed Lily off to the New England Hospital, and looked about at houses. She decided on a red-brick one on a quiet street in Brookline, and bought it through a profiteering agent. She ordered atrocious furniture on the credit plan (Lily returned it piece by piece later), and awaited the birth of her grandchild in grim satisfaction.

To the triumphant Lily the world existed for two golden babies. These were her lives to shape and guide. These were her souls to expand. She, with her constant faith, must quicken their geniuses.

So the years passed. Jamie and John were three and able to read. Then John at four could bang out a harmony on the upright piano. Jamie at six was doing third grade lessons. . . .

They were nine. And Lily's pride, and joy, and love, and life.

33

They had not cried in their cradle. They had never been jealous of each other. They had given her and Luke wholeheartedly their love. They wrote regularly and beautifully to their grandmother. Their teachers adored them. Despite their talents, they were manly, and popular with children. They had never been ill. They were growing like weeds. John, at the Boston Conservatory, had been singled out as an extraordinary pupil. His little sensitive face had stared out of many daily papers. Jamie, in the seventh grade, leading his class, was the marvel of his school. He could solve the mathematical problems of high school students. He could also discuss his future with calm assurance. . . .

Lily was thirty-two now, and a housewife. Occasionally she swept into the shop which had been yearly enlarged until it comprised three wide windows and twenty-two tables. The doctors and lawyers who frequented the place would rise and eagerly greet her. She was completely complacent. She was fat, but her skin was firm and soft to Luke's touch. Her eyes were clear and content. There were always tender anecdotes about her boys, Jamie and John. The realization of her dreams, the growing fulfillment of her hopes. The latent genius quickening.

She walked in peace. She knew ten years of utter harmony. She was therefore totally unprepared for any swift disruption.

In 1908 the twins were ten. Though they were young men now with certain futures, they were still very charming, and went swimming or skating with the boys on their block whenever they were called for. . . .

It was on the last day of March, going all too meekly like a lamb, that Lily, in her kitchen, making the raisin-stuffed bread pudding the twins adored, sat down suddenly with her hand to her throat, and her heart in a lump against it. She was alone, but she knew she was not ill. She made no attempt to cry out to a neighbor. She could see, as clearly as though she stood at the pond's edge, the twins, their arms tight about each other, crashing through the treacherous ice, making no outcry, their eyes wide with despair, dragged swiftly down, brought up again to break her heart forever, and Jamie's red scarf, that Ma Manda had knitted for him, floating. . . .

Within twenty minutes three frightened children brought her the news. Two days later their bodies were found. Lily identified them in a dim dank morgue.

The twins lay together in a satin-lined casket in the flower-filled parlor. They were very lovely in their last sleep. The undertaker's art had restored them and enhanced them. There was about their mouths that too exquisite beauty that death brings to the mouths of children who die in pain. Dead, they were more similar than living. And it was James who looked like John. . . .

James and John were Lily. James and John were dead. Only the fact that she had watched her heart and soul flung into the earth with her sons kept Lily's body alive. She was spiritually a dead woman walking in the patent hope of physical release. There was no youth in her anymore. Her body was no longer firm, but flabby. Her eyes were lusterless. Her lips that had always been a little too thin were a line now that went sharply down at each corner. And the voice that had bantered richly with her boys, that had thrilled like a girl's at the intimate bass of a man, was quavering, and querulous, and, all too often, still. . . .

Ma Manda stayed on. Lily wanted it. They were held by their mutual bereavement. The twins, dead, were more potent than ever they could have been, living. Now Lily and Ma Manda knew there was nothing these boys could not have done, no world they would not have conquered, had they lived.

Ma Manda one weekend returned to Springfield, sold her house and the two fine mares, and her business and her lease to a prosperous German. Her only sentimentalities were two ribboned packets of letters.

Luke was sorry that the twins were dead, but his heart was not broken. Lily was his world. While she lived there was hope, and love, and life. He had no real conception of the genius of the twins. He had always thought of them as smart little boys. Now death had shattered their spell for him. He even wondered vaguely why it did not occur to Lily she might have another child.

One night, after a silent meal that Luke had cooked himself to tempt the too light appetite of his women, Lily rose abruptly from the supper table, and with the knuckles of her clenched fists showing white, said in a voice that she tried to keep steady: "Luke, I'm sleeping in the twins' room tonight. I—I guess I'll go up now. G'night, Ma Manda. 'Night Luke."

An hour later, when he softly tried the door, it was locked.

A year passed. Lily, a little mad in her constant communion with her dead, had grown somehow hauntingly lovely, with her loosened hair always tangled, her face thin and pale and exquisite, and her eyes large and brightly knowing. Now she was voluble with Ma Manda, though there were no notes in her voice. She kept up a continual stream of pathetic reminiscences. And she went about her house with her hands outstretched briefly to caress some memorial to her boys.

Ma Manda indulged her. To her there was only beauty in Lily's crazy devotion. She had loved Luke's golden sons more than she had ever loved Luke. As with Lily, throughout their growing, they had become her sole reality. With the accident's idea of duty, she kept their memory fresh, her sorrow keen. She went regularly to a Baptist church and wailed when the preacher harangued the dead.

And always for Luke, in his starved normal passion, suprisingly not the brute, Lily's light body was a golden mesh.

Lily had sat by an open window, staring up at the stars, her bare feet on a chilled floor, her nightgown fluting in the wind. Presently she had begun to sneeze. Soon her eyes and her nose were running. when she got into Jamie's white bed, she felt a great wave engulf her. In the morning, she was very ill.

Lily felt that she was dying. And she was afraid to die. She hated pain. She had given no thought to death before the death of her twins. After that she had thought of her going as only a dreamless sleeping and a waking with her sons. Now there was something in her that was making her last hours torture. And a cough that tore her from the hot pillows and started that jerk and pull in her heart. Sometimes her breath was a shudder that shook her body.

In the first few hours of the third night, she clutched at Ma Manda and stared up at her with eyes so full of piteous appeal that Ma Manda said sharply and involuntarily: "Lily, my child, you better let Luke in. He's a great one for healing. There's the power of the Almighty in his hands."

Lily made a little gesture of acquiescence. Ma Manda went softly, fumbling in her tears.

Luke bent over Lily. His blue eyes burned. They were dark and deep and glowing. She felt her own eyes caught in them. Felt her senses drowning. He flung one hand up to the sky, the fingers apart and unbending. The other he pressed against her chest till his flesh and her flesh were one.

He was exalted and inspired. The muscles leaped in his arm. He was trembling and black and mysterious.

"Lily, my girl, God's going to help you. God in His heaven's got to hear my prayer! Just put your faith in me, my darling. I got my faith in Him. I got a gift from the heavenly Father. Praise His name! Lily, my Lily, I got the power to heal!"

Strength surged out of him—went swinging down through the arm upraised, flashed through his straining body, then shot down and tingled his fingers which had melted into her breasts. They were like rays, destroying. Five streams of life, pouring into her sick veins, fierce, tumultuous, until the poison and the pain burst into rivulets of sweat that ran swift and long down her quivering body, and presently left her washed clean and quiet and very tired.

Then Luke's words came in a rush, in the voice of one who had fought a hard fight, or run a long race, yet deep and tremblingly beautiful.

'God, be praised! God, the Maker, we humbly thank Thee! Thou heard! Thou heard! Thou gave me strength to heal! O God, this poor child—my Lily—she's well! She can rise and take up her bed and walk! O God, Thou art the Father of all living! Thou art life! Thou art love! Thou art love! Thou art love!!!"

He slumped down on his knees and burst into wild tears. His head went bumping against Lily's breast.

In her relief and gratitude and wonderment, she felt her first compassion for her husband. In his weakness she was strong. She was a mother.

He clung to her. He was a man sick with passion.

Presently she said: "Lie with me, Luke," and drew him up into her arms.

For Lily, and for Luke, and for Ma Manda, after a week or two, that night crowded out of their consciousness might have never been. Lily went back to her inner life; Ma Manda to the spiritual needs of her daughter-in-law and the physical needs of her son; Luke to the old apathetic content in Lily's apparent contentment.

But one Sunday morning as he lay staring at a bright patch of sunlight on the wall and hearing faintly the bells of the Mission Church without emotion, the door creaked sharply.

Lily came in and stood at the foot of his bed.

He sat up in real surprise and made a vague gesture toward his bathrobe.

Her eyes were level into his and full of scorn. Her face was pale and proud. Her lips were a thin twist of contempt.

She was so lovely and so terrible in her fury that he caught his breath.

He scuttled down to the foot of the bed and gripped her wrist tight.

"Lily, you sick? For God's sake, what ails you?"

She flung her arm free. 'I'm going to have a child. Another child! Well, it's yours. I've borne my babies. And I've buried them. This is your little black brat, d'you hear? You can keep it or kill it. If it wasn't for my babies in heaven, I'd get rid of it with the deadliest poison. But I can't damn my soul to hell for a wretched child that may be born dead. And if it lives"—her voice was a wail—"I curse it to your despair!"

For the first time since his childhood, Luke flung himself down full length on the bed and cried. . . .

In the months that followed, Ma Manda and Luke, in their terrific watchfulness, had a nine months' travail, too.

Lily's child was born on a spring morning in a labor so fierce that both of them, after hours of struggle, lay utterly spent; the child in the big white crib that had been the twins', the other, for the last time, on her own great mahogany bed.

Lily was conscious and calm. She was dying, as she had wanted to die, painlessly. She felt no curiosity about her baby. She had heard a sharp whisper, "It's a girl,' which she had half expected, and had turned her face from the sound of it to summon all of her strength for a bitter chuckle.

Presently Luke came to stare down at her. His eyes were filled with great desperation. He, too, had forgotten the new baby. Lily was dying.

"Lily"—his voice was deep and tender—"just put your faith in God. My Father has never failed me. He'll pull you through."

She was quietly exalted. "I have come through."

"Lily, I love you. Don't act that way. Put your hand in mine. Let me help you, my darling."

His hand went out to her. She saw the fingers stiffen, straighten, and the muscles pulling in his arm.

But she made no move.

"Are you too weak? Let me raise you hand. The power of God is in me. It leaps like a young ram. Only touch my, Lily!"

Ma Manda, kneeling at the foot of the bed, wrung her hands and wailed, "Only touch him, Lily."

Her eyes were wide and seeking. Her mouth was tremulous and beautiful. With a tremendous effort she raised herself up from her pillow. Her braids went lopping over her breasts.

Her hands went out, slowly, and gropingly. Luke waited, quivering, his heart in his mouth.

But then she sighed sharply. Her hands clasped tightly. Her eyes were passionate. Her face was glorious.

It was Ma Manda who scrambled to her feet and laid her back on the pillow and knew that she was dead, and gently brushed the lids over her eyes. In the instant when her soul leaped to the sun, the new baby whimpered, once, then again, and was still. Luke turned toward it with a furious oath. He bent over the crib and looked down at the tiny dark bundle that was scarcely anything at all, with its quiet hands and shut eyes.

In the sudden hope that it had died, he put his hand over its heart.

The baby opened its eyes. They were blue—as deeply blue as his own, but enormous and infinitely sad. It was their utter despairing that moved him. He felt for this child a possessive tenderness such as the twins had never inspired. It was a woman-child. He understood her frailty.

So he knelt and slapped her face hard, and breathed into her mouth and cried out *Lily! Lily!* naming her. He urged the strength in his spatulate fingers to quicken the beat of her heart. He prayed, "God, be merciful!" again and again.

She broke into a lusty wail and fell into a normal sleep, with the tears still wet on her cheeks.

Lily was dead, and Lily was not dead. A mother is the creator of life. And God cannot die.

Cook

Miss Lavinia Williams had grown past middle age in the kitchen of the Tuckers. She had come as cook when Blake was five, and now he was twenty-five.

Cook was colored a beautiful shade of warm brown. Her grandmother face was quite unlined. Her dark eyes, behind the gold-rimmed glasses, did not twinkle, but they were kind. Her sweet unsmiling mouth talked common sense. But it did not talk very much. Mostly it hummed sad slave songs. Her soft hair with its touches of gray was parted down the center and rolled in a neat knob. There were little curls in her nape, and sometimes over steam, a fuzz on her forehead. She was middling tall and middling broad. Her hands and feet were large.

None of the Tuckers knew much about cook. To the elders, she was a colored person quieter than most, and never giving trouble, nor asking for more money. They didn't like Negroes, particularly, and had no interest in cook's inner life. They only wanted fidelity and servility, and both they got.

But Blake knew this about her, that she had a house in Harlem, to which she went whenever she could, and where she was now going for over Sunday, since he and his parents were spending the day with Grandfather.

He fancied it was a boarding house that she had bought with her savings to keep her declining years in comfort. For the Tuckers discharged old servants without pension or pity.

It was autumn. The oak in the backyard had one orange branch of great beauty. Sometimes a few dry leaves fell on the bulkhead. There were not so many birds. Two very tiny squirrels played happily all day long. The motionless cat lay and looked at them. At night the harvest moon rode swiftly over the sky, more luminous and lovely with each hour. The city stars shone bright for city stars.

Cook was ready. The bus left at ten. It was nine. Mr. Tucker and Blake were at their respective offices. Mrs. Tucker was downtown to catch a Saturday sale. The second girl had gone to market. Cook had made up the menus. There was only dinner that evening and breakfast Sunday. She would leave New York Sunday night and be back in Boston in time for breakfast Monday.

She was alone in the house. She had tidied her room and drawn the shades so that the afternoon sun would not shine on the mirror. At two o'clock each bright afternoon she came upstairs and drew her shades. She was careful of the fine old-fashioned bureau, not because it was Mrs. Tucker's, but because it was beautiful.

Cook came downstairs carrying the overnight bag her niece had given her last Christmas. She was dressed in dark blue and a becoming hat that Mrs. Tucker had got through with. In the bag, in addition to changes of clothing, were a Bible, a modest insurance policy, and a packet of bank notes of the higher denominations worth more than two thousand dollars.

She got her lunch box out of the Frigidaire. There were two minced ham sandwiches, two of egg and olive, two of peanut butter, and a bar of chocolate with nuts that Blake had given her two days ago, and which she had saved for this journey.

She carried a collapsible drinking cup, for she felt it improper to suck tonic through a straw. And she could not bring herself to drink from a glass that the soda jerk simply rinsed in a little clear water.

One last thing, her umbrella in the back vestibule. This she got. And this morning she would go out the front door, because the back door did not lock of itself, and there was no one to lock it after her. She quitted the kitchen and went through the halls. The house was quietly elegant, but she was unimpressed. There was nothing in sight she wanted or did not have.

There was quite a walk to the car line. A cruising cabby accosted her, but she stomped on stolidly. Why should she pay a dollar to go the identical distance she could go for a dime? Money was got by the sweat of one's brow; or at least the dependable part of it.

The bus was on time. Presently the seats were all full, with cook in the uncomfortable one over the wheel, where almost inevitably, as if by design, except that there is no prejudice in Boston, the colored passenger is put.

She leaned back and relaxed. She was one of these people who never get used to travel. It was always an enormous strain until she was settled in her seat, and it began to be a strain again when she was near her destination.

The driver came to hoist up baggage. He bent to cook's valise, but she gripped it firmly.

He argued mildly. "You gotta keep it outta the aisle, lady."

She put it between herself and her seatmate. The lady was Jewish and friendly and did not mind. Later they would share the lunch box, and the Jewish lady would pay for the pop.

But for the moment there were no words between them. Cook, with the bus in motion, knew that she would nod. It was funny to see her catch herself out of sleep, and then slide back again, and again jerk awake, until finally and soundly she slept, with her hat awry.

It was noon when she roused. The passengers were piling out for refreshments. The Jewish lady's "Poddun me!" awoke her. She took her bag and her lunch box and followed her.

They both talked with little grunts and soft groans and vast gestures.

It was early evening when cook reached New York. She knew the way from bus stop to subway. The push and bustle bothered her, but did not overly confuse her. Soon she was through the turnstiles and in the crowded train, hanging on to a greasy strap, and peering anxiously at the flying platforms.

At the 135th Street stop she got out, walked one block west and four blocks north, and there she was on Strivers' Row, the 200 block of 139th Street.

She stopped before an imposing house, mounted the stone steps, rang the bell beneath the doctor's plate, and waited in warm anticipation.

A black maid opened the door and beamed broadly.

"Welcome home, Miss Williams!"

"It's nice to see you, Annie! All you all well?"

"Well, Henry was having a baby, and it made him nervous, but it's twins, and they're doing nicely, and so is Henry."

Somebody shouted down, "Aunt Viney, Aunt Viney! Bless your old heart!"

It was young Lestra. She flew downstairs and gathered Viney in her arms.

"I met two trains, and I've been upstairs listening for taxis. Did you fly, funny woman?"

"I came by bus and took the subway. All told two dollars and five cents."

One might have said she smiled sardonically.

Lestra laughed, and they went upstairs with their arms around each other. Annie put the umbrella in the stand and followed with the bag. She thought Miss Williams was very eccentric.

Dell Clement in a becoming negligee met them under the flattering hall light. She was beautifully imposing as the house. Education had worked its usual miracle. She and Viney were sisters. But Viney, the elder, had slaved and saved to send Adele through grade school and high school and college. And now Dell stood in her mellow yellow loveliness as unlike Viney, her sister, as Mrs. Tucker was unlike Viney, her cook.

"Dear, dear Viney!" she exclaimed, with an elegance that was becoming in her drawing room, but before Viney was simply putting on airs. For the first duty of the gracious is to put the awkward at ease. And Viney was always uncomfortable around Dell.

She offered, "Well, you look well, Dell!" and dared not disarrange that crimson mouth, and brushed Dell's bloodless cheek.

"'Age does not wither nor custom stale—'. Don't gape, Annie. Viney, let her have your things, and come along with me. I want a visit with you before the guests arrive."

She stood divested and dismayed. "You all having a party?"

Lestra was resentful, too. "Darling, Dad and I begged her to postpone it when we knew you were coming. But there's a bird in town who's being partied. And you know Dell."

She was unperturbed. "If someone asks you to play tonight, Lestra, mind you be nice about it."

"I hate playing for a parcel of drunks. They only ask to be polite, and nobody pays attention. And when I play, I sweat blood, and I hate to sweat blood to no purpose."

But Dell was disdainful. "You're only putting on because Viney's here to take your part. Come along with me, Viney. I want to rest my face before the evening starts."

They went into Dell's bedroom. It was in excellent taste, without frills and with subdued lights.

"Ah, but perhaps you want to rest your face, too? Shall we go into your room? Or will the chaise longue do?"

"It'll do," said Viney, going to sit bolt upright on the edge of it. "I had a good sleep coming. And I don't know how to rest my face unless you mean by yawning."

Dell, lying flat on the bed, looked at her critically. "Viney, why is it you haven't a line or wrinkle, and you're fifty? And you've worked like a dog all your life, and I've been a lady since you sent me to boarding school when I was seven, and you were seventeen, and already a cook in the white folks' kitchen."

She said without sadness, "Because I was so tired after supper that I went straight to bed and straight to sleep, while the rest of the world was sitting up studying."

Dell lit a cigarette with a lovely gesture. "Did you ever envy me, my poor Viney?"

"When I sent you to boarding school, I didn't. You were so lost looking and little. And then when I sent you up north to college, I was glad you was getting out of the South. And when you married

Neil, I just couldn't envy no woman no man. Not that Neil ain't the nicest, and I was happy to help him get started. But I guess I'm a born old maid.

"But when Lestra was born, and I come north to see her, I cried. I loved her so much I almost hated her because she wasn't mine. I'd had something to do with everything else, but I hadn't had nothing to do with that. And she was the first and only thing I'd ever really wanted."

"Darling, Lestra loves you as much as she loves me."

"All this house means to me is that it's a roof over her head. I guess that's how come God gave me this power to foresee. I don't never selfishly use it. I got a considerable sum in my suitcase right now. And I reckon before morning the Lord'll direct me how best to bestow it."

Dell got terribly excited. She sat up straight. Her face was no longer resting.

"Viney, have you hit the number again? Good God, when? For how much?"

Viney enjoyed it. "Well, now, Dell, I guess it's too late for you to give a more elaborate party. And what else do you ever want money for? If you'd followed Lestra's mind and put off your doings, I reckon we could have scraped up a hundred or so for a fancy frock."

Dell was utterly dismayed. She made a disdainful gesture. "And I've already worn that wretched dress four times. And there was such a bargain at a shop on 57th Street. Ninety-eight dollars, and too too divine." She cast a sidelong glance at Viney. "But the Carters' dinner is Wednesday."

"Well, said Viney indulgently, "if the Lord directs me to make you a present, it'll be a party frock."

Dell was satisfied. She drew a long breath and settled back. Viney saw with surprise that her face did seem to be resting. There was even something pathetic about her. She was like a child who has been appeased with the promise of a toy. And out of her loins had come the miracle, Lestra, who was so removed from trivialities. Well, Lestra was of Dell's body, but her soaring spirit was of God.

"Viney, what on earth did you dream this time?"

"Well, seems like I saw a man standing on a precipice like he was fixing to fall. So I started running toward him. And when I come up close I called, and he turned and it was Neil.

"Well, I just stopped dead, and I said, 'Oh, oh!' and I woke myself up saying it. And there I lay with my mouth wide open. And that was another o."

"ooo," said Dell. "What a crazy number."

"Dell, I hit it just the same. Next day. And happen the Merivales was leaving that morning. They'd been the Tuckers' guests two weeks. And Mrs. Merivale, she come and give me five dollars. And, of course, that was the Lord's direction. Because all along the Merivales had been planning to leave Saturday. And here they was going unexpected Friday."

"Wouldn't your Lord like it if you sometimes played with your salary?"

"I ain't a gambler. I've seen too many folks go clean fool playing them numbers every day. Me, I follows my dreams, and plays with change I pick up here and there. If I don't get a hit but once in six months, I'm satisfied. I was cooking for my living before numbers was ever thought of. And I ain't going to sit down now and let 'em support me."

"Well, darling, go on about its being Friday and the five dollars."

"Well, seemed like I'd never get through serving breakfast. First there was one thing wanted, then another. Working for second-class white folks! Lord, lord! But finally I was free with my table cleared and my dishes stacked. And I run on down to the cobbler's. Sam is a right enough bootblack there, but it's mostly a blind, and he does more business than Toney.

"It was past twelve already and Sam leaves around one to collect the rest of his numbers. You'd be surprised at the parcel of white folks that play with him. Why, our policeman hit three times last month for fifty cents each time."

Dell cried out impatiently, "Viney, don't talk around! So you put five dollars on ooo, and oh, my God, you must have over two thousand dollars! Viney, where's that money right now?"

"In my bag 'long with my papers. I always carry my insurance papers with me 'cause you never can tell where death'll overtake you. And I want whoever finds me to see I've got enough for a proper burial. I've lived decent and I'll lie in my coffin likewise."

"Viney, will you march yourself to your room and get that money and bring it here to me to put in my safe? My God, you know a hundred niggers will be running amuck here tonight. And there isn't one of them who couldn't use two thousand dollars."

Viney escaped rather gratefully. There just wasn't an atmosphere of righteousness in Dell's room. She was not at all sure that Dell's thoughts dwelt much on her Maker. She understood how white folks could forget God. They had so many other things to study. But colored folks were too few generations removed from sorrow songs and slavery. How could they forget the God of deliverance? Why, she well remembered when Dell would boast that Lestra had never heard a spiritual sung or been inside a Negro church.

Viney's room was at the farthest end of the hall. Adjacent was a French door that opened onto a little balcony. Not until she had almost reached it was she aware that the door was open and a man stood in a silhouette.

"Oh," she cried. "Oh, my goodness!" and her mouth was agape.

The figure turned and came forward. It was Neil in tuxedo with both hands outstretched.

"Lavinia! I was waiting to welcome you. I didn't want to disturb you and Dell."

He kissed her cheek and pressed her hand warmly.

Viney fluttered. "You gave me a start, but I'm real glad to see you. Let's go in my room and sit down a spell. I want a good look at you."

Neil locked the door and followed her into the cheerful room that Dell had told the decorator was to be her elderly mother's; and was therefore not a terrifying place with newfangled furniture, but was instead expensively arranged with fine old-fashioned pieces.

There was a dreamy light over everything. Viney sank into a rocker, and Neil went to stretch his long body in a wide-armed chair.

He was still alert and lean. Lestra had got his sensitive hands and head of wild curls. His eyes had seen much suffering and mirrored it. He was a very beautiful pale ivory man who had never been a gay boy, and had loved no woman but Dell, and Dell not very much, having loved humanity too largely, and not any one woman's glowing body.

Tonight his mouth was tired, and his hands were making his hair more unruly than ever. Now he slumped forward and stated unseeingly at the overnight bag at his feet.

"Neil, you worried 'bout some patient?" asked Viney gently.

"Why do people go on having children? Why in God's name don't they stop it? Babies are born, and babies die, and why should they live so briefly? Suppose my Lestra had been stillborn, and her gift gone with her? And there are other infant Lestras, dead with their songs in their silent throats. Oh, God, Negro children die in droves, and they are all our hope."

"You're a great doctor, Neil, and you heal with love as well as learning. So if you can't save 'em nobody can. And there ain't no use your worrying."

"I ought to take it up with your God. He's known to keep an eye on sparrows. I wish He'd stretch out a hand to these little blackbirds."

"My God is ever mindful of the least of His flock. And the children of Ham ain't least. The meek will inherit the earth. And the Ethiop will wipe out his oppressors."

He smiled at her unshakable faith. It made his face softer. He straightened up and stuck his hands in his pockets.

"Well, I'd like to see some quicker action. I hate to wait for the coming of the Ethiop. Couldn't I take it up with your God right now? I say, man to man, our Father in Heaven, give me a hospital to give to the sick children. For I cannot bear any longer the lame and the halt and the blind."

He swung out his feet as he settled back. The overnight bag toppled over with a bang.

"Well, I didn't expect such a speedy reply!"

But Viney was ashen and reverent.

"Don't mock! Don't dast! God has answered!"

He looked at her searchingly. "What does He say?"

"I hear Him like He was speaking inside me. Here is My House. Take it." She said apologetically, "I reckon that's a parable."

But Neil jumped up and began striding up and down. His shadow leaped along the wall. It was gigantic.

"Oh, my God, Lavinia, don't you see? This house. This fine big house. Oh, my god. I can make it a fine big hospital. Here in this room there'll be four little beds and four little boys. Lavinia! But this is your room. This is your house."

She said very simply, "Take it."

He halted before her and stared down at her hard.

"Your God is human," he said humbly.

But he began to tear about again.

"Lavinia, you're not a young woman. And there's Dell, who's got used to this way of living. And Lestra, who will never go to business."

"About me, Neil, I'm the kind what dies in harness. I ain't one that'll ever be a dependent. And my little insurance ain't life. It's an endowment, come due in fifteen years. And I reckon with careful managing I can make it last till the chariot swings low, with enough left, God willing, for a funeral with flowers.

"And Dell, she's my own sister, but she ain't the type to shed tears about. I reckon you'll always have a hundred for a party frock. And as long as you're a doctor, she'll be a deity. And there ain't nothing else she worries about.

"And Lestra, as long as she has her piano, you can give her dry bread and water, and she'd still be fed of the spirit wine and wafer."

Neil stopped his walking and leaned against the wall. His face was young and full of faith.

"Few men see their dreams come true, and mine was a very vast vision. Monday I've a million things to do. I think I can get hold of a thousand dollars. The few I have are tied up in that bank."

"Neil, there's twenty-five hundred dollars in that bag."

"What—? Lavinia! Have you won again? And you'd give it to me? In God's name, who are you?"

"I'm the lowliest of the flock. I'm a servant to second-class white folks"

"I'm a servant, too. Only my humans are called humanity."

The little clock struck the hour tunefully. Neil lagged about.

"This is my last night to be a proper husband. I'll go and be a gracious host, and let you dress. Shan't I send Lestra to help you?"

Viney, left alone, sighed and wriggled her feet. She had been all day in street shoes, and she yearned for her kitchen comforts. And now she must put on her high Cuban heels and go sit in a corner of Dell's drawing room with silly young men saying silly things in affected voices.

She was tired, because there is no hardship to be compared to riding nine hours in a bus. There was also a little gnawing in her stomach. The Jewish lady had eaten largely of her lunch. But even if she hadn't, cold sandwiches at twelve and two are not a hot dinner at six.

Someone knocked at her door.

"Come!" she called.

It was Annie.

"Miss Lestra says please can you come up to her studio if it isn't any trouble?"

Viney got up. "Any company come yet, Annie? I don't want to run into anybody."

"Lordy, no! They're s'pose to come at nine, so the bell'll start ringing good at ten. Guess you'll never get used to New York folks, Miss Williams. I ain't used to 'em myself. T'aint much like down home."

Viney went upstairs to the big attic room that had been converted into a studio for Lestra and the grand piano that she had given her.

She knocked and entered.

"Lestra?"

She sat at her piano in the far end of the attic. A floor lamp made a circle of light around her. The rest of the room was in shadow.

Lestra was now in slender and shimmering white. Her hair that had been carefully combed and brushed was beginning to curl again. It was Neil's magnificent head. She was utterly like him, except that, being darker, she was lovelier.

She struck a chord for the express purpose of startling Viney, then wheeled about and faced her.

"Father says I've got to get out. What's this about a hospital?"

She was severe and aggrieved.

Viney sat down in an uncertain chair.

"Lestra! You know your father never told you to get out like that. I reckon he'll get you all a nice little flat on Sugar Hill."

"And will it have an attic room like this, please tell me? Don't you know, dear aunt, that this is two houses?"

She was not afraid of Lestra. "It'll make a nice big hospital."

Lestra was suddenly as young as she was. "Don't I matter? Is it because Father's proved his genius? But I have potentialities. My hands can work wonders, too. My fingers can perform miracles."

She turned back to her piano, because she was ever too proud to show tears.

"Play something sweet," said Viney complacently. "Lands! I don't hear nothing but jazz, jazz, jazz! Black and his old radio."

But she was yet too troubled. "But Aunt Viney, suppose they

won't let me play after ten? They'd call it 'no noise'! And suppose I feel like playing at one? Oh, God, Oh, God!"

"I declare," said Viney nervously, "you all in this house are forever calling 'Lord, Lord!' and not one of you ever goes inside a church."

"Oh, church! I am God. You are God. Father's God. Only mother is mortal."

"Lestra!" She was wholly aghast.

Lestra swung up, quickly crossed the floor, and knelt at Viney's feet with her fine white frock a silver spray around her.

"Forgive me, darling! I, too, live by faith. But I believe in beauty and fire and truth. And I will be these things. And I will sing them in songs of myself. There is a maestro in Italy. Would God he knew I was on earth."

It was funny. It was solemn and beautiful.

"What is a maestro, lamb?"

"A master."

"Way yonder in Italy? There's a sight of sea between you. That's sure enough one more river to cross."

"Aunt Viney, people go to Europe every day."

"Your pa and ma wouldn't hear of it, with you still in college."

"Father's forgotten I'm on earth, what with his old hospital. And mother would love to tell all the 'dicties she had a daughter studying abroad."

"Lestra, lamb," said Viney helplessly, "all that'd take a heap of money."

"Father says you've got some for him. Can't you spare me enough for my passage? He won't mind. Third class is less than a hundred. And if you'll give me a hundred more to carry me awhile, why if my master believes in my ability, he'll find a way to keep me."

"If your master believes in your ability, my Master will find a way."

There was a burst of blatant music from below.

"Lord," said Viney, scrambling up, "lemme go see 'bout that money."

Lestra got up, too. She was very excited. "I'll go and get drunk to celebrate."

But she was only teasing Viney.

Viney hurried downstairs ahead of her and scuttled past Dell's open door before any of the luxurious ladies could spy her. She possibly knew a few of them by sight and small talk was ever pure agony to her.

She reached her room, locked the door, and drew a long breath of relief. There lay the bag. She fetched her purse from the bureau, got out her key and opened it.

Her nightgown lay on top. It twinkled up at her. She was not surprised to hear it say, Put me on.

Well, if she just loosened her stays and lay across the bed for a minute. Right now they were probably dancing downstairs. She would be in the way, or what was worse, some young man might ask her to dance. When the buffet was served, she'd go down. For Dell might'nt like it if she didn't. Or Neil mightn't like it. Or maybe Lestra mightn't.

But she knew she was not really on their minds in this moment. Not that they loved her less, but there were larger problems of introducing people, and passing drinks, and matching partners.

She took off her glasses and slipped off her dress to loosen her stays. And what with thinking on this and that, she was undressed and in her gown before she knew it.

Well, she might as well brush her teeth and in general freshen up. She went into the bathroom. Above the running of the bath-water her voice soared in unmusical lament.

She came back sparkling and sweet, and turned down the bed, and puffed up the pillow. It was past her usual bedtime. At the white folks' she would have been asleep an hour ago. But this was holiday. She would snatch forty winks and rise and shine.

She got her insurance papers and carefully placed them under her pillow, giving them a loving little pat. She left the money in the unlocked bag. There was wisdom in this. She would rather steer a thief to an obvious cache than have him strangle her life out for a packet of greenbacks under her head.

She snapped out the light and slipped in the cool clean bed.

The harvest moon put patches on the wall. Music and laughter drifted up. Viney smiled and wriggled her toes. She wondered if Dell would mind very much having to give up the house. She her-self lived with white folks so long she had no feeling about front doors. Having had so little all her life, she had got used to having nothing. She knew without resentment that what the Lord gave, He could take away. And she blessed the name of the Lord.

Lestra was going to Europe. Lestra was setting sail on an un-known sea. God, guide her craft. Bring her safe to some shore. For Lestra is my life. I began to live when Lestra was born. I was a slave unmindful of my chains. But with Lestra's birth I began to be. Lestra was born of Dell's body, but of my desires that were buried in me with all my bright youth when Mama died.

I'm an ignorant old woman. I will leave no monument. There is only my blood in Lestra's young body. Maybe I, too, might have something wonderful. Education is everything.

She wanted to pray. She wanted to pray that Lestra might live long, and continue well, and grow into greatness, and not forget God.

She got up and knelt by the side of the bed. Her thin plaits hung over her breasts. Her face was infinitely pure.

After a long time she got back in bed, and knew rather guiltily that she would not get up again. So she found the most comfortable spot, settled herself, slept, and after a little, snored.

The Five Dollar Bill

Judy could read before she was seven. Mother said that when she was four she could read the weather reports to her father. The only one she fell down on was the variable wind one. Only she didn't really fall down, for when she came to that difficult word and got it out somehow, the father caught her up in his arms and hugged and kissed her hard.

Judy loved the father. She did not know very much about him. She guessed he was her relative because they had the same name. She would have liked to know if this kinship were closer than an uncle; or was it like a grandfather, for the father was much older than mother, with the top of his head broken and wrinkles around his kind eyes.

But Judy was a shy child who did not like to ask questions, for either the grown-up people said, run and play, or gave you ridiculous answers with superior smiles.

Judy could answer the little questions herself. It was the big questions about babies and God, and telling a lie for your mother that grown-up people were never truthful about.

The stork did not bring babies. It was not true about a stork flying over clouds and dropping babies down chimleys. Santa Claus could come down a chimley because he was a man and wouldn't get hurt. But would God let a stork drop a dear little baby down a dirty chimley?

No, a woman prayed God very hard for a baby. Then it began to grow in her stomach. When it was quite grown a doctor cut a hole in her side and the baby came out. After that the woman stayed in bed until the hole healed up. In that moment of the baby's birth the woman became a mother. But how a man became a father Judy did not know.

And about God: did He really punish people in a fire with a pitchfork? Did He stick them with the pitchfork *Himself*? Why Judy could not have hurt a fly. She could kill a mosquito all right because it was teenier. Sometimes though when you killed a mosquito a lot of blood squished out. That made your stomach feel queer for a minute. But then mother said, Got him good, didn't you darling, and everything was all right.

Mother could kill anything without feeling queer. She killed flies and ants and even big roaches, and put down traps for mice. She said anything that belonged outdoors should stay outdoors if it didn't want her to kill it. And she would grab up a wad of paper and go banging at a fly, which was fun to watch if you did not think too hard about the fly's family.

God was supposed to be better than Mother. God was not supposed to have Mother's temper. She would say God damn to the father. Then she would have a temper when the father reproached her for saying such words before Judy.

They would begin the queer thing called quarreling. The words would fly between them and it would seem to Judy that her mother's words hit hardest. Yet at such times, as fond as she was of the father, she would want to run to her mother, saying protectively, there, there, my darling.

Judy often wondered if the father lived with them. She always went to bed while he was still sitting up and he was never there in the morning like her mother. There were only two bedrooms, hers and her mother's. And once she had heard her mother say to the college man, Jim and I have not lived together as man and wife for months.

Mother was careless with money. She was always losing it. Judy never saw her lose it really, but she would tell Judy about it and after a while Judy would remember exactly how it happened. When the father sat down to dinner, Mother would tell him about it, too, adding, Judy remembers. Judy would say proudly, yes, Mother.

Mother always lost the money on the day the college man came. Mother said he was poor and came to sell things to help him through college. She said Judy had better not tell the father because he was not a college man and got mad if anybody mentioned college men to him.

Judy did not know what the college man sold and she would not ask her mother. It always cost just what the father had left for the gas bill or the milk bill, and once even what the father had left for a birthday frock for Judy.

When the college man came, Mother would let Judy take her dolly out in its carriage. But it would not be the same as on other days. She would dress her doll hurriedly, and it would not seem to be a real baby, but just an old doll. She would feel silly, and would just want to get away from the college man and his teasing voice.

Then one night the Father and Mother had a terrible quarrel

about Mother losing money. You could hear their voices all over the house, only this time it was the father's words hitting hardest. Neither Judy nor her mother had ever mentioned the college man to him, but he knew all about him just the same, and called himself a fool and the college man a rat and said he was going to divorce mother and take Judy away from her.

Judy did not know what divorce meant, but when the father said he would take her away from her mother, she knew that as mad as he was he would take her for keeps, and never let them see each other.

She got out of bed and ran into the kitchen, and threw herself into her mother's arms. She was sobbing wildly and saying hysterical things. Her mother held her close and began to cry, too, saying there there, my precious, just like Judy had always wanted to say to her.

After a long time she felt the father's hand on her head. She heard him say something about the child's sake, and knew he meant he would let her stay. All in a moment she fell asleep, with her hand sliding down her mother's soft cheek.

After that the father didn't leave any more money for bills. The college man came once and said where was the money for his books. He looked very scornful while he said it, and he kept his hat in his hand.

Mother forgot about Judy and cried and clung to the college man. He pushed her away and said she knew where to reach him when she had the money for his books. The outer door slammed after him.

Then Judy knew that the college man sold books and was mad because mother would not pay him. Still it was strange. She had never seen her mother so heartbroken. Even with the father it had not been like that. For she had never heard her proud mother plead. She had never seen her stalwart mother cling to anyone.

Judy had to say it. Give him back his old books.

Her mother stopped in the midst of a sob. You go and play, she said coldly.

After a while Judy almost forgot about the college man and the money her mother owed him. It was only when her mother walked up and down and around the room looking burningly beautiful, that Judy felt sick and afraid and saw the college man's image.

Then it was that Judy, who could read almost anything at seven, read in the Sunday supplement about the moving picture machine. You sent away for some reproductions of famous paintings. When they came you sold them. When you had sold them all you sent the money to Mr. Fisher in Chicago, and he sent you a moving picture machine. If you put up a sheet and charged a penny to all the children in the neighborhood once a week, pretty soon you'd have enough money to give your mother to pay the old college man for his old books.

Judy talked it over with the father, except the part about the college man. He said he was proud of his little businesswoman and helped her write the letter to Mr. Fisher. He took her out and lifted her up to the mailbox so she could post it herself.

In less than a week the pictures came. The father said they were beautiful and made the first purchase himself. There were twenty to dispose of at a quarter apiece.

Judy sold one to her teacher, one to the barber who cut her hair, one to the corner grocer, at whose store they had an account, one to kind Mr. McCarthy who ran the pool room, one to an uncle, one to an aunt, and two to company ladies. The father said she had done simply wonders and took the rest of the pictures to the office building, where he was superintendent, and sold them.

He brought her the money in silver. Judy was very excited. She counted out her money and wanted to have all changed to a five dollar bill.

Mother got up and said she would take Judy to the corner grocer's right now. And tomorrow they would go to the post office where Judy was to send the money order herself.

Mother held out her hand and was radiant. Judy slipped her small palm into hers. They smiled at each other and shut out the male, their husband and father. In this moment Judy was saying, It is for your sake, my darling. Her mother's mounting excitement answered, I know it, my sweet, my precious.

They went to the corner grocer's, still holding hands. Judy skipped along. It was seven o'clock of a winter's evening. The stars were shining. The snow crunched under her feet. Everything was dear and familiar, the car line, the icicles on the cables, the signboards with their bright illustrations luminous under the electric lights, the vacant lot with the snowmen silent and stout, the fire alarm, the post box. All things good, and best of all her mother's bright and beautiful face, her mother's parted red-lipped mouth, with breath on the winter night.

The corner grocer rang up No Sale and gave Judy a five dollar bill. Judy said, You take it for me, Mommy, with the same indulgence that mothers used in saying to small children, you may carry the package, dear.

Mother opened her purse and fished around in it. After a while she looked her amused surprise at Mr. Brady and gave him a lovely, humble smile full of sweet pleading. She took Mr. Brady into her confidence and said she must make an urgent call. Would Mr. Brady give her a nickel and put it on the bill.

All of a sudden Judy felt sick. She knew her mother's burning beauty had not been for her, nor was it now for Mr. Brady. She did not want to hear her mother make the telephone call. She went and stood at the door and stared up at a star snug among its elders. The star began blinking so hard that it made her eyes water.

When she heard the nickel ring in the telephone box, she began to sing shrilly and kept on singing until her mother came out of the booth and bade Mr. Brady a wonderful good night.

All the way home Judy would not look at her mother. She played a skipping game that kept her a pace ahead. Her mother kept saying loving things, but Judy pretended not to hear and would give no loving answers.

At the door her mother reminded her, "My precious, don't bother to mention to your father about the telephone call. I dialed the wrong number and lost my nickel, so I really didn't make it after all."

When Judy went in she said, Good night, Father, with her head hanging down. She hated him, too, and ran off to bed without once begging to stay up.

In the morning Judy made herself believe that last night had been a bad dream. She ran all the way home from school. Her mother greeted her with a hug and kiss. She looked very alive and kept smiling at Judy with the blood flooding her cheeks and her eyes star bright in her head.

Judy ate her lunch. The table was pretty but there was unwashed china in the sink. The plate her mother placed before her was not a company plate.

The lunch was soft things but they stuck in Judy's throat. She felt excited and sad. Suddenly her mother was saying, Darling, I sent your money off myself. I was passing the post office this morning and it seemed rather silly to make a second trip this noon. You won't tell your father, will you? He thought it would please you to send it yourself. But you're Mother's big girl, aren't you, my precious? And you aren't disappointed, are you?

No'm, said Judy, and she never said No'm. Her heart was standing in her throat. She thought it would burst.

That night she went to bed before the father came for dinner. She said she felt sick in her stomach, and in fact, she did. She did not want the light, nor a book, nor her doll. She shut her eyes tight. The father tiptoed into the room. She lay very still. His lips brushed her forehead. He tiptoed out. She put her mouth in the pillow and sobbed herself to sleep.

It was not so bad the first week. After every mail, she would make herself believe the moving picture machine would surely come on the next. But the week passed. Another week began. The father said, It ought to come this week anyway. Her mother added cheerfully, oh, yes.

The second week ended. The third week began. Then the father said, Shall I help you write them a letter, Judy?

Her eyes met her mother's bright unwavering ones. I forgot the address, she said.

Thereafter the father did not speak of the matter again. He said Judy must just consider it an unfortunate experience and profit by it.

Saturday morning of the fourth week it was Judy who got the mail that the elevator boy had pushed under the doorsill. There was a letter addressed to herself. It bore Mr. Fisher's return address. The other letters fell from her hand. She stumbled blindly into her room and opened the envelope.

It was not really a letter. It was a newspaper page. There was a picture of a little girl and a story with easy words about how she had kept some pictures that belonged to Mr. Fisher, though he had written her twice to return them. The police had come and taken her to jail, where she had stayed forever and ever. Her mother got sick and died from worrying. Her father lost his job because his daughter was a thief and had to beg on the streets.

Judy was terrified she could not stir. Her eyes dilated. She could not swallow. She began to itch all over.

After a long time she folded the newspaper page and hid it under her mattress. She flung herself across the bed, quivering and unable to cry. She would suffer like this at the peal of a bell, at an unfamiliar voice, at an unexpected sound, and she would share this pain with no one. For she knew even if she screwed up the courage to go to a grown-up, she would get the untruthful answer, children don't go to jail, when there was that picture of that little girl which proved that they did.

The doorbell jangled. Judy jumped off the bed, scuttled under it, and drew herself up into a ball, banging her head against the floor, and holding her breath hard.

God, she prayed, let me die.

But children do not die. They grow up to be the strange things called mothers and fathers. Very few parents profit by childhood experiences. When they look back they do not really remember. They see through a sentimental haze. For childhood is full of unrequited love, and suffering, and tears.

TWO

The WPA Years

My Baby...

One day during my tenth year a long time ago in Boston, I came home from school, let myself in the backyard, stopped a moment to scowl at the tall sunflowers which sprang up yearly despite my dislike of them, and to smile at the tender pansies and marigolds and morning-glories which Father set out in little plots every spring, and went on into the kitchen.

The back gate and back door were always left open for us children, and the last one in was supposed to lock them. But since the last dawdler home from school had no way of knowing she was the last until she was inside it was always Mother who locked them at first dark, and she would stand and look up at the evening stars. She seemed to like this moment of being alone, away from the noise in the house.

We were a big house. Beside the ten rooms, and the big white-walled attic, there were we three little girls and the big people, as we used to call them. Father, our mothers, Grampa, and the unmarried aunts. Presently, as I shall tell you, there were two more little ones. Grampa used to say that if we lived in the Boston Museum, which was the biggest building Grampa had ever seen, we'd still need one more room. That was a standing joke in our house. For besides this permanent collection, there were always visiting relatives and friends, for we had a nice house, and we were a hospitable family.

My room was the big third-floor front bedroom. Mostly I shared it with Mother. I remember everything in that room, the big brass bed that had been Father's wedding present to Mother, the wicker settee and the wicker rocker and the wicker armchair, that had once seen service in the parlor until superseded by mahogany, and now creaked dolefully on damp nights, making me think of ghosts. There was a built-in marble washstand in the room, and I think Mother was very proud of this fixture. There were taps for running hot and cold water, and on Saturdays and Sundays and holidays the hot tap was really hot. The New England winters were cold then, and although our old-fashioned house had a furnace that sent up some semblance of heat through the registers, there were coal stoves in nearly all the rooms. In my room was a little pot-bellied stove, and I knew how to tend it myself. At night I would sift the ashes and bank the fire, and in the mornings I would scoot out of bed onto the freezing carpet, run to the stove, bang the door shut, open the drafts, race back to bed and lie on my belly doing my algebra until the room had warmed enough for me to dress. My room, for some reason, became the hub of the house. I think it was because that little pot-bellied stove was one of the only two on the top floor. And whereas I left my window for Mother to open, so I wouldn't cool off the house before it was bedded down for the night, my cousin, in whose room was an ancient, evil, ugly stove, let her fire go out, flung open her window, and shut her door against intruders. At night everyone came into my room to warm himself before going to bed, and an aunt stopping in to toast for a moment before my banked fire and finding another aunt present would fall into conversation, and by and by all the other members of the family, except Father and Grampa who couldn't come in their nightshirts, would drift in and settle in the wicker furniture, and the rocking chair would sing back and forth, and someone would ask, Is that child asleep? And someone would answer, if she isn't, she'd better be.

They would sit there until the banked fire gave out no more heat. Then they would sigh and heave themselves up, and their heavy bodies would pad out of the room. Mother would crack the window and let in the stars and turn out the flickering gaslight. Sometimes she slipped in beside me, sometimes not. I would lie and listen to the creaks and groans of the many bedsteads, and it seemed to me a fine and safe thing to have a big family.

That day in my tenth year when I came home from school, my mother was not in the kitchen. This seemed odd, for the children in our Irish neighborhood were often bellicose, and Mother stood ready at all times to rush out and rescue us. I could not fight when I was a child. I shook too much and was too ashamed. But my mother and the cousin who was eleven months older than I were great battlers. It was wonderful to hear my mother tearing into an Irish termagant with a sailor's tongue, and to see my girl cousin triumphantly straddling a thirteen-year-old bully.

My mother and my cousin were so much alike that sometimes I had the mean thought that I was not really my mother's child. And oddly enough, my mother's sister was shy and soft and dark like myself. My cousin and I used to wonder quite seriously if our mothers, for some reason, had switched us.

When I could not find my mother in the kitchen, I went softly down the hall to the parlor. I did not call her in the fear that if there were company, I would be summoned. The parlor door stood open but my cautious peeking revealed no one inside. Suddenly, I heard movement in the upstairs sitting room. I went back down the hall and up the back stairs, and sitting down on the top step, I had a clear view of the front room.

Now, looking back, I do not remember the room's furnishings. I can only recall that almost center in the room was a big table-desk that had once been in Father's office, and beside this desk sat a strange white woman with a little brown girl in her arms. I could not see my mother, but I was aware of her presence in that room. Grampa was probably in the grandfather chair, chewing tobacco, spitting into a tin can when it was summer and into the stove when it was winter, not listening to the conversation of the women. My father and my widowed aunts were at work.

My mother and the woman spoke in low voices, and I did not hear anything they said. I wished I could see the baby more clearly, for I loved babies. She was good, hardly stirring, and never uttering a sound. Presently the woman rose. I scrambled down the back stairs as quietly as I could.

That night at supper my mother asked us how we would like a baby boy and girl to play with. We were wildly excited, for we were beginning to think we were too big to play with dolls and it was hard not to have something to fondle. Well, we'll see, said my mother and sent us out front to play, with Grandfather at the parlor window to watch us so that the roving bands of Irish boys from Mission Hill way would not bother us. We knew that the big people were going to talk about the white lady and wanted us out of earshot.

The day the babies came is as clear in my mind as if it were yesterday. It was a Saturday. We had not come home from dancing school, held in the spacious home of a Negro woman who had known a better day, where we were taught parlor prancing by a young and lovely Irish girl, whose mother accompanied her to class because some of the seniors were boys of eighteen, and our teacher was only twenty-one. She was engaged and was not interested in the boys at all except as one boy danced better than another. Nor were the boys interested in her since they were all in school and there were several prettier girls in the class. Now it seems strange that we had a white dancing teacher, but in those days it was the fashion. If you went to a Negro teacher, it was an admission that you could not afford to pay a white one.

When we rang the front bell, Mother came to the door. She smiled and said that the babies had come, and that they were to sleep with me because my bedroom was the biggest. My cousins raced upstairs to see the newcomers. I stayed behind to ask questions. Actually I could not bear the exquisite moment when I would hold two real babies in my arms. I asked my mother how long they would stay. She said they would stay indefinitely for their mother had gone to work to support them. She was, in fact, going to work as nursemaid for a friend of my unmarried aunt's employer. I asked my mother where their father was. She hesitated for a moment, then said that their father had not been very good to them, and that was why they were here, and I must love them a lot so they would not miss their mother too much.

With my heart bursting with love for these babies, I went slowly upstairs. Finally, I reached my room, and I heard my cousins crowing delightedly. At the foot of my bed sat a little boy in pajamas. He looked about three. His hair was very blond and curly, his skin very pink and white. He looked like a cherub as he bounced about outside the covers and chattered in utmost friendliness to my cousins. I started toward him, for I wanted nothing so much as to hug him tight. My cousins began telling me excitedly what a darling he was.

I was almost upon them when suddenly I stopped. I did not do it willfully. Some force outside me jerked me to a halt. The smile left my face and involuntarily I turned and looked toward the head of the bed.

There was that baby girl, staring solemnly at me. I went slowly toward her. I had forgotten the boy was on earth. I stood above her. She was no more than two. Her hair was as curly as the boy's but softer and longer and brown. Her wide serious eyes were brown, too. She was copper-colored. In all of my life I have never seen a lovelier child. I do not know how long we stared at each other unthinkingly. As clearly as if I had spoken aloud, I heard a voice inside myself say to the inward ear of that child, I am going to love you best of all. Then I turned away without touching her and in a minute had joined my cousins who had already decided the boy would be the most fun.

The months passed, and the girl and I became inseparable. When I came home at half-past two there was her little face pressed to the windowpane, and no one had told her the time. From the moment I entered the house, I was her mother and she was my child.

Their own mother came to see the children on the one day a week that she was free. But she was so young, only twenty-one and she had been caring for babies all week, and so after a few minutes with them, Mother sent her out to see her young friends. My mother treated her like a child which seemed odd to me then.

I learned that my mother was her aunt by marriage, and that she remembered the day she was born. I was told she had played with us when we were babies just as we played with her children now. I knew then that she was not white.

The hard winter had set in when Father had to shovel a path from the house to the sidewalk before we children could leave for school. The snow was banked as high as our shoulders. There are no such winters now. We were little girls and we wore boys storm boots that laced to our knees as did all the other little girls. We wore flannel shirts and drawers that made us itch like mad and red flannel petticoats. Some bitter mornings the bells sounded over the city which meant it was snowing too hard for school.

The babies scarcely left the house that winter, for Mother said they were packed with cold. I think the house was warmer than it ever had been, and sometimes Father grumbled about the cost of coal. Grampa gave the babies a mixture of white Vaseline, lemon juice, and sugar. Mother borrowed my allowance money regularly for patent medicines. They worked on those children all winter. When it was spring, it seemed that Grampa and my mother had succeeded, for the children had gained and grown taller.

The girl was as much a part of me now as my arm. She had grown even closer to me after the long, uncertain winter. I had forgotten the years when she had not been with me. I could not imagine a life without her. As young as she was, and as young as I was, there was an understanding between us of amazing depth. The family remarked our oneness. Her own mother knew without jealously that the baby loved me best.

Death came on her quietly, and on what mild spring breeze it could have blown we never knew. There was a day when she whimpered and sucked on her thumb, a habit we had broken. I do not remember if the doctor came; I only remember that it seemed to me I could not bear to see her lying there, not whimpering now, but still sucking on her thumb with nobody telling her not to, and her eyes enormous and with a look of suffering.

Then one day—it may have been the next day, it may have been the next year, for the pain I suffered with her—my mother wrapped her up and took her to the hospital.

When Mother had gone, I slipped out of the house and trailed her like a little dog. It was a short walk from our house to the Children's Hospital. Mother went inside, and I stood on the sidewalk opposite and stared up at the hospital windows.

I guess the waiting room was on the second floor, for suddenly I saw my mother in line at a second-floor window. She did not see me, and I cannot say if the baby saw me or not. She lay listlessly in Mother's arms pulling on her thumb. I stared at her with my hands pressed tight in prayer until they had passed out of sight. Then I ran home and crawled under the bed and lay there quivering, unable to cry, until I heard Mother's weary step in the hall.

We children ran to her, and when we saw she had returned without the baby, we could not bear to ask her what the doctor had said. She would not tell us. She only said the doctor would take good care of her and that she would soon be well.

It is so long now that I cannot remember how long it was. Perhaps a week passed, perhaps a month. One night in my sleep I heard the front doorbell or the telephone ring. The next thing I remembered was the soft sound of my mother's sobs. I sat up and stared at her. The boy's blond head lay on the pillow, his face sweet in sleep. My mother looked at me. I do not know why she had come into my room unless to reassure herself that there was life in death. She came to me and hugged me tight, and said in a choked whisper that the baby was dead. Then she straightened almost sternly and told me to go back to sleep. I did not cry. I just felt surprised for a minute and then went to sleep almost instantly.

I was ten and I was smart for my age. I had been told that the baby was dead, and I had seen the grown-ups' strained faces, but did not know what death was. The last time I had seen the baby she had been alive. It was not until I looked down at her little white coffin that I knew that she was not. Had she died without pain, she might have looked otherwise. But the sudden swift disease had ravaged her. A bandage covered her eyes, and the agony had left its mark on her mouth. She did not look like a sleeping child. Perhaps the undertaker had not yet perfected his art. This was death unbeautiful and unmistakable. The only mourners were my family.

The mother came home with us that night. I remember her white, frightened, little-girl's face, and my mother's tenderness. She did not go back to work. There was a week of family conferences, for we children practically spent the whole week outdoors.

Then one day we came home from school, and the boy and his mother had gone. My mother said they had gone far away to another city. She talked to us very seriously, and her eyes were filled with sadness and something that looked like shame. Her words came out slowly, as if reluctantly. Sometimes she could not look at us.

She said the boy and his mother would never come back. They had gone away to begin a new life. If anyone asked us about them, we must say we had never known them. We knew by her face that we must not ask any questions. We went away from her, and we could not play, nor could we look at each other.

So summer came again, and an aunt from the South came to visit us, bringing her two little boys. My cousins had a child apiece and were wildly happy. Mother and the aunts were happy, too, for they had not seen their sister in years.

One day a strange dark man came to our house and talked in an angry voice to my mother. She talked back to him the same way she talked to the Irish termagants. I heard her tell that man that his baby had died because he had neglected it. She told him that his wife and son had gone away, and thrust him out of the house.

Sometime after that a letter came for my mother. I saw her hands tremble when she opened it. She did not say anything to us, but that night she read it aloud to her assembled sisters. My cousins were in the attic playing with the two little boys, and my mother thought I was with them. Actually I was lying underneath my bed, crying for that dead baby. There was not a night for a good six months that I did not cry for her. When I heard my mother and my aunts, I crammed my fist into my mouth. How could I tell them I was crying for a child I was supposed never to have heard of?

My mother and the aunts settled in the wicker furniture. Somebody carefully shut the door. Then Mother read the letter. I do not remember everything it said. All that I remember is something about a marriage, and something about a new life, and something about a husband's being white. Mother opened my little pot-bellied stove, thrust the letter in, and struck a match to it. Suddenly the sisters silently converged and watched the letter burn. When the letter was ashes, mother shut the stove door. I heard my unmarried aunt murmur, God help her to be happy. Then they filed out, and one of them called upstairs sharply for the children not to make so much noise. They went back down-stairs.

I took my fist out of my mouth, and I cried even harder, for now there was much more to cry about.

Ghosts

This bizarre story was told by a Harlem woman identified only as Mrs. Laura M. She was interviewed in her apartment at 300 West 114th Street over a period of several days. Mrs. M. was a woman who had none of the personality traits which one ordinarily expects to find in a person who relates personal experiences of the kind given in this interview.

She is phlegmatic, unimaginative, practical, and apparently a materialist, except for the variations imposed upon her by the set of events which she has described. She is a staunch churchgoer, a Presbyterian, but shows and expresses no preoccupation with the supernatural. She has a high school education and has none of the attitudes toward the supernatural that is often found among ignorant and uneducated persons.

No doubt her stoicism caused her to act as she did under the circumstances which she described. After a discussion of the possibility that aliens from Mars had invaded Earth (as described in an Orson Welles' radio broadcast), she said she believed the behavior of those who were frightened as "stupid" and "ridiculous."

"I didn't hear it," she said, "but if I had, I wouldn't have been frightened. And even if it had been true, I wouldn't have run out of the house. I would have just waited. If a catastrophe is coming, it's coming."

I went to see Mrs. Laura M. with whom I once roomed, and during a conversation that somehow got around to ghosts, I expressed the opinion that I hoped my luck would continue and that I would never see or hear anything that might be described as a ghost. Mrs. M. looked at me curiously, as if she might say something on the subject, but apparently changed her mind. A neighbor who'd been visiting Mrs. M. and was on the verge of going, was persuaded by the sudden turn in the conversation to tell about a strange thing that had happened to her.

In the apartment in which she had lived before moving to her present address, Mrs. M. had had a strange experience upon moving. She had placed her baby's playpen in a certain corner in her living room. Soon after she had settled in the apartment, she noticed that the baby began to cry a lot, unnaturally, as if in terror.

She would go to the playpen, and none of the physical things, which irritate a baby to the point of crying, would be apparent. The baby was in good health and there was nothing to cause the constant terrified screaming. Mrs. M. found it very difficult to understand the change in the baby's disposition as it had formerly been an even-tempered child.

One day she mentioned the baby's behavior to her next-door

neighbor. This friend listened, and then with some reluctance, asked where the baby's playpen was. Mrs. M told her. The neighbor then explained that another baby's crib had stood in that identical spot. The mother of this child had died, and the family had moved away. Mrs. M. had almost immediately moved in.

The neighbor's explanation was that the dead woman, the baby's mother, was coming back to see her child, not knowing that it had been taken away, and that it was this strange spirit form that was frightening Mrs. M.'s child. She advised Mrs. M. to move her baby's playpen to another corner of the room. She did and the baby did not cry anymore.

Mrs. M. sat down again and looked at me in a strained way. Then she blurted out, "I've had a similar experience. Not long after we moved"—she was then living with a brother—"to 117th Street, I had a funny thing happen to me. It was a seven-room apartment, and I had one of the rooms on the street fixed up as a sewing room. The sewing room, bathroom, and kitchen were on one side of the hall, the storage room"—a small room which she used for trunks and suitcases—"and two bedrooms were on the other side. My living room was at the end of the hall and there was a bedroom off from that.

"Well, one day I was sitting in the sewing room when I heard a rustle in the hall. It sounded like the swish of a taffeta skirt. I looked up at the door and saw the figure of a woman go past. She had on a black taffeta dress and I didn't see any head. I called out, 'Who's there?' Of course, nobody answered. I jumped up and looked down the hall. Just as the figure reached the door of the living room, it disappeared. I went in and looked around, but I didn't see anything.

"I went back to the sewing room and picked up my work. I just shrugged my shoulders and said I was seeing things. Nothing else happened like that for a long time. Then one day, a friend was sitting in the sewing room with me, and I heard the rustle again. I looked up and saw the figure again. My friend saw it, too, and she said, 'Good God, L.! What's that?' I laughed and said, 'What's what?' She told me what she had seen.

"I told her that it was just her imagination, that she had seen a reflection from the street. She insisted that she had seen the headless figure of a woman. She was nervous for about ten minutes, then she quieted down, but she kept insisting that she had seen something. She said that it must have been somebody who had died in the house, and was coming back to look for something. Well, I know that I had seen something, so I said to myself that it must have been a good spirit since it hadn't bothered me, so I didn't worry about it anymore while I was in that house.

"Then a woman who lived across the street came over and said, 'You've stayed in this house longer than the last three families.' I asked her what she meant, and she said that she had lived in the house when it was first opened to Negroes, but that she had lived in an upstairs apartment. The first family that had my old apartment in that house on the first floor had stayed there a long time, and so had the people who had lived in there after that. Then she had moved downstairs into the apartment I then had.

"She had put her bed in a certain place in one of the bedrooms and she felt like she was choking to death in the middle of the night. She didn't know what to do at first, but finally she had moved her bed to another position. After that she didn't have that choking sensation. But other little things happened, and she moved out.

"She said that the next two families had moved in and stayed a month or two and had then moved out. I'd been in that apartment about a year and a half when she told me that. She asked me if I had had any experiences in that room. I told her that I hadn't heard my brother speak of anything funny happening. She just shook her head and said it was queer.

"I used to hear sounds like steps very often. At first I thought it was my brother coming in from work. He didn't get in then until one thirty or two in the morning. I used to call out but there'd be no answer, so I just thought I was mistaken and I'd go back to sleep. One night in particular I remember hearing the steps very distinctly. I thought maybe he'd had an accident, so I got up and went to the door of my bedroom and called out. There wasn't a soul there, so I went back to bed.

"Then you remember"—she turned to me—"you used to hear little noises which you thought were mice. Well, some of them were and some of them weren't. I didn't want to frighten you, so I just let you think that every sound you heard was a mouse scampering around."

I remember hearing noises in the closet of the bedroom which I had, heavier than the sound a mouse makes, but I finally decided that it was Mrs. M. moving around in her bedroom next door.

"When you used to ask me what I was doing up so late at night"—I heard the noises as late as three o'clock in the morning—"I gave you some kind of answer because I was always asleep at the hour you mentioned. Before you moved up with me, I had the bedroom you had. I used to hear noises in that closet, too. One night the door kept swinging and I got up and shut it. The latch clicked and I got back in bed. Before I could get the covers up over me again, the door was open and swinging a little again. Now, I know that door latch was caught. But I went on to sleep. There wasn't anything I could do.

"While I slept in that room, I had another experience. One night I got in bed and after a while I felt something that felt like somebody trying to stand up under the bed. It was pushing right in the center of the bed. I reached up and turned the light on and looked under the bed. There wasn't a thing there, so I turned off the light, and in a little while, the pushing stopped, and I went to sleep.

"After you moved up there, I shifted the bedrooms. I took the room my brother had had, the room where the woman across the street had felt like she was choking in, and my brother took the next room. I didn't ever feel anything choking me, but I did feel that pushing again. Again I got up and turned on the light, but there wasn't anything there. I never felt it again.

"Then once after you moved up, too, I was coming down the hall—you were in the bathroom—and it felt like somebody come along behind me and blew my hair up.

"It felt like a breeze that a human being makes, not like the wind. Like this"—she pursed her lips and blew as one blows up a balloon—"I brushed my hair down but it wouldn't stay." (Mrs. M. has very light, thin hair). "All of it in the back stood straight out from my scalp. I kept brushing it down but it wouldn't stay. After I had brushed it down about a dozen times, it returned to normal.

"There wasn't any draft, and the front door wasn't open to let air blow down the hall. And what little air comes in the cracks wouldn't have been strong enough where I was standing in front of the living room almost to blow my hair up like that. I never believed in anything like ghosts or things like that. I don't know how I feel now except that I do think whatever it was meant no harm to me, so that's probably why I didn't get frightened."

I asked her if she moved because of those experiences.

"Goodness, no. After you moved, and my brother moved, I just didn't need a seven-room flat."

Pluto

Prominent on my bookcase stands a collapsible wooden image of the long-eared, sad-eyed hound known as Pluto, and immortalized by Mr. Walt Disney. There is no child, and almost never an adult, who does not, upon entering my house, immediately pick Pluto up, pull the strings that make him flop, and play happily for at least five minutes or at most to the end of the visit.

Today though, a child came to my house who did not run straightaway to Pluto. Maybe it was because he was a hungry child. And when is a child not a child? When he's hungry. This one had hollows under his eyes, and his body was too thin, and his clothing was not much comfort against the wind.

My apartment house has a prosperous exterior. Several times a week somebody comes to your door with a hard-luck story. Generally it's a man, and so because I'm a woman, I simply say I'm sorry through a crack in the door, and shut the door quickly. In New York you have to be on the lookout for stick-up men.

But today it was a woman who answered my "Who is it?" There

was something about her plaintive, "Me, lady," that made me open the door wider than I usually do when the voice is unknown.

I saw them both then, the thin little black boy and the thin black woman, both staring anxiously, and neither looking as if they had the strength or will to harm the most helpless female.

"Yes?" I said.

The woman swallowed hard and said, "Could you give me a quarter, missus, to buy something to eat for the boy?"

"Why aren't you on relief?" I asked suspiciously, although in my heart I was disarmed by her Southern accent.

"They said I'd get a check next week," she said helpfully. "They was nice to me," she added.

My neighbor opened her door. She was smartly dressed. Her little boy ran across the hall and stared up at the ill-clad child. I was ashamed of all of us.

"Come inside," I said coldly.

The boy and his mother entered and stood awkwardly in the center of my floor, the boy clinging to his mother's hand as if my sunny room were a dungeon.

"Sit down," I said.

They sat down together on the couch and Pluto was plainly visible. I saw the little boy look at it, and then he looked at me.

For a moment I started to urge him to pick it up and play with it. But then I remembered he had come begging for bread and I could not offer him a toy.

The boy's grave eyes turned back to Pluto. I wanted him to get up and go to it. It made me mad that he recognized the place of his poverty. And then I remembered again that he had come for a quarter and not for a plaything.

I didn't have a quarter to spare. I had only sufficient carfare until payday.

"I don't have a penny in the house," I lied. "But I'll be glad to give you something to eat. You like bacon and eggs?"

"Yes, missus," she said, and then reluctantly, "But I hates to put you to that bother."

"Not at all," I said shortly, because it was a bother. She had interrupted me in the middle of an excellent story. It was about poor people, too; a good proletarian short story.

I banged about the kitchenette, and after a while the living room was fragrant with steaming coffee and sizzling bacon. I found some cold potatoes and fried them. I sliced my last tomato. I piled some slices of bread on a plate and then I felt guilty and toasted them.

All the while I was humming to myself because I did not want that woman to tell me her story. I could have told it to her myself. It would be no different from a hundred others.

It wasn't I could not hum at the table. I spooned a cup of coffee while they ate. Inevitably, the woman in return for the meal told me the facts that led up to it.

She was widowed when the boy was a baby, knocking about with him from pillar to post, coming North so that he could go to a Northern school, sleeping-in and sleeping-out for a string of slave-driving tyrants, farming the boy out to one indifferent slattern after another, never earning much, never saving anything, keeping body and soul together through sheer determination to survive. Now two weeks out of the hospital after a major operation, she was still too frail for domestic work, and her cousin by marriage, who was on relief, was letting her sleep in the living room and forage for food as best as she could. The slattern who had been keeping the boy gave him back to her yesterday. She had put him to bed without any supper.

She had brought him out this morning without any breakfast. She was on her way to the relief people now to ask them if they could hurry. As for herself, she could wait, but a boy gets hungry.

The boy had already eaten more than his share of the platter, and was draining his second cup of diluted coffee. He had not said a word. He had simply looked from his mother to me during his intervals of swallowing, throughout her drab recital. It was not surprising that what she was saying evoked no response in him. He knew all about it. It was as much his life as it was hers. His life in fact was harder, for there was no way for him to know with certainty that she would come once weekly to see him, or that the slattern who beat and neglected him would be replaced by one who only neglected him.

They finished their meal, or rather the platter was clean and the coffeepot empty. Light had come into the woman's face, and the boy did not look quite so much like a wizened old man.

I got up, and the woman understood the signal. She jumped up and thanked me profusely. She prodded the boy. He did not speak, but he smiled, and suddenly he looked seven and no longer an undersized seventy.

I made a package of the odds and ends in my icebox, and after a little struggle with myself, slipped my half-dollar into the woman's hand. I could borrow carfare from a friend. Obviously she could not.

I led them to the door, but the boy broke away and ran across the room to Pluto and lovingly touched him. Pluto fell over and the boy laughed aloud. He gave him a final affectionate pat, and trotted back to his mother. He looked up at her with a face full of eager confidence.

He pronounced solemnly, "I'm gonna ask Sandy for one of them dawgs."

She looked at me almost apologetically. "He believes in Sandy Claus," she said. She hurried on proudly, defensively, "He ain't failed him yet."

"That's fine," I said and shut the door. I could hear them going down the hall, and the boy was talking volubly. I guess he was telling his mother what else he was going to ask "Sandy" for.

For a moment I wanted to believe that I had been taken in, for I am perhaps the poorest tenant in my fine apartment house. I live on the fifth floor in a tiny rear apartment, and why should she have come first to me. And then I realized that in all probability she had not.

I turned back into my room and crossed the floor to put Pluto back on his feet. It has become an automatic act when my door closes after a visitor.

The sad-eyed hound looked up at me, and his tail drooped wistfully. He did not look funny, and I did not want to laugh at him, and he is supposed to make you laugh.

I moved away and cleared the table. I was thinking that it is not right to take a child's joy away and give him hunger. I was thinking that a child's faith is too fine and precious for the dump heap of poverty. I was thinking that bread should not be bigger than a boy.

I thought about those things a lot.

Amateur Night in Harlem: "That's Why Darkies Were Born"

The second balcony is packed. The friendly, familiar usher who scowls all the time without meaning it, flatfoots it up and down the stairs, trying to find seats for the sweethearts. Through his tireless manipulation, separated couples are reunited, and his pride is pardonable.

The crowd has come early, for it is amateur night. The Apollo Theater is full to overflowing. Amateur night is an institution. Every Wednesday, from eleven until midnight, hopeful aspirants come to the mike, lift up their voices and sing, and retire to the wings for the roll call, when a fluttering piece of paper dangled above their heads comes to rest—determined by the volume of applause—to indicate to whom the prizes shall go.

The boxes are filled with sightseeing whites led in by swaggering blacks. The floor is chocolate liberally sprinkled with white sauce. But the balconies belong to the hardworking, holidaying Negroes, and the jitterbug whites are intruders, and their surface excitement is silly compared to the earthy enjoyment of the Negroes.

The moving picture ends. The screen shoots out of sight. The orchestra blares out the soul-ticking tune, "I Think You're Wonderful, I Think You're Grand."

Spontaneously, feet and hands beat out the rhythm, and the show is on.

The regular stage show precedes Amateur Hour. Tonight an all-girls orchestra dominates the stage. A long black girl in flowing pink blows blue notes out of a clarinet. It is a hot song, and the audience stomps its approval. A little yellow trumpeter swings out. She holds a high note, and it soars up solid. The fourteen pieces are in the groove.

The comedians are old-timers. Their comedy is pure Harlemese, and their prototypes are scattered throughout the audience. There is a burst of appreciative laughter and a round of applause when the redoubtable Jackie Mabley states that she is doing general housework in the Bronx and adds, with telling emphasis, "When you do housework up there, you really *do* housework." It is real Negro idiom when one comedian observes to another who is carrying a fine fur coat for his girl, "Anytime I see you with something on your arm, somebody is without something."

The show moves on. The girls of sixteen varying shades dance without precision but with effortless joy. The best of their spontaneous steps will find their way downtown. A long brown boy who looks like Cab Calloway sings, "Papa Tree-Top Tall." The regular stage show comes to an end. The acts file on stage. The chorus girls swing in the background. It is a free-for-all, and to the familiar "I Think You're Wonderful, I Think You're Grand," the blackface comic grabs the prettiest chorine and they truck on down. When the curtain descends, both sides of the house are having fun.

A Negro show would rather have the plaudits of an Apollo

audience than any other applause. For the Apollo is the hard, testing ground of Negro show business, and approval there can make or break an act.

It is eleven now. The house lights go up. The audience is restless and expectant. Somebody has brought a whistle that sounds like a wailing baby. The cry fills the theater and everybody laughs. The orchestra breaks into the theater's theme song again. The curtain goes up. An announcer talks into a mike, explaining to his listeners that the three hundred and first broadcast of Amateur Hour at the Apollo is on the air. He signals to the audience and they obligingly applaud.

The emcee comes out of the wings. The audience knows him. He is Negro to his toes, but even Hitler would classify him as Aryan at first glance. He begins a steady patter of jive. When the audience is ready and mellow, he calls the first amateur out of the wings.

Willie comes out and, on his way to the mike, touches the Tree of Hope. For several years the original Tree of Hope stood in front of the Lafayette Theater on Seventh Avenue until the Commissioner of Parks tore it down. It was believed to bring good fortune to whatever actor touched it, and some say it was not Mr. Moses who had it cut down, but the steady stream of down-and-out actors since the depression who wore it out.

Willie sings "I Surrender Dear" in a pure Georgia accent. "I can' mak' mah way," he moans. The audience hears him out and claps kindly. He bows and starts for the wings. The emcee admonishes, "You got to boogie-woogie off the stage, Willie." He boogie-woogies off, which is as much a part of established ritual as touching the Tree of Hope.

Vanessa appears. She is black and the powder makes her look

purple. She is dressed in black, and is altogether unprepossessing. She is the kind of singer who makes faces and regards a mike as an enemy to be wrestled with. The orchestra sobs out her song. "I cried for you, now it's your turn to cry over me." Vanessa is an old-time "coon-shouter." She wails and moans deep blue notes. The audience gives her their highest form of approval. They clap their hands in time with the music. She finishes to tumultuous applause, and accepts their approval with proud self-confidence. To their wild delight, she flings her arms around the emcee, and boogie-woogies off with him.

Ida comes out in a summer print to sing that beautiful lyric, "I Let a Song Go Out of My Heart," in a nasal, off-key whine. Samuel follows her. He is big and awkward, and his voice is very earnest as he promises, "I Won't Tell a Soul I Love You." They are both so inoffensive and sincere that the audience lets them off with light applause.

Coretta steps to the mike. Her first note is so awful that the emcee goes to the Tree of Hope and touches it for her. The audience lets her sing the first bar, then bursts into catcalls and derisive whistling. In a moment the familiar police siren is heard off-stage, and big, dark brown Porto Rico, who is part and parcel of Amateur Night, comes on stage with nothing covering his nakedness but a brassiere and panties and shoots twice at Coretta's feet. She hurriedly retires to the wings with Porto Rico switching after her, brandishing his gun.

A clarinetist, a lean dark boy, pours out such sweetness in "Body and Soul" that somebody rises and shouts, "Peace, brother!" in heartfelt approval. Margaret follows with a sour note. She has chosen to sing "Old Folks," and her voice quavers so from stage fright that her song becomes an unfortunate choice, and the audience stomps for Porto Rico who appears in a pink and blue ballet costume to run her off the stage.

David is next on the program. With mounting frenzy he sings the intensely pleading blues song, "Rock It for Me." He clutches his knees, rolls his eyes, sings away from the mike, and works himself up to a pitch of excitement that is only cooled by the appearance of Porto Rico in a red brassiere, an ankle-length red skirt, and an exaggerated picture hat. The audience goes wild.

Ida comes out. She is a lumpy girl in a salmon pink blouse. The good-looking emcee leads her to the mike and pats her shoulder encouragingly. She snuggles up to him, and a female onlooker audibly snorts, "She sure wants to be hugged." A male spectator shouts, gleefully, "Give her something!"

Ida sings the plaintive, "My Reverie." Her accent is late West Indian and her voice is so bad that for a minute you wonder if it's an act. Instantly here are whistles, boos, and hand-clapping. The siren sounds off stage and Porto Rico rushed on in an old-fashioned corset and a marabou-trimmed bed jacket. His shots leave her undisturbed. The audience tries to drown her out with louder applause and whistling. She holds to the mike and sings to the bitter end. It is Porto Rico who trots sheepishly after her when she walks unabashed from the stage.

James comes to the mike and is reminded by the audience to touch the Tree of Hope. He hasn't forgotten. He tries to start his song, but the audience will not let him. The emcee explains to him that the Tree of Hope is a sacred emblem. The boy doesn't care, and begins his song again. He has been in New York two days, and the emcee cracks that he's been in New York two days too long. The audience refuses to let the lad sing, and the emcee banishes him to the wings to think it over.

A slight, young girl in a crisp white blouse and neat black shirt comes to the mike to sing "Tisket, Tasket." She has lost her yellow basket, and her listeners spontaneously inquire of her, "Was it red?" She shouts back dolefully, "No, no, no, no!" "Was it blue?" No, it wasn't blue, either. They go on searching together.

A chastened James reappears and touches the Tree of Hope. A woman states with grim satisfaction, "He teched de tree dat time." He has tried to upset a precedent, and the audience is against him from the start. They boo and whistle immediately. Porto Rico in red flannels and a floppy red hat happily shoots him off the stage.

A high school girl in middy blouse, jumper, and socks rocks "Froggy Bottom." She is the youngest thing yet, and it doesn't matter how she sings. The house rocks with her. She winds up triumphantly with a tap dance, and boogie-woogies confidently off the stage.

A frightened lad falls upon the mike. It is the only barrier between him and the murderous multitude. The emcee's encouragement falls on frozen ears. His voice starts down in his chest and stays here. The house roars for the kill, and Porto Rico, in a baby's bonnet and a little girl's party frock, finishes him off with dispatch.

A white man comes out of the wings, but nobody minds. They have got accustomed to occasional white performers at the Apollo. There was a dancing act in the regular stage show which received deserved applause. The emcee announces the song, "That's Why"—he omits the next word—"Were Born." He is a Negro emcee. He will not use the word "darky" in announcing a song a white man is to sing.

The white man begins to sing, "Someone had to plough the cotton, Someone had to plant the corn, Someone had to work while the white folks played, That's why darkies were born." The Negroes hiss and boo. Instantly the audience is partisan. The whites applaud vigorously. But the greater volume of hisses and boos drown out the applause. The singer halts. The emcee steps to the house mike and raises his hand for quiet. He does not know what to say, and says ineffectually that the song was written to be sung and urges that the singer be allowed to continue. The man begins again, and on the instant is booed down. The emcee does not know what to do. They are on a sectional hookup—the announcer has welcomed Boston and Philadelphia to the program during the station break. The studio officials, the listening audience, largely white, have heard a Negro audience booing a white man. It is obvious that in his confusion the emcee has forgotten what the song connotes. The Negroes are not booing the white man as such. They are booing him for his categorization of them. The song is not new. A few seasons ago they listened to it in silent resentment. Now they have learned to vocalize their bitterness. They cannot bear that a white man, as poor as themselves, should so separate himself from their common fate and sing paternally for a price of their predestined lot to serve.

For the third time the man begins, and now all the fun that has gone before is forgotten. There is resentment in every heart. The white man will not save the situation by leaving the stage and the emcee steps again to the house mike with an impassioned plea. The Negroes know this emcee. He is as white as any white man. Now it is ironic that he should be so fair, for the difference between him and the amateur is too undefined. The emcee spreads out his arms and begins, "My people—."

He says without explanation that "his people" should be proud of the song. He begs "his people" to let the song be sung to show that they are ladies and gentlemen. He winds up with a last appeal to "his people" for fair play. He looks for all the world like the plantation owner's yellow boy acting as buffer between the black and the big house.

The whole house breaks into applause, and this time the scattered hisses are drowned out. The amateur begins and ends in triumph. He is the last contestant, and in the lineup immediately following, he is overwhelmingly voted first prize. More of the black man's blood money goes out of Harlem.

The show is over. The orchestra strikes up, "I Think You're Wonderful, I Think You're Grand." The audience files out. They are quiet and confused and sad. It is twelve on the dot. Six hours of sleep and then back to the Bronx or up and down an elevator shaft. Yes sir, Mr. White Man, I work all day while you-all play. It's only fair. That's why darkies were born.

Temple of Grace

Twenty West 115th Street is the New York stamping ground of Daddy Grace, the self-styled rival of Father Divine. It was to this building that he came roaring out of Washington, with the as yet unfulfilled promise of dethroning the Father. Divine's lease on this property had expired, and at renewal time it was discovered that Daddy Grace had signed ahead of him. Divine's prestige tottered briefly, for it was a test of faith to his followers to accept the forced removal of God from His heaven by a mundane piece of paper. However, through an act of a diviner God, the Father acquired Crum Elbow as well as a handsome property on West 124th Street, and it was Daddy Grace whose triumph was now scarcely more than hollow.

The Grace Temple on 115th Street, still surrounded by various flourishing business establishments of Father Divine, is a red-brick building plastered over with crude angelic drawings and pious exhortations. The entrance hall leads directly to a flight of descending stairs over which is the inscription "Grace Kitchen," or across a narrow threshold into the auditorium. This auditorium is of good size, seating possibly two hundred people. The floor is plain, reverberating board. The seats appear new and are cushioned in red leather of good quality. The walls are blue, with gilt borders and two-foot bases painted red. At the rear, to the right, are elevated rows of seats which the choir of fifteen lusty white-robed women occupy. On a platform above them is an upright piano.

At half-past seven the choir began to drift in and until eight they sang unfamiliar hymns grouped around the piano. Occasionally the pianist quickened the tempo into swing, and the choir swayed and shuffled and beat out the rhythm with their hands and feet.

In the place occupied by the pulpit in the average church is an elevated, wooden enclosure, most nearly resembling the throne room of a maypole queen. Six graded steps lead up to it, and most of the incoming congregation knelt briefly at the foot of the stairs before settling in their seats. In the absence of Daddy Grace, who did not appear all evening, they made obeisance to the covered throne chair which stood center in the enclosure and was not uncovered at any time during the proceedings.

To the left of the throne room was the orchestra space. There was a piano, a trombone, a drum, two sousaphones, and two trumpets. At half-past seven a child less than two was beating without reprimand on the drum. He played unceasingly until the orchestra members entered at past eight, and the drummer smilingly relieved him of the sticks.

The auditorium filled slowly. In all there were about seventy-five people. Most of the congregation came singly or in groups from the dining room, and many continued to munch after they were seated. There were at first no ushers. Toward the end of the evening a young man in a smart uniform with "Captain" lettered on an armband and "Grace Soldier" lettered on his breast stood at stiff attention at the rear of the temple. His one duty was to admonish the half-dozen nonparticipants, a row of high-school boys, not to whisper. Oddly enough, at that time the place was bedlam.

The crowd gathered informally. There were as many young children as adults. The grown-ups visited with each other. The children played up and down the aisles. There was unchecked laughter. There were only two or three men with poverty and disinterest in their faces, who spoke to no one and appeared to have come in to escape the cold.

In contrast to the Divinites, who are for the most part somberly and shabbily dressed, the Grace cohorts, though apparently poor, follow their own fashion dictates. The older women were plainly and poorly costumed, but the younger women wore skillful makeup, cheap hats smartly tilted, intriguing veils, and spike heels. One young woman who came in street clothes disappeared down the stairs and returned in an ankle-length dinner dress of black taffeta. It was she who accepted the offerings which white-frocked women brought her after each collection.

At eight the choir took their proper seats, and for half an hour sang familiar hymns, with frequent interpolations of praise to Daddy Grace. The congregation meanwhile had settled and quieted. No one joined in the singing, but there was perfunctory applause at the conclusion of each song. Occasionally a member turned to look up at the choir with mild interest.

When the choir service ended, a slim light brown man in a business suit appeared. At his entrance the orchestra began to play an unfamiliar tune, a variation of four notes, in swing tempo.

The man said there would be a short prayer. His voice rose in illiterate and incoherent prayer with frequent name coupling of "God" and "Daddy Grace." At their mention, there were murmurs of "Amen" and "Praise "Daddy."

The prayer concluded and the orchestra continued to play. Now the unchanging beat of the drum became insistent. Its steady monotone scraped the nerve center. The Africanesque beat went on . . . tom . . . tom . . . tom . . . tom . . . A woman in the front row rose. She flung out her arms. Her body was slim and strong and beautiful. Her delicate-featured dark face became ecstatic. She began to chant in a vibrant unmusical voice, "I love bread, sweet bread." She clapped her hands in four-four time. Presently she began to walk up and down before the throne, swaying from her hips, her feet shuffling in dance rhythm, singing over and over, "I love bread, sweet bread."

A man rose and flung his hands in the air, waving them from the wrists. He began to moan and writhe. The monotonous beat of the drum was the one dominant note now, though the other instruments continued to play. Others rose and went through the motions of the woman. Children rose, too, children of grade school age, their faces strained and searching. A six-year-old boy clapped and stomped until his dull, pale, yellow face was red and moist.

When a shouting, shuffling believer was struck by the spirit, his face assumed a look of idiocy, and he began to pivot slowly in a circle. Tender arms steadied him, and he was guided along by outstretched hands until he reached the milling throng before the throne, where he whirled and danced and shrieked in the whirling, dancing, shrieking mob until he fell exhausted to the floor. When he revived, he weaved back unsteadily to his seat and helped to steer others to the throne.

Finally both drummer and dancers were weary. The space before the throne cleared. A big pompous dark man in a business suit who had been sitting in one of the elevated seats in the rear, looked on with quiet approval, descended and came down the aisle, mounted the stairs leading to the throne, walked to a table to the right of the throne, and put on a gilded crown with a five-pointed star in its center. He advanced to the front of the dais and read briefly from the Bible. The reading concluded, he began to address the congregation as "dar ones" and "beloved." His voice was oily, his expression crafty. His garbled speech played on the emotions. He spoke feelingly of the goodness of Daddy, of Daddy's great love for his flock. He called them Daddy's children and urged them to obey and trust Daddy, and reminded them that they were part of a United Kingdom of Prayer. When the swelling murmurs of "Amens" and "Praise Daddy" indicated their revived strength and ardor, he bent to the woman who had first started the singing and asked in his smooth voice, "Sister, will you start the singing again?"

She rose and began to moan and sway. The orchestra took up her tune, but this time the drum did not beat, and suddenly a tambourine was heard, then another, and then another, until there were four or five. The beat was the same as the drum's had been, steady, monotonous, insidious, and far more deafening. When the open palms and closed fists slapped the center of the tambourine, the little disks jangled and added to the maddening sound.

The crowd's frenzy mounted. Their hysteria was greater than it had been before. They crowded to the space before the throne and their jerking bodies and distorted faces made them appear like participants in a sex orgy. Their cries were animal. When the young girls staggered back to their seats, they lay exhausted against the chair backs, tearing at their hair, with uncontrollable shudders shaking their bodies.

The mad dance went on for forty minutes, twice as long and twice as terrible as the first had been. When the man in the gilded crown felt their frenzy had reached its peak, he came to the front of the platform and stood silently until their awareness of his big, overbearing presence slowed their pace, muted the tambourines, and finally hushed the auditorium.

When they returned exhausted to their seats, he immediately asked them if they loved Daddy enough to keep his temple going by the purchase of his various products. There was no attempt to gloss this bald question. When there were sufficient murmurs of "Amen" and "Praise Daddy," he blew a police whistle and up and down the aisles went the white-frocked women hawking "Daddy Grace" toothpaste, hair pomade, lotions, and toiletries of every kind. One young woman was selling the *Grace Magazine,* fifteen cents for the current issue, and five cents for back numbers.

The sales were few, and the man in the gilded crown tried to encourage the buying by telling the congregation that soon Daddy Grace planned to open shops of every description all over Harlem, and there would be work for everybody.

When the last purchase had been made, the pompous man asked the first spokesman to read the list of trinkets available for Christmas presents. The list included a cross bearing Daddy Grace's picture for $1.50, a combination pen and pencil for a like sum, other articles at various prices, most of them with Daddy's picture as special inducement. The devotees signified their promise to purchase these trinkets by fervent "Amens."

This business concluded, the oily tongue called for the tithe offerings. Those with tithe money were asked to form a line in the center aisle. Half of the congregation got in line. The oily tongue asked for a march. The orchestra struck up. The whistle blew, and the marchers advanced to the front of the throne where they dropped their tithe money in the proffered baskets.

The sum collected totaled only a dollar and some odd cents. The man in the gilded crown concluded that there were some who had tithes but were disinclined to march. Thereupon he dispatched the white-frocked women down the aisles with baskets. They bent over the rows, asking persuasively, "Help us with the offering, dear heart."

When they had returned to the throne, there was a short speech about pledge money, and they were dispatched again. Again they bent down, begging as persuasively as before, "Help us with the offering, dear heart."

When the copper and silver pledges were brought for his approval, the smooth tongue asked for offerings for the House of Prayer. His voice filled with entreaty. He talked of the Grace temples in other cities and implored the congregation to gladden Daddy's heart by making this temple "the best of all." It could only be done with money, he said. His language was plain and his appeal was not garnished by spiritual references. Rather, he fixed them with his eye and flatly informed them that the temple could not run without money, and it was money that he wanted. He then asked the pianist for a march. The pianist who was leaning indolently against the piano with his collar open and his tie loosed, said wearily, "I'm tired." One of the women in white ran down the aisle and returned with the man who had played for the choir. He obligingly swung into a march.

The police whistle blew. The people with pledges were asked to line up in the center aisle. Happily and proudly they lined up in double file. Their manner of marching was different now. It was a shuf-fling strut, and their arms were bent up at the elbows and held firmly against the side. The line marched down the center to the throne, then divided and in single file shuffled up the two side aisles, met again at the rear of the hall, and then one after one went down the center aisle again and placed their pledge money in the basket.

The man in the gilded crown announced that the offerings had reached the total of $5.06. He said that he did not want to take up their time by begging since the hour was growing late, but he wondered if there was anyone present who would raise the total to $5.25. A man came forward immediately. Thus en-couraged, the pompous leader asked if there was another beloved heart who would increase the sum to $5.50. The woman who had led the singing promptly gave a quarter. The leader begged for another quarter for three or four minutes, but no one came for-ward. Abruptly he ended his plea and announced that he would now preach the sermon.

As he spoke a woman screamed, and her arm shot stiffly up into the air while her body grew rigid. Three women laid her on the floor in the aisle. She continued to scream and moan, and then be-gan to talk unintelligibly in a high-pitched, unnatural voice.

The man in the gilded crown announced his text. His voice grew deep and stern. "I'll tell my story about the cow and the sheep who told on the man."

He paused, and then waved his arm dramatically at the pros-trate woman.

"Oh, my beloveds," he said, "sometimes I tremble in fear at the power, the wonderful, mysterious power."

He shook himself in semblance of terror, but it was not funny to the congregation. They stirred uneasily.

"You must fear the power, the wonderful power," he exhorted them. "You must fear and follow Daddy. You must have fear."

A man shot out of his seat and began to moan and sob, flinging his arms around in the air. Smooth tongue looked at him with satisfaction. The congregation strained forward, a concerted sigh escaping from them. Others began to scream and moan. In a few minutes half the flock was on its feet, beginning again that stupefying, tireless dance. In a few minutes more almost every man, woman, and child was dancing, this time without music but with a uniformity of shuffling step and weaving arms.

The man in the gilded crown retired to the rear of the platform, his performance over.

The crazy dance went on. In the street the sound was audible a half block away.

Cocktail Party

The party was on the fifth floor, but even as we entered the lower hall, we could hear the shouts and laughter. It was a successful party then, for, judging by the volume of voices, the four-room flat was packed. That meant that all invitations had been accepted.

The elevator bore us up and let us out. Our smiling hostess stood in her open door. Behind her was a surge of vari-colored faces, the warm white of fair Negroes, the pale white of whites, through yellows and browns to rusty black.

We brushed cheeks with our hostess, and our mutual coos of endearment fell on the already false air. We entered the smoke-thickened room, brushed cheeks with a few more people, shook hands with some others, and followed our hostess into the bedroom.

A visiting Fisk professor, already bored with the party, had got his length somehow into a boudoir chair and sat pulling on his pipe. He could not leave because he had come with his wife, who would not leave until all the important people had come.

Gloomily he uncoiled himself when we entered and, after greetings, assured his hostess in sepulchral tones that he was perfectly happy.

We laid our coats as carefully as we could on the pile of wraps on the bed. Our hostess fingered a soft brown fur. "Mink," she sighed. "Real mink." She blew on it for our inspection, then rubbed a fold of it over her rump. "The closest I'll ever get to it, I guess."

She was on the city payroll, had graduated from a first-class Negro college, belonged to a good sorority, had married respectably, and was now entrenching herself in New York Negro Society. There had been one or two flamboyant indiscretions in her past and so every once in a while, to assure herself and her hometown that she had lived them down, she entertained at a lavish party. She was not yet sufficiently secure to give a small affair. And of all the people lapping up her liquor, hardly one would have come to an intimate dinner. As yet it was necessary for her to give large, publicized affairs so that everyone felt bound to come out of fear that it might be thought he was not invited.

As we returned to the main room, a woman in cap and apron shuffled up, inexpertly balancing a tray of cocktails. We had not known that our hostess had a maid. Yet the woman's harassed dark face was familiar. We remembered that once before, while we visited with our hostess, there had been a ring at the door, a voice had called that it was the janitor's wife with a package, and presently this woman's face had appeared.

Our hostess found places for us on the already populated divan. We sat among acquaintances, balancing our drinks. To our left were a public school teacher, two Department of Welfare investigators, two writers, a "Y" worker, a white first-string movie critic, a white artist and his wife. To our right were two Negro government officials, two librarians, a judge's daughter, a student red-cap, a Communist organizer, an artist, an actress. There were others. In this room and in the inner room were crowded fully sixty in-coming and out-going people.

With the exception of the Communist organizer, all of the Negroes were members of Harlem society. Some of their backgrounds began with their marriages or their professions. One or two were the unimportant offspring of earnest men who had carved small niches in the hall of fame. Two or three were as celebrated as their fathers. Some of them were well-to-do, most particularly where both husband and wife held well-paid jobs. Others had fallen on lean times, but family connections and Home Relief kept them in circulation.

The women in general were light-colored, one of the phenomena of Negro society. Their dress was smart, their makeup skillful. The men were varying colors and soberly dressed. Our hostess had no reputation as a conversationalist, and our host, of better reputation where social talk was concerned, was already in his cups. There was no attempt by either to marshal their guests into interesting groups. The crowd was too unwieldy, and our hostess had only probed beneath the surface of a half-dozen men who thought her pretty. She could only dump a newcomer into whatever space was available, and introduce him to the nearest of the sitters. Whereupon the ensuing conversation was either polite or flirtatious, depending upon sex and preference. When a friend found a friend's face in the crowd, navigation was too difficult, and the greetings were confined to a shouted, "How are you?"

We listened to live conversation around us. A tall unattractive girl on our right had assumed an affected pose. She languished on the divan and blew puffs of smoke through a cigarette holder. Her large foot pivoted on its ankle. She surveyed it dreamily. Her father was a man of importance, and although she had neither beauty nor charm, she had constituted herself the year's number one Negro debutante.

The young leftist writer was talking to her around our backs. He had brought her to the party. Generally one of the artist group squired her. They were indifferent to her lack of prettiness and liked her father's liquor. She boasted of her escorts to her sorors who expressed no envy. They were quite content with their younger beaux who were marrying men.

The writer said, "Will you serve as a sponsor for the dinner then? Your name will look good on the stationery. I can come up tomorrow and go over a guest list with you."

She smiled at the toe that protruded through the space in her shoe for its protuberance.

"I've two other dinners that week, you know. Three will give me such a crowded calendar. But for you—and your guest of honor is quite celebrated, isn't he?"

"Very," he said enthusiastically. "He's been in the papers and a lot. The critics rave about him. I'm going to read his book as soon as he gives me the copy he promised me."

"I'll expect you tomorrow night," she said. "Come at dinnertime. Father will want you to sample his latest concoction. Keep the rest of the evening free, will you? My sorority is—ah—having a dance at the Renaissance. There's no tax, maybe you'd like to look in."

"I'd love to," he exclaimed, "but I can't! I've a meeting at nine, important. Anyway," he added helpfully, "I haven't got a tux." Her eyes returned to her toe, but this time they were sorrowful.

Cocktails, little sausages on toothpicks, black and green olives, cheeses with crisp little crackers, two-inch sandwiches, went in continuous file around the room. Our hostess had a fine array of liquor with impressive labels on the improvised bar. Once she had recommended her bootlegger to us, but we had stopped his visits when we found his labels were often not yet dry and no two like bottles had similar tastes. Since most of the people were connoisseurs no more than we were, they eagerly drank the badly cut liquor and got high.

The actress, from a chair-backed hassock, surveyed the room with disdain. She was playing in a downtown hit! Her hair went up and her nose turned up, and even her lips were slightly curled. She was light-skinned and lovely and remote as a queen among her subjects. Ten years ago she had been a gamin and her accent had been Harlem. Now offstage she was indistinguishable from a throaty Englishman.

We bent to flick our ashes in the tray she was holding in a graceful hand, our mouths open for a pretty compliment. She withdrew her hand in horror and we let our ashes fall on the floor. Her eyes asked us elegantly, "Have we met?"

The white movie critic started toward her, the white artist's wife on his arm. The actress smiled and smiled.

The woman said, "My husband and I saw your show last night. We thought you were marvelous."

"How kind!" said the actress.

"My paper gave you quite a plug," said the movie critic proudly.

The actress smiled and smiled again. All of them beamed at each other.

"I'm so-o-o sorry," the actress murmured, "that we haven't been introduced. May I have the pleasure of your acquaintance?"

The movie critic told her his name and introduced the artist's wife. In a moment they were as chatty as old friends.

We had come at a late hour, and when it was an hour past the scheduled time for the party's end, the crowd gradually began to thin. Our hostess's hair-up had drifted down and her trailing gown had been trampled on. She struck a graceful pose at the door, and her meticulous phrases sped each departing guest.

We had not seen our hostess in several months. She urged us to stay for a little chat. When the last guest had gone, she dispatched her husband and the janitor's wife with borrowed chairs and hassocks and end tables and ashtrays to various flats in the house. She sat down, shook her shoes off, and pulled the rest of her hair down. She lifted her arms and wrinkled her nose.

"I put four on the card, 'cause I know colored folks, and I knew they'd start coming around six. I didn't even plan to take my bath until five. I start sweating so quick. And then at four sharp here come two white folks. I forgot they don't keep c.p. time. Well, I jumped into this, and did my hair and face, and I know they thought my party was a flop, because nobody else came until around five, and they left before six."

We said it was the best attended party we'd been to in a long time.

She fanned herself under the arms.

"It was kinda nice, wasn't it?" she agreed. Then she chuckled softly. "You notice how Doctor Brown's wife kept looking at me? She knows he likes me. She only came to keep her eye on him. She'd have to go some to keep her eye on me! You notice that good-looking chap with his wife, one wore the sleazy green dress?" She smiled meaningfully. "Well, she's just up for the holidays, but he's here for the winter."

The janitor's wife came back. She was frankly dragging now. Her cap was at a comic angle, but she did not look funny. She stood respectfully before our hostess. I could see that one of her shoelaces was black and the other was white, ink-stained black.

"I'll see you Saturday," said our hostess to her cheerfully, though this was Sunday. "That all right? I won't have a penny until then. Pouring liquor down all these darkies cost a lot. They'll talk about you if your drinks are scarce. Saturday noon, I'll see you, Flora."

The woman covered her embarrassment with a painful smile. "That's all right," she said.

She turned to go. When she reached the door, our hostess jumped up suddenly, called to her to wait, rummaged in her bathroom, returned and thrust some silk pieces in the woman's hands.

"Will you do these for me, Flora? I'll pick them up Saturday when I pay you."

When the door shut behind Flora, our hostess came back and said triumphantly, "I'll give her a few cents extra, and I'll save a dollar's washing. We're going to two affairs this week, and that dollar'll mean taxi fare. I hate to come home late at night in a subway with a lot of funny looking derelicts."

We said we hadn't been anywhere in weeks and hoped that she'd have a good time.

Our hostess said we ought to get out more, and she tried to interest us in the affairs she was planning to attend. One was for Spain, the other for China, both causes worth supporting. She spoke with feeling of the pogroms in Germany. It was obvious that she kept abreast of the international situation.

We asked her what she thought of the Gaines decision.

She said she hadn't seen any reference to it in her paper, and she read the paper daily.

We said it had been given front-page space in the Negro week-lies for the past two weeks.

She laughed and answered that she only read the society pages of the Negro papers because of their poor journalism. The society reporters were no better, but at least you kept up with what the darkies were doing. As an afterthought she asked us what the Gaines decision was.

We explained that it was a Supreme Court decision whereby a Southern state must either admit a Negro student to its university or build a university of equal standards for him.

She laughed and said she hoped they'd build one. She was tired of her present job and she was a qualified teacher. She'd like to go South to teach a group of good-looking male students.

Her husband returned. It was obvious that he had had another drink or two in somebody's flat. It had made him hungry.

"Any food, female?" he addressed his wife. "None of these scraps." He surveyed with distaste the dainty sandwiches. "Got any greens left?"

"Greens and spare ribs, have some with us?" she asked.

We thanked her but said we really should go.

Her husband looked at us a little belligerently. He was born in the South, and he said that he yearned for it, but he never got any farther than his government job in Washington even on holidays.

"You don't like colored folks cooking?" he asked.

We said that we loved greens and spare ribs and named all the other Southern dishes and said that we loved them, too.

He smiled at us paternally and said that he wished we were all down South, celebrating the New Year right, with black-eyed peas and hogshead.

"My mother," he reminisced happily, "would turn her house

inside-out for my friends. You folks up North got a lot to learn about hospitality. You all buy a quart of gin, a box of crackers, and a bottle of olives, and throw a couple of white folks in, and call it a cocktail party."

Our hostess stood in her stocking feet and drew herself up grandly. "You're drunk," she said coldly. "Go and eat."

Gravely he bade us good night and walked away with unsteady dignity.

Our hostess went to the door with us in her stocking feet. Again we thanked her for a lovely party.

She surveyed her tumbled rooms complacently.

"I'll clean up and take a bath, and turn on the radio and do my paper. I'm speaking Wednesday at the Young Matrons' meeting. I'm going to talk on the evil of anti-Semitism. There is some anti-Semitism in Harlem which should be scorched at the start. How you like that for a subject?"

We told her we didn't think there was any anti-Semitism in Harlem as such. There was only the poor man's resentment of exploitation by the rich. It was incidental that in this particular instance that one was black and one was Jewish. Black workers and Jewish workers did not hate each other.

"Maybe," she said brightly. "But I still think it's a good topic for a paper. Last month some dumb cluck read a paper on child care. Who can afford to have a child now anyway? I want to give 'em a paper on something current."

We urged her to go and put her shoes on before she caught cold. We brushed cheeks all around.

When we got back home, we wondered as usual why we had gone to a cocktail party.

THREE

Pulp Fiction

Jack in the Pot

When she walked down the aisle of the theater, clutching the money in her hand, hearing the applause, and laughter, seeing, dimly the grinning black faces, she was trembling so violently that she did not know how she could ever regain her seat.

It was unbelievable. Week after week she had come on Wednesday afternoon to this smelly, third-run neighborhood movie house, paid her dime, received her beano card, and gone inside to wait through an indifferent feature until the house lights came on, and a too jovial white man wheeled a board onto the stage and busily fished in a bowl for numbers.

Today it happened. As the too jovial white man called each number, she found a corresponding one on her card. When he called the seventh number and explained dramatically that whoever had punched five numbers in a row had won the jackpot of fifty-five dollars, she listened in gnawing disbelief that there was that much money in his pocket. It was then that the woman beside her leaned toward her and said excitedly, "Look, lady, you got it."

She did not remember going down the aisle. Undoubtedly her neighbor had prodded her to her feet. When it was over, she tottered dazedly to her seat, and sat in a dreamy stupor, scarcely able to believe her good fortune.

The drawing continued, the last dollar was given away, the theater darkened, and the afternoon crowd filed out. The little gray woman, collecting her wits, followed them.

She revived in the sharp air. Her head cleared and happiness swelled in her throat. She had fifty-five dollars in her purse. It was wonderful to think about.

She reached her own intersection and paused before Mr. Spiro's general market. Here she regularly shopped, settling part of her bill fortnightly out of her relief check. When Mr. Spiro put in inferior stock because most of his customers were poor-paying reliefers, she had wanted to shop elsewhere but she could never get paid up.

Excitement smote her. She would go in, settle her account and say good-bye to Mr. Spiro forever. Resolutely, she turned into the market.

Mr. Spiro, broad and unkempt, began to boom heartily from behind the counter. "Hello, Mrs. Edmunds."

She lowered her eyes and asked diffidently, "How much is my bill, Mr. Spiro?"

He recoiled in horror. "Do I worry about your bill, Mrs. Edmunds? Don't you pay something when you get your relief check? Ain't you one of my best customers?"

"I'd like to settle," said Mrs. Edmunds breathlessly.

Mr. Spiro eyed her shrewdly. His voice was soft and insinuating. "You got cash, Mrs. Edmunds? You hit the number? Every other week you gave me something on account. This week you want to settle. Am I losing your trade? Ain't I always treated you right?"

"Sure, Mr. Spiro," she answered nervously. "I was telling my husband just last night, ain't another man treats me like Mr. Spiro. And I said I wished I could settle my bill."

"See," he said, triumphantly, "it's like I said. You're one of my best customers. Worrying about your bill when I ain't even worrying. I was telling your investigator . . ." he paused significantly ". . . when Mr. Edmunds gets a job, I know I'll get the balance. Mr. Edmunds got himself a job maybe?"

She was stiff with fright. "No, I'd have told you right off, and her, too. I ain't one to cheat on relief. I was only saying how I wished I could settle. I wasn't saying that I was."

"Well, then, what you want for supper?" Mr. Spiro asked soothingly.

"Loaf of bread," she answered gratefully, "two pork chops, one kinda thick, can of spaghetti, little can of milk."

The purchases were itemized. Mrs. Edmunds said good night and left the store. She felt sick and ashamed, for she had turned tail in the moment that was to have been her triumph over tyranny.

A little boy came toward her in the familiar rags of the neighborhood children. Suddenly Mrs. Edmunds could bear no longer the intolerable weight of her mean provisions.

"Little boy," she said.

"Ma'am?" He stopped and stared at her.

"Here." She held out the bag for him. "Take it home to your mama. Its food. It's clean."

He blinked, then snatched the bag from her hands, and turned and ran very fast in the direction from which he had come.

———

Mrs. Edmunds felt better at once. Now she could buy a really good supper. She walked ten blocks to a better neighborhood and the cold did not bother her. Her misshapen shoes were winged.

She pushed inside a resplendent store and marched to the meat counter. A porterhouse steak caught her eye. She could not look past it. It was big and thick and beautiful.

The clerk leaned toward her. "Steak, madam?"

"That one."

It was glorious not to care about the cost of things. She bought mushrooms, fresh peas, cauliflower, tomatoes, a pound of good coffee, a pint of real cream, a dozen dinner rolls, and a maple walnut layer cake.

The winter stars were pricking the sky when she entered the dimly lit hallway of the old-law tenement in which she lived. The dank smell smote her instantly after the long walk in the brisk, clear air. The Smith boy's dog had dirtied the hall again. Mr. Johnson, the janitor, was mournfully mopping up.

"Evenin', Mis' Edmunds, ma'am," he said plaintively.

"Evening," Mrs. Edmunds said coldly. Suddenly she hated Mr. Johnson. He was so humble.

Five young children shared the uninhabitable basement with him. They were always half sick and he was always neglecting his duties to tend to them. The tenants were continually deciding to report him to the agent, and then at the last moment deciding not to.

"I'll be up tomorrow to see 'bout them windows Mis' Edmunds, ma'am. My baby kep' frettin' today and I been so busy doctorin'."

"Those children need a mother," said Mrs. Edmunds severely. "You ought to get married again."

"My wife ain' daid," cried Mr. Johnson, shocked out of his servility. "She's in that T.B. home. Been there two years and 'bout on the road to health."

"Well," said Mrs. Edmunds inconclusively and then added briskly, "I been waiting weeks and weeks for them window strips. Winter's half over. If the place was kept warm—"

"Yes'm, Mis' Edmunds," he said hastily, his bloodshot eyes imploring. "It's that ol' furnace. I done tol' the agent time and again, but they ain' fixin' to fix up this house 'long as all you all is relief folks."

The steak was sizzling on the stove when Mr. Edmunds' key turned in the lock of the tiny three-room flat. His steps dragged down the hall. Mrs. Edmunds knew what that meant. "No man wanted." Two years ago, Mr. Edmunds had begun doggedly to canvass the city for work, leaving home soon after breakfast and rarely returning before supper.

Once he had had a little stationery store. After losing it, he had spent his small savings and sold or pawned every decent article of furniture and clothing before applying for relief. Even so, there had been a long investigation while he and his wife slowly starved. Fear had been implanted in Mrs. Edmunds. Thereafter she was never wholly unafraid. Mr. Edmunds had had to stand by and watch his wife starve. He never got over being ashamed.

Mr. Edmunds stood in the kitchen doorway, holding his rain-streaked hat in his knotted hand. He was forty-nine, and he looked like an old man.

"I'm back," he said. "Cooking supper."

It was not a question. He seemed unaware of the intoxicating odors.

She smiled at him brightly. "Smell good?"

He shook suddenly with the cold that was still in him. "Smells like always to me."

Her face fell in disappointment but she said gently, "You oughtn't to be walking 'round this kind of weather."

"I was looking for work," he said fiercely. "Work's not going to come knocking."

She did not want to quarrel with him. He was too cold and their supper was too fine.

"Things'll pick up in the spring," she said soothingly.

"Not for me," he answered gloomily. "Look how I look. Like a bum. I wouldn't hire me myself."

"What you want me to do about it?" she asked furiously.

"Nothing," he said with wry humor, "unless you can make money, and make me just about fifty dollars."

She caught her breath and stared at his shabbiness. She had seen him look like this so long that she had forgotten that clothes would make a difference.

She nodded toward the stove. "That steak and all. Guess you think I got a fortune. Well, I won a little old measly dollar at the movies."

His face lightened and his eyes grew soft with affection. "You shouldn't have bought a steak," he said. "Wish you'd bought yourself something you been wanting. Like gloves. Some good warm gloves. Hurts my heart when I see you with cold hands."

She was ashamed, and wished she knew how to cross the room to kiss him. "Go wash," she said gruffly. "Steak's 'most too done already."

It was a wonderful diner. Both of them had been starved for fresh meat. Mrs. Edmunds' face was flushed, and there was color in her lips as if the good blood of the meat had filtered through her skin. Mr. Edmunds ate a pound and half of the two-pound steak and his hands seemed steadier with each sharp thrust of the knife.

Over coffee and cake they talked contentedly. Mrs. Edmunds wanted to tell the truth about the money, and waited for an opening.

"We'll move out of this hole someday soon," said Mr. Edmunds. "Things won't be like this always." He was full and warm and confident.

"If I had fifty dollars," Mrs. Edmunds began cautiously, "I believe I'd move tomorrow. Pay up these people what I owe, and get me a fit place to live in."

"Fifty dollars would be a drop in the bucket. You got to have something coming in steady."

He had hurt her again. "Fifty dollars more than you got," she said uneasily.

"It's more than you got, too," he said mildly. "Look at it like this. If you had fifty dollars and made a change, them relief folks would worry us like a pack of wolves. But say f'instance you had fifty dollars, and I had a job, we could walk out of here without a howdy-do to anybody."

It would have been anticlimactic to tell him about the money. She got up. "I'll do the dishes. You sit still."

He noticed no change in her and went on earnestly, "Lord's bound to put something in my way soon. Things is got to break for us. We don't live human. I never see a paper 'cept when I pick one up in the subway. I ain't had a cigarette in three years. We ain't got a radio. We don't have no company. All the pleasure you get is a ten-cent movie one day a week. I don't even get that."

Presently, Mrs. Edmunds ventured, "You think the investigator would notice if we get a little radio for the bedroom?"

"Somebody got one to give away?" His voice was eager.

"Maybe."

"Well, seeing how she could check with the party what give it to you, I think it would be all right."

"Well, ne' mind—" Her voice petered out.

It was his turn to try. "Want to play me a game of cards?"

He had not asked her for months. She cleared her throat. "I'll play a hand or two."

He stretched luxuriously. "I feel so good. Feeling like this, bet I'll land something tomorrow."

She said very gently, "The investigator comes tomorrow."

He smiled quickly to hide his disappointment. "Clean forgot. It don't matter. That meal was so good it'll carry me straight through Friday."

She opened her mouth to tell him about the jackpot, to promise him as many meals as there was money. Suddenly someone upstairs pounded on the radiator for heat. In a moment someone downstairs pounded. Presently their side of the house resounded. It was maddening. Mrs. Edmunds was bitterly aware that her hands and feet were like ice.

"'Tisn't no use," she cried wildly to the walls. She burst into tears. "'Tisn't nothing no use."

Her husband crossed quickly to her. He kissed her cheek. "I'm going to make all this up to you. You'll see."

By half-past eight they were in bed. By quarter to nine Mrs. Edmunds was quietly sleeping. Mr. Edmunds lay staring at the ceiling. It kept coming closer.

Mrs. Edmunds woke up first and decided to go again to the

grand market. She dressed and went out into the street. An ambulance stood in front of the door. In a minute an intern emerged from the basement, carrying a bundled child. Mr. Johnson followed, his eyes more bleary and bloodshot than ever.

Mrs. Edmunds rushed up to him. "The baby?" she asked anxiously.

His face worked pitifully. "Yes, ma'am, Mis' Edmunds. Pneumonia. I heard you folks knockin' for heat last night but my hands was too full. I ain't forgot about them windows, though. I'll be up tomorrow bright and early."

Mr. Edmunds stood in the kitchen door. "I smell mean in the morning?" he asked incredulously. He sat down, and she spread the feast, kidneys, and omelet, hot buttered rolls and strawberry jam. "You mind," he said happily, "explaining this mystery? Was that dollar of yours made out of elastic?"

"It wasn't a dollar like I said. It was five. I wanted to surprise you."

She did not look at him and her voice was breathless. She had decided to wait until after the investigator's visit to tell him the whole truth about the money. Otherwise they might both be nervous and betray themselves by their guilty knowledge.

"We got chicken for dinner," she added shyly.

"Lord, I don't know when I had a piece of chicken."

They ate and the morning passed glowingly. With Mr. Edmunds' help, Mrs. Edmunds moved the furniture and gave the flat a thorough cleaning. She liked for the investigator to find her busy. She felt less embarrassed about being on relief when it could be seen that she occupied her time.

The afternoon waned. The Edmunds sat in the living room and there was nothing to do. They were hungry but dared not start dinner. With activity suspended they became aware of the penetrating cold and rattling windows. Mr. Edmunds began to have that wild look of waiting for the investigator.

Mrs. Edmunds suddenly had an idea. She would go and get a newspaper and a package of cigarettes for him.

At the corner she ran into Mr. Johnson. Rather he ran into her, for he turned the corner with his head down and his gait was as unsteady as if he had been drinking.

"That you, Mr. Johnson?" she said sharply.

He raised his head and she saw that he was not drunk.

"Yes, ma'am, Mis' Edmunds."

"The baby is worse?"

Tears welled out of his eyes. "The Lord done took her."

Tears stood in her own eyes. "God knows I'm sorry to hear that. Let me know if there's anything I can do."

"Thank you, Mis' Edmunds, ma'am, but ain't nothing nobody can do. I been pricin' funerals. I can get one for fifty dollars. But I been to my brother, and he ain't got it. I been everywhere. Couldn't raise no more than ten dollars." He was suddenly embarrassed. "I know all you tenants is on relief. I wasn't fixin' to ask you all."

"Fifty dollars," she said strainedly, "is a lot of money."

"God'd have to pass a miracle for me to raise it. Guess the city'll pay to bury her. You reckon they'll let me take flowers?"

"You being the father, I guess they would," she said sadly.

When she returned home the flat was a little warmer. She entered the living room. Her husband's face brightened.

"You bought a paper!"

She held out the cigarettes. "You smoke this kind?" she asked lifelessly.

He jumped up and crossed to her. "I declare I don't know how to thank you! Wish that investigator'd come. I sure want to taste them."

"Go ahead and smoke," she cried fiercely. "It's none of her business. We got our rights same as working people."

She turned into the bedroom. She was utterly spent. Too much had happened in the last twenty-four hours.

"Guess I'll stretch out for a bit. I'm not going to sleep. If I do drop of, listen out for the investigator. The bell needs fixing. She might have to knock."

At half-past five, Mr. Edmunds put down the newspaper and tip-toed to the bedroom door. His wife was still asleep. He stood for a moment in indecision, then decided it was long past the hour when the investigator usually called, and went down the hall to the kitchen. He wanted to prepare supper as a surprise. He opened the window, took the foodstuffs out of the crate that in winter served as an icebox and set them on the table.

The doorbell tinkled faintly.

He went to the door and opened it. The investigator stepped inside. She was small and young and white.

"Good evening, miss," he said.

"I'm sorry to call so late," she apologized. "I've been busy all day with an evicted family. But I knew you were expecting me and I didn't want you to stay in tomorrow."

"You come on up front, miss," he said. "I'll wake up my wife. She wasn't feeling so well and went to lie down."

She saw the light from the kitchen, and the dark rooms beyond.

"Don't wake Mrs. Edmunds," she said kindly, "if she isn't well. I'll just sit in the kitchen for a minute with you."

He looked down at her, but her open, honest face did not disarm him. He braced himself for whatever was to follow.

"Go right on in, miss," he said

He took the dish towel and dusted the clean chair. "Sit down, miss."

He stood facing her with a furrow between his brows and his arms folded. There was an awkward pause. She cast about for something to say, and saw the table.

"I interrupted your dinner preparations."

"I was getting dinner for my wife. It's chicken."

"I looks like a nice one," she said pleasantly.

He was baffled. "We ain't had chicken once in three years."

"I understand," she said sincerely. "Sometimes I spend my whole salary on something I want very much."

"You ain't much like an investigator," he said in surprise. "One we had before you woulda raised Ned." He sat down suddenly, his defenses down. "Miss, I been wanting to ask you this for a long time. You ever have any men's clothes?"

Her voice was distressed. "Every once in a while. But with so many people needing assistance, we can only give them to our employables. But I'll keep your request in mind."

He did not answer. He just sat staring at the floor, presenting an adjustment problem. There was nothing else to say to him.

She rose. "I'll be going now, Mr. Edmunds."

"I'll tell my wife you was here, miss."

A voice called from the bedroom, "Is that you talking?"

"It's the investigator lady," he said. "She's just going."

Mrs. Edmunds came hurrying down the hall, the sleep in her face and tousled hair.

"I was just lying down, ma'am. I didn't mean to go to sleep. My husband should've called me."

"I didn't want him to wake you."

"And he kept you sitting in the kitchen."

She glanced inside to assure herself that it was sufficiently spotless for the fine clothes of the investigator. She saw the laden table, and felt so ill that water welled into her mouth.

"The investigator lady knows about the chicken," Mr. Edmunds said quickly. "She—"

"It was only five dollars," his wife interrupted, wringing her hands.

"Five dollars for a chicken?" The investigator was shocked and incredulous.

"She didn't buy that chicken off none of your relief money," Mr. Edmunds said defiantly. "It was money she won at a movie."

"It was only five dollars," Mrs. Edmunds repeatedly tearfully.

"We ain't trying to conceal nothing," Mr. Edmunds snarled. He was cornered and fighting. "If you'd asked me how we come by the chicken, I'd have told you."

"For God's sake, ma'am, don't cut us off," Mrs. Edmunds moaned. "I'll never go to another movie. It was only ten cents. I didn't know I was doing wrong." She burst into tears.

The investigator stood tense. They had both been screaming at her. She was tired and so irritated that she wanted to scream back.

"Mrs. Edmunds," she said sharply, "get hold of yourself. I'm not going to cut you off. That's ridiculous. You won five dollars at a movie and you bought some food. That's fine. I wish all my families could win five dollars for food."

She turned and tore out of the flat. They heard her stumbling and sobbing down the stairs.

"You feel like eating?" Mrs. Edmunds asked dully.

"I guess we're both hungry. That's why we got so upset."

"Maybe we'd better eat, then."

"Let me fix it."

"No." She entered the kitchen. "I kinda want to see you just sitting and smoking a cigarette."

He sat down and reached in his pocket with some eagerness. "I ain't had one yet." He lit a cigarette, inhaled, and felt better immediately.

"You think," she said bleakly, "she'll write that up in our case?"

"I don't know, dear."

"You think they'll close our case if she does?"

"I don't know that neither, dear."

She clutched the sink for support. "My God, what would we do?"

The smoke curled around him luxuriously. "Don't think about it till it happens."

"I got to think about it. The rent, the gas, the lights, the food."

"They wouldn't hardly close our case for five dollars."

"Maybe they'd think it was more."

"You could prove it by the movie manager."

She went numb all over. Then suddenly she got mad about it.

It was nine o'clock when they sat down in the living room. The heat came up grudgingly. Mrs. Edmunds wrapped herself in her sweater and read the funnies. Mr. Edmunds was happily inhaling his second cigarette. They were both replete and in good humor.

The window rattled and Mr. Edmunds looked around at it lazily. "Been about two months since you asked Mr. Johnson for weather strips."

The paper shook in her hand. She did not look up. "He promised to fix it this morning but his baby died."

"His baby! You don't say!"

She kept her eye glued to the paper. "Pneumonia."

His voice filled with sympathy. He crushed out his cigarette. "Believe I'll go down and sit with him a while."

"He's not there," she said hastily. "I met him when I was going to the store. He said he'd be out all evening."

"I bet the poor man's trying to raise some money."

She let the paper fall in her lap, and clasped her hands to keep them from trembling. She lied again, as she had been lying steadily in the past twenty-four hours, as she had not lied before in all her life.

"He didn't say anything to me about raising money."

"Wasn't no need to. Where would you get the first five cents to give him?"

"I guess," she cried jealously, "you want me to give him the rest of my money."

"No," he said. "I want you to spend what little's left on yourself. Me, I wish I had fifty dollars to give him."

"As poor as you are," she asked angrily, "you'd give him that much money? That's easy to say when you haven't got it."

"I look at it this way," he said simply, "I think how I'd feel in his shoes."

"You got your own troubles," she argued heatedly. "The Johnson baby is better off dead. You'd be a fool to put fifty dollars in the ground. I'd spend my fifty dollars on the living."

"'Tain't no use to work yourself up," he said. "You ain't got fifty dollars, neither have I. We'll be quarreling in a minute over make-believe money. Let's go to bed."

Mrs. Edmunds woke at seven and tried to lie quietly by her husband's side, but lying still was torture. She dressed and went into the kitchen and felt too listless to make her coffee. She sat down at the table and dropped her head on her folded arms. No tears came. There was only the burning in her throat and behind her eyes.

She sat in this manner for half an hour. Suddenly she heard a man's slow tread outside her front door. Terror gripped her. The steps moved on down the hall, but for a moment her knees were water. When she could control her trembling, she stood up and knew that she had to get out of the house. It could not contain her and Mr. Johnson.

She walked quickly away from her neighborhood. It was a raw day and her feet and hands were beginning to grow numb. She felt sorry for herself. Other people were hurrying past in over-shoes and heavy gloves. There were fifty-one dollars in her purse. It was her right to do what she pleased with them. Determinedly she turned into the subway.

In a downtown department store she rode the escalator to the dress department. She walked up and down the rows of lovely garments, stopping to finger critically, standing back to admire.

A salesgirl came toward her, looking straight at her with soft expectant eyes.

"Do you wish to be waited on, madam?"

Mrs. Edmunds opened her mouth to say "Yes," but the word would not come. She stared at the girl stupidly. "I was just looking," she said.

In the shoe department, she saw a pair of comfort shoes and sat down timidly in a fine leather chair.

A salesman lounged toward her. "Something in shoes?"

"Yes sir. That comfort shoe."

"Size?" His voice was bored.

"I don't know," she said.

"I'll have to measure you," he said reproachfully. "Give me your foot." He sat down on a stool and held out his hand.

She dragged her eyes up to his face. "How much you say those shoes cost?"

"I didn't say. Eight dollars."

She rose with acute relief. "Oh, I didn't bring that much with me."

She retreated unsteadily. Something was making her knees weak and her head light.

Her legs steadied. She went quickly to the down escalator. She reached the third floor and was briskly crossing to the next down escalator when she saw the little dresses. A banner screamed that they were selling at the sacrifice price of one dollar. She decided to examine them.

She pushed through the crowd of women, and emerged triumphantly within reach of the dresses. She searched carefully. There were pinks and blues and yellows. She was looking for white. She pushed back through the crow. In her careful hands lay a little white dress. It was spun gold and gossamer.

Boldly she beckoned a salesgirl. "I'll take this, miss," she said.

All the way home she was excited and close to tears. She was in a fever to see Mr. Johnson. She would let the regret come later. A child lay dead and waiting burial.

She turned her corner at a run. Going down the rickety basement stairs, she prayed that Mr. Johnson was on the premises.

She pounded on his door and he opened it. The agony in his face told her instantly that he had been unable to borrow the money. She tried to speak, and her tongue tripped over her eagerness.

Fear took hold of her and rattled her teeth. "Mr. Johnson, what about the funeral?"

"I give the baby to the student doctors."

"Oh, my God, Mr. Johnson! Oh, my God!"

"I bought her some flowers."

She turned and went blindly up the stairs. Drooping in the front doorway was a frost-nipped bunch of white flowers. She dragged herself up to her flat. Once she stopped to hide the package under her coat. She would never look at that little white dress again. The ten five dollar bills were ten five-pound stones in her purse. They almost hurled her backward.

She turned the key in her lock. Mr. Edmunds stood at the door. He looked rested and confident.

"I been waiting for you. I just started to go."

"You had any breakfast?" she asked tonelessly.

"I made some coffee. It was all I wanted."

"I shoulda made some oatmeal before I went out."

"You have on the big pot time I come home. Bet I'll land something good," he boasted. "You brought good luck in this house. We ain't seen the last of it." He pecked her cheek and went out, hurrying as if he were late for work.

She plodded into the bedroom. The steam was coming up fine. She sank down on the side of the bed and unbuttoned her coat.

The package fell on her lap. She took the ten five dollar bills and pushed them between a fold of the package. It was burial money. She could never use it for anything else. She hid the package under the mattress.

Wearily she buttoned up her coat and opened her purse again. It was empty, for the few cents remaining from her last relief check had been spent indiscriminately with her prize money.

She went into the kitchen to take stock of her needs. There was nothing from their feasts. She felt the coffeepot. It was still hot, but her throat was too constricted for her to attempt to swallow.

She took her paper shopping bag and started out to Mr. Spiro's.

Papa's Place

Mama helped her daughter with the dinner dishes. Bessie washed and Mama wiped. It had been a very good dinner, and Mama felt as full and content as a kitten. Bessie looked perfectly furious. She was Mama's own child, but Mama had to resist an impulse to run.

It was hard to remember that Bessie had been a fat jolly baby. She tried to remember when Bessie had stopped being her daughter. It was so long ago, thirty-five-years. Mama had just been widowed, and Bessie was only twelve years old. All of Mama's friends had said that Bessie was wonderful. Overnight, she turned into a little woman. Only Mama could see Bessie turning into something else.

At Papa's funeral she did not shed a tear. Instead she took command and comforted Mama, and led Mama's friends up to see the remains. Indeed, she took Papa's place with Papa hardly cold in his coffin.

She had never liked Papa. Papa never knew it, but Mama did. All day long Bessie was one way, but when Papa came home Bessie was another way. She was quiet, never chattering to Papa like she did to Mama about the wonderful things she would do for him someday. She was touchy, slipping like an eel from Papa's side whenever he tried to caress her.

She was calm as an oyster when Papa fell ill. When she watched by the bedside, while Papa lay a long time dying, her expression was one of exasperation. When Papa breathed for the last time and Mama flung herself across his body Bessie pulled Mama away and said in a clear triumphant voice, "You've got me to take care of you now."

Mama stacked the dishes carefully giving them pats to keep them even the way Bessie wanted them. She stole a glance at her daughter. Bessie had not unbent. She was attacking the copper pots and pans as if she saw reflected the image of her enemy. Yet Mama knew the shining copper gave back the image of Bessie's own face.

Mama had left the kind and loving home of her parents and gone to the kind and loving home of her husband. She was not grown-up when she married. She was not really grown-up when Papa died. She was thirty, but she was gentle and clinging because first there had been her parents, and then there had been Papa to cling to.

Mama, however, had character and hadn't at all expected to cling to Bessie. She knew perfectly well that Bessie was only twelve and that she must be both father and mother to her fatherless child. Nothing surprised and baffled Mama more than to find Bessie being father and mother to her.

It was Bessie, it transpired, who was bent on making a happy home for Mama. Papa had been thrifty and there was a nice account in the bank. But Bessie got a job. After school she tended a neighbor's baby. Everybody said Bessie was a wonderful girl to work while other children were playing. Everybody wished they had a daughter as loving as Bessie. Everybody said that Mama was blessed.

When Bessie brought her first pay home and dropped it in her mother's lap, as Papa had done before her, Mama found herself saying, too, what a blessing Bessie was. And then Mama wept, not because she was happy and proud, but because Bessie looked so smug.

Mama put the silver in the table drawer. She blinked her lashes. Here she was, doing things the way Bessie wanted them done. Here she was as she had been since Papa died, under Bessie's thumb, and still unable to wriggle out from under.

Even when Bessie married, she had not been able to wriggle out. Bessie's meek little husband stood in such awe of his wife that he wanted Mama around as an ally. All of Mama's urgings that the newlyweds go their way without her met a refusal as firm as a rock. Who would look out for you? asked Bessie. What is home without a mother? asked Bessie's silly husband.

Bessie had had other chances. She did not have to marry a fool. Mama remembered two before Charlie. They had been big and dominant, and they had reminded Mama of Papa. But Bessie had been cool to them. She said they did not show proper respect for Mama. As far as Mama could tell, it was only that they did not want to marry her along with Bessie.

Charlie did not want to be the head of the house. He thought Bessie was more excellent in every way than he was. He let Bessie keep her excellent job and admired her tremendously because she earned more than he did. When he lost his own job, he bought a cookbook, and was better than Mama at preparing nice dishes.

Bessie broke her record of never indulging in sickness the day her baby was born. She had to go to bed in a hospital and lie like a lump on a log for two weeks. She was certain poor Mama could not manage without her. And indeed Mama, who had had so many years of being managed by Bessie, was like a forlorn orphan.

Bessie got the baby she wanted, a girl who obliged her by growing daily in soft and gentle ways. Charlie took care of her while Bessie was at work. He was better at it than Mama, who had lost her confidence in her ability to bathe a baby or mix a formula.

It was his being better that brought about Charlie's downfall. The child very naturally looked to him for everything. He was her infant world. He taught her her first word, which turned out to be "Daddy." It was then that Bessie divorced him for nonsupport.

When Marilyn grew old enough to understand, she understood perfectly that her daddy had never given her as much as a five-cent handkerchief, while her dear wonderful mummy had given her everything.

Mama glanced at the kitchen clock. It was nearly seven. At seven she would speak. She, who had had so many years of not speaking until spoken to, was going to have her say at last.

Marilyn, thought Mama tenderly, and saw the girl as clearly as if she stood before her. Soft and sweet and twenty-one. Young for twenty-one, still tangled up in Bessie's apron strings, still unable to choose between her mother and her heart.

If I'm not home by seven at the latest, Marilyn had said. The clock chimed softly. Well, it was seven, and there was a train speeding west at seven, too. Marilyn had made her choice.

Mama said, "Bessie," in a voice so soft and scared that Bessie did not hear her at all. So Mama said, "Bessie!" in a loud fierce voice to give her momentum to go on with the rest.

Bessie turned and stared with stern surprise. "Mama, I'm not deaf."

"No," said Mama stoutly, "but you're blind."

"What are you talking about?" said Bessie severely.

Mama sat down. She was beginning to be scared again. But having sat down, she found she could release her strength to her backbone.

"About Marilyn and that [. . .] man."

"Fiddlesticks," said Bessie calmly. "A girl brought up like Marilyn doesn't leave her home and mother for a penniless young doctor."

"If she's in love, she does," said Mama firmly.

"Marilyn knows whom she loves," said Bessie complacently. "She's a grateful child. She knows how I've sacrificed for her."

"Then I wouldn't doubt she's tired of being a burden," said Mama stolidly.

Bessie fixed Mama with her eye and made her mouth a long thin line. "What have you and Marilyn got up your sleeves? You've both been acting odd. Why is Marilyn late tonight? She knows I insist on dinner at six. Other girls her age have to work. I've kept my nose to the grindstone to keep her in college. The least she could do is obey me. And why did you stay in the park so long? I've told you time and again one hour in the sun is long enough."

"I didn't go to the park this afternoon," said Mama.

Bessie caught her breath in surprise. "But I sent you to the park. Why did you disobey me?"

"I went to the bank," said Mama excitedly. "I drew out my

money, Papa's money that you were too mean to touch. I gave it to Marilyn."

Bessie stepped back as if she had been struck.

"What for?"

"To get married on," said Mama coldly. "She's on a train now, going somewhere west to help her husband set up his practice."

Bessie looked helpless and bereft. "How could my own mother send my own child away from me?"

"It was my bounded duty," said Mama gently. "Marilyn was too much like me, too much like putty in your hands. You could turn and twist us how you liked. You led and we followed. You held the hoop and we jumped."

"It was because I always knew best," said Bessie with stubborn despair.

"It was because you were the big frog in our little pond," said Mama without reproach. "You never loved Papa because he was head of the house. You were jealous of Papa, Bessie. You think you love me, but it's just because I'm not anybody for you to be jealous of.

"When you see your child again, hard knocks will have made her a woman, and she'll be your equal like you never let me be. And you'll say she's not as lovable as she used to be. You shielded me, Bessie. You wrapped me in cotton; I'm too old to want to get out of my wrappings. But I couldn't bear to see Marilyn not knowing whether she wanted to get out either."

Bessie sank down on the edge of a chair. She twisted the corner of her apron. Her mouth hung lax, and her lower lip trembled. Her eyes were full of frustration and pain.

"Mama," said Bessie, "tell me what to do."

Mama's heart leaped to her throat. Bessie had uttered a cry for help. Bessie wanted her mother to tell her what to do. Mama got up and cradled Bessie's head against her breast.

"Just cry," said Mama sensibly. "All mothers cry when their daughters get married. You'll feel wonderful after."

Bessie's tears wet Mama's dress just like when Bessie fell off the tricycle. Mama felt wonderful, too.

Bessie

Mr. Bannister came home from Bessie's funeral and went straight upstairs to his room. He stretched himself full length on his bed and stared up at the ceiling. Below the stairs he heard the muted voices of his new young wife and his children.

The voices sounded alien. Mr. Bannister was suddenly overwhelmed with his loss. He had lost his best friend. Indeed, he had lost his right arm.

Mr. Bannister remembered the first time he had seen Bessie Hobbs. She was seventeen and as shy as a bird. It was quite a month before he realized how pretty she was. By that time, however, he was head over heels in love with a widow ten years his senior, and anyone as young as Bessie simply didn't count.

Bessie had come to work for his mother when his father was ill and required his mother's constant attendance. Bessie's own father had just died, and however regrettable it was to leave school, her earnings would feed the numerous younger Hobbses.

In no time at all she was rock and anchor to Mr. Bannister's mother. When his father died, it was Bessie who saw his mother through her bitter bereavement. She was like a devoted daughter. And it was natural that Mr. Bannister should give her the teasing affection he would have given a younger sister.

Sometimes he went into the kitchen to help her with the dishes. He had got over the widow, and he told her how silly he had been, and how he would marry a simple home girl someday. Bessie would listen gravely. The color would glow in her cheeks and he would tease her about having a beau. Bessie would deny it hotly, often with tears springing to her eyes. Mr. Bannister would be glad though he did not really know why.

In the fall Mr. Bannister went away to college. In his letters to his mother there was always some little message for Bessie. In his mother's letters to him there was always some little message from Bessie. With him always at school, his mother and Bessie ate together and sat together and took their infrequent excursions together.

At Christmas, Mr. Bannister brought a college friend home with him. Bessie set the table for three. Mrs. Bannister went into the kitchen to talk to her. She said that Bessie was her companion now and entitled to a place at the table. When Bessie sat down at dinner, Mr. Bannister was surprised and embarrassed. He stole a quick glance at his college friend. The boy's eyes were wide with admiration and Mr. Bannister felt a prick of jealousy that he could not explain.

After dinner he followed Bessie to the kitchen. Diffidently he asked if she had a beau yet. When she assured him with blushes that she hadn't, he sternly advised her to wait for Mr. Right, and not to let a fickle college boy turn her head.

For summer vacation, Mr. Bannister joined his mother and

Bessie at his mother's seashore cottage. It was the happiest summer he had ever known. He and Bessie were constantly together. He taught her to swim, he took her fishing, they went on long hikes. He had a few summer crushes, but somehow none of these smartly dressed girls was quite what he wanted.

As his college friendships multiplied, Mr. Bannister did not always come home for the winter and spring vacations. In summer he went to the seashore only for weekends. Through the week he read law in his uncle's office in town. He was maturing rapidly, and as his world broadened, his mother and Bessie seemed dear and sweet but a little too old fashioned.

The summer after he finished college, he got desk space in his uncle's office and the promise of steady advancement. Labor Day weekend he arrived at his mother's cottage with a new suit, a broad smile, and a bride.

The young couple lived with the senior Mrs. Bannister. Mr. Bannister could not yet afford a maid, and his bride had never learned to keep house. When the junior Mrs. Bannister learned Bessie was not a poor relation but a paid servant without even a high school diploma, she had a scene with her mother-in-law.

The scene upset Mrs. Banister so that she took to bed with a fluttering heart. When she was able to be up again, Bessie's kitchen status was settled. She spoke to her son, but he said that he wanted no part of a woman's fuss. Mrs. Bannister began to spend most of her time in her bedroom. And as her frailty increased, so did her dependence on Bessie.

At the end of the year Mr. Bannister's son was born. He was a fine average baby with the average baby's many demands. Young Mrs. Bannister was ready to scream inside of a month. She found an escape by getting a job.

There came a catastrophic month for Mr. Bannister. His wife's employer moved his business to another city. Young Mrs. Bannister kept her job. She did not write her husband for two weeks. When she did, it was to ask for a divorce.

Mr. Bannister rushed off to see her. His mother went to bed with shock. He found Bessie's telegram on his return to his hotel, after his humiliating session with his wife and her employer, so obviously the man she planned to marry next. He returned home alone to his mother's funeral.

He walked straight through the house to the kitchen. Bessie was feeding the baby. He knelt and put his face in Bessie's lap. No words passed between them and Mr. Bannister wished he could stay in the kitchen with his face in Bessie's lap forever.

All that week Mr. Bannister tried to find words to ask Bessie to take her meals with him. At night when he sat in the living room alone, he longed to ask Bessie to join him. But however hard he tried, the words would not come.

One night he rode home on the bus behind two of his neighbors. The most voluble one was telling her friend that young Mrs. Bannister had left her husband because of the long relationship between him and Bessie, which relationship Mr. Bannister had tried to hide by relegating Bessie to the kitchen.

It did not take young Mrs. Bannister long to see that Bessie was crazy about her husband. After the birth of the baby, she had gone to work to regain her self-respect. Now she was in another city getting a divorce, so that Mr. Bannister would be free to marry Bessie.

Mr. Bannister was upset but the only thing on his mind was that he was compromising Bessie.

There was but one thing Mr. Bannister could do. The next day he invited his secretary to lunch. He had never paid any particular attention to her. Now he saw that she was charming and amusing and kind. They went to lunch rather constantly after that and then they began to go to dinner and the theater, and on Sunday outings.

When his wife received her divorce, Mr. Bannister realized suddenly and sharply that for some time now he had monopolized most of Miss Taylor's evenings, and that his only honorable course was to propose to her.

They were married one Saturday afternoon. Bessie did not know they were married until they walked into the house as man and wife. She murmured her congratulations through bloodless lips.

The new Mrs. Bannister liked Bessie at once. She did not try to usurp Bessie's place with the child. Instead she tried very hard to be a good housekeeper that Bessie might devote more of her day to the baby.

When her own child was born, she regained her strength very slowly. Bessie took care of both babies and the ailing mother and the house. When Mr. Bannister came home from work, the house was cleaner and dinner better than they had been when his wife was well and able to help.

When Mrs. Bannister was strong again, she made few bungled efforts to care for her child. But soon she surrendered her baby to Bessie and decided to do all the housework by herself.

Dinner was not always on time, and sometimes the roast was not quite done. In her last minute scramble to gather the laundry, Mrs. Bannister would often overlook her husband's favorite shirts.

Gradually, and with tact, Bessie began to relieve Mrs. Bannister of her duties. Mr. Bannister was aware of the difference but he did not mention it. He felt as if Bessie had been away and had come back. He knew that nothing would be the same if she ever went away for good.

Mrs. Bannister's second baby was born, then her third. She did not mend after her child's birth, but death did not free her for seven long years.

For those seven years, Bessie kept house for Mr. Bannister and the children. She sat at table with them. It came about very naturally when the children were small and needed instruction in table manners. They called her Aunt Bessie because she was the nearest thing to a mother that any of them could remember.

The oldest boy was fourteen when his stepmother died. He loved Bessie more than anyone in the world. He knew that his mother had deserted him, and that Bessie had not.

He was too young to be tactful and told his father that he owed it to Bessie to marry her for her years of faithfulness. His father was furiously resentful. He saw Bessie as a scheming woman who had let slip her chances to marry, and now, in her middle thirties, had sent a sentimental boy to plead for her.

It was in this state of anger that was really guilt that Mr. Bannister met Peggy Hollis. She was everything that Bessie was not. In short, she was twenty-one.

There was a whirlwind courtship. Mr. Bannister had never acted so silly in his life.

For the third time and with no forewarning, Mr. Bannister brought his bride to Bessie. As he looked from the young, trim girl at his side to the worn and gentle woman before him, he was filled with a sense of intolerable loss, and his triumph turned to ashes.

Bessie went to bed that night with a blinding headache. She could not raise her head from the pillow the next morning. The children were late for school. The beds went unmade. The third Mrs. Bannister burned her hands at the stove.

Toward noon Bessie fell into delirium. The doctor was called. He was very grave when he left her room. He said she did not seem to have the will to live. . . .

Mr. Bannister lay on his bed and stared up at the ceiling. Below the stairs he heard the alien voices. Mr. Bannister rolled over and muffled his mouth in the pillow. The marriage bed shook beneath his sobs.

Mother Love

The maternal instinct, Leila always insisted, was something you had or you hadn't. You didn't acquire it by having a child. Leila felt that she could speak with authority for all her life she had had the examples of her mother and her maiden aunt.

Pat—Leila rarely called her Mother—was sweet and all that but she just wasn't maternal. On the other hand, Aunt Clara had been mother in everything but name.

From the first, Pat hadn't wanted a baby. Leila had heard the story often from Aunt Clara. Pat had been planning her first trip to Europe. She and her husband Terry had never had a proper honeymoon, just a week that began and ended in a downpour and a touch of the grippe for Pat. For two years she and Terry had saved for a second honeymoon abroad. A week before their scheduled sailing Pat was taken sick suddenly. Only this time it was not the grippe. It was a baby.

Pat stormed and wept and said she did not want a baby. She wanted to go abroad. And now all that lovely money that she and

Terry had saved would have to be spent for hospitals and doctors and diapers. For a month, Pat's rebellion continued. After that she began to feel wonderful and excited. She made the most extravagant plans for Junior's future.

Leila was born, and Pat turned her face away and wept. A girl after all those months of waiting for a son. When she came from the hospital Pat was still not reconciled. It was quite two months before she stopped minding. If Aunt Clara hadn't been on hand to love and want her, Leila was sure she would have grown up with all kinds of complexes.

Clara had come to stay with Pat during the last weeks before Leila's birth. Clara was Pat's eldest sister. She had raised Pat and her other brothers and sisters after their mother died. She had been only sixteen, but a born mother in every way.

By the time Pat was of an age to marry, Clara was well along in her thirties. She had raised a houseful of children. It had kept her busy and happy. Her father, until his death, had been her beloved companion. She had not lacked a man's advice in the children's upbringing. In addition, her father had considerately remained alive until his youngest child, who was Pat, was grown up and working. His insurance, wherein Clara was sole beneficiary, would provide her with a modest income for life. Marriage, therefore, had never held out sufficient enticement to make Clara want to change her way of life.

With her father's death, and Pat's marriage a year later, Clara became aware of her solitude and her spinsterhood. She began to realize that her married brothers and sisters no longer came to see her. On birthdays and vacations they visited their in-laws because their in-laws were the grandparents of their children.

When Pat wrote Clara a tearful little note, decrying her canceled trip and the reason for it, Clara felt the first surge of happiness she had known in three years. Pat was going to have a child, and Terry had no living parents to have first claim on it.

Clara began to dream about Pat's baby while Pat was still hating the whole idea. When Pat wrote that she wanted a boy, Clara wrote back that she hoped the baby would be a dear little girl. She wanted to make adorable dresses again. Did Pat remember her own dear little dresses? Pat did. She had always hated homemade clothes.

When Leila was born and Pat could not bear the sight of her, Clara stayed on. Leila knew—Aunt Clara had once told her—that she probably would have died of neglect if her aunt hadn't been there to care for her. Of course, her mother had nursed her but a child needed affection as much as food. After a month or so her mother had got used to her, and had even begun to view her with pride.

It was a little selfish of Pat, Leila always thought, to wrest her out of Aunt Clara's arms just when Aunt Clara was beginning to think of her as her very own. Literally, of course, Pat assumed full charge of her child, because her full strength was restored and because she absorbed all the advice in the baby books and could follow it efficiently. That didn't alter the fact that it was a terrific wrench to Aunt Clara's heart.

Pat didn't seem to notice. She did not urge Clara to make her home with her. She took it for granted that Clara was ready and anxious to return to her own house. But to Clara, the thought of going away, and leaving Leila to Pat's inexpert hands, was more than she could bear. She went in secret to the landlord and leased a small flat across the hall. She told Pat that she was too young to stay tied to a house all day and all night. She, Clara, would always be happy to mind the baby. Pat was more than grateful. She and Terry hadn't been out in ages.

Leila didn't know who would have dried her tears when she was small if Aunt Clara hadn't been next door with comforting arms and candy. Pat let her take the bumps from the time she first began to walk and lay in a sprawling sobbing heap. Through her first years at school when she sometimes came home in tears, Pat just said she must fight her own battles.

For the first eight years of Leila's life practically everything she wore was something Aunt Clara made. Pat was always too busy to sew. Sewing by hand took too much time. She would add also, unnecessarily, that she hated her own homemade dresses, and saw no reason for Leila to suffer similarly.

When Leila was eight, she began hating homemade dresses, too. Aunt Clara still thought the old styles were prettiest, and Leila grew self-conscious about looking different.

Leila was willing to admit that she adored the dresses Pat bought for her. But she never forgot that Aunt Clara said that anybody could go downtown and buy a dress.

Pat had some good points. For one thing, she kept up with things, and could always answer Leila's questions. She read a good deal. That was fine, but she never let Leila interrupt her. She said that she and Leila were two separate individuals and each should respect the rights of the other. Aunt Clara said that was stuff and nonsense. A mother's life was inseparable from her child's.

When Leila reached her teens, she began to grow a little tired of spending so much time with Aunt Clara. She found that it was nicer in her mother's flat, where she could go off to dream in her room without Pat coming in every five minutes to ask if she felt ill.

When she and her girlfriends giggled over their fudge making, Pat didn't want to come into the kitchen to join in the fun. Pat didn't mind when you raced out of the house, leaving her alone. She didn't get excited when she saw you walking home from school with a boy.

All of Leila's friends adored Pat, though Leila couldn't see why. They said she was understanding, not a bit like their mothers. Their mothers, they said, were as bad as Leila's Aunt Clara, quite unable to grasp the idea that they were grown up.

Leila felt that her friends were being unfair to their mothers. Only an unnatural mother like Pat would placidly accept her child's growing up. Aunt Clara simply couldn't. She cried on Leila's birthdays because she was a year older and a year nearer independence.

Leila told Aunt Clara about Larry before she told Pat. She kissed Larry good night, and flew across the hall to her aunt's apartment. The ring on her finger felt unfamiliar and wonderful.

Aunt Clara came to the door in her bathrobe. She looked at Leila's shining eyes, then down at the jewel on her outstretched hand. Aunt Clara burst into tears. There were not tears of joy. She was inconsolable. Leila held her in her arms, patting her into quiet, assuring her that she had not lost a niece, but had gained a nephew. It was obvious that Aunt Clara did not consider the gain of any importance.

Leila went back to her own flat with a terrible let-down feeling. Aunt Clara had not wanted to share her happiness. Instead, she had wanted Leila to share her grief. Leila decided to go and wake Pat. If Pat was going to be troublesome, too, she might as well be troublesome now and get it over with.

She called Pat into her bedroom. She heard Pat close her book.

Pat would probably ask why she should be dragged away from her book to be shown a ring that she could have seen some other time. Diffidently, Leila held out her hand.

Pat gave a little aching cry, opened her arms. Leila felt happy and love inside them. Then Pat released her and searched her eyes and was satisfied. For a moment Pat's lips trembled but before Leila's own eyes could fill, Pat was making a joke about weeping and making wrinkles.

"I didn't think you'd take it like this," said Leila. "I thought you'd either not care or you'd carry on like Aunt Clara did."

"So you told Clara first," Pat said quietly.

Leila dropped her eyes. "You know how she is about me," she said hastily.

"Yes, I know," Pat said gently. "She lives for you."

"But I don't want her to," Leila burst out passionately, remembering that scene with Aunt Clara. 'I'm only her niece, and anyway, marrying isn't the same as dying!'"

"To Clara it's almost the same. Don't forget she raised me and my brothers and sisters, but she wasn't our mother. When we married, our children weren't her grandchildren. Sometimes we forgot Clara was on earth. I was never sorry to see you make up for our omissions."

"You let her love me more than you loved me," Leila cried jealously.

"I let her spoil you," Pat said. "That isn't the same thing."

Leila looked surprised. "I guess it isn't," she said slowly.

"I've always known," said Pat, and her voice broke a little, "that you thought me an unnatural mother. Clara, bless her heart, never wanted to be married that she could not understand that I could love Terry so much that at first, your coming seemed an intrusion. Nor could she know that almost every woman wants to give her husband a son, not because she loves boys best, but because she thinks her husband does."

Leila gave a guilty start. Tonight when she had looked at Larry, she had thought about a son in his image.

"If sometimes I seemed cold," Pat went on, "it was because I was preparing myself—and you—for this moment. Clara would never face it. I faced it the first day you went to school. Every real mother does, Leila. Every mother who places her child's future self-sufficiency before her own present delight in that child's independence."

"If I ever have a child," said Leila defiantly, "I won't let Aunt Clara come near it."

"Don't say that, darling," Pat pleaded.

"She's an overindulgent maiden aunt," said Leila firmly.

In the flat across the hall, Clara lay sobbing into her pillow. Larry had a perfectly good set of parents and so had Leila.

The Puppy

When twelve-year-old Johnny Barrow drowned on a summer's day, nobody thought John, senior, would survive the shock. The two had been inseparable. They had been perfect companions.

Margaret had stayed outside their charmed circle, for Margaret had never wanted children, and had never forgiven Johnny for making her a mother. Yet it was she who went to pieces and turned into an old woman.

John and Margaret Barrow had been married fifteen years. Six months after their marriage, John knew he should never have married Margaret, and Margaret should never have married anyone.

The young bride took her marriage lightly. She seemed to delight in her inability to make a bed decently, or broil a chop, or hold a serious conversation. At first he had laughed at her bedmaking, and kissed the finger that she had cut trying to get a dinner out of cans, and teased her because she read nothing but the funnies and the ads, and caught her up and danced her around the room when she switched from a quiet symphony to a blast of jazz.

But when six months later she was still a sophomore on holiday, John decided that men were fools who want the honeymoon to last forever. The day that he was notified of a promotion and raise in pay, he went to see a doctor. He was afraid of his ability to handle his new job because of his steady loss of weight and nervous fatigue. The doctor found that he was suffering from nothing more than undernourishment, and advised him to get married and stop eating in restaurants.

John went straight from the doctor's office to a glittering restaurant where he was reproachfully assured that nothing served came out of cans. He ate two enormous dinners without stopping. Over coffee he thought with grim amusement of Margaret's happy satisfaction that marriage was not making her fat.

He felt wonderful on his way home, and stopped to buy flowers for Margaret. After all, he had got a promotion and a raise. It was a cause for celebration. For with a fat raise he was going to hire a cook-housekeeper. He knew that Margaret would be happy about that as he was. She would poutingly protest that he spoiled her. He should make her learn to do things, she would insist, letting herself look small and young and helpless. And he would feel that he was a brute to expect her to be anything but beautiful.

Margaret's beauty would make his heart miss a beat. She could make all other women seem shadows that his hands had no wish to touch. He could not yet live without her, he was ready to admit. And if he lived with her, he would have to be the homemaker. A hired housekeeper would have to be his proxy.

At the end of two years, Margaret's beauty disturbed John only when other men drifted toward her and away from their plain wives. For Margaret had not matured! Her mouth still wore a childish pout. She was exactly the same as she was when they married, which was no credit to himself.

He was lonely. He lived with a child whose whole life was spent in having fun. And, because Margaret was a child, her fun was entirely innocent, and he could not even expend his passion in jealousy.

It was then that John began to want a son. He felt that where he had failed, a baby might succeed in making Margaret a woman. It would be something smaller and frailer than herself, dependent on her for everything. Surely in that moment when she saw her son for the first time, Margaret's eyes would flow and soften and her lips would curve into tenderness.

But, Margaret's eyes filled with angry tears, and she turned her face to the window. The nurse assured the discomforted father that many young mothers reacted like that. They got over it, she said heartily. John knew that Margaret would not. In a flash he realized that she was jealous. Her son's tiny hand made her own look enormous, his doll-sized body made hers seem immense. It was a contrast she hated.

Margaret was more thistledown than ever after Johnny's birth. It was as if she sought by this means to prove to herself and the world in general that motherhood had not changed her. John was the stay-at-home with his son when Margaret plunged back into gaiety. John wheeled the baby in the park while Margaret went riding with unmarried friends who had no tiresome bassinet on the backseat. When she was cornered by expectant parents, she sent a frantic signal to John, who joined the conversation and talked with ease and eloquence about infant care.

As Johnny grew it began to appear that he was to be like his

mother in looks and like his father in ways. It was a long time before he realized that the flyaway Margaret was his mother. Even
when he knew, it did not matter. He continued to prefer the
motherly housekeeper, and would go to Margaret only when
coaxed with candy.

But the housekeeper filled only a physical part of his life. It
was his father who was the beginning and end of his inner world.
His love for his father was an incandescent light that gave him a
beauty beyond Margaret's. What John could not kindle in Margaret for all his trying was a radiance in Johnny's eyes whenever he
lifted his face to his father.

So Johnny took that place in his father's heart that Margaret
had not even wanted to fill. And John was no longer lonely. Margaret's persistent youth was no longer terrifying. Johnny was adult
beyond his years. At eight he could talk about things with his father of which Margaret hadn't the vaguest notion. At ten a bril-
liant future was already predicted for him. John settled down to
the long rich years of his son's companionship. At twelve Johnny
Barrow was dead.

Margaret had never known death. She had never before been
close to it. She had never been summoned by a screaming child to
a stretch of white beach and given a lifeless body to hold. She had
never had to tell a man that his son was dead through her selfishness. She had never had to lie awake living over and over that afternoon when Johnny flung in from a taxing game of tennis, and
downed two glasses of ice water, and she shooed him out to take
a swim, because it was much too hot to have a boy tramping
around the house.

Everybody thought that Johnny's death would very nearly kill
his father. And everybody was shocked when Margaret seemed to

take it harder. She collapsed at the funeral, and for weeks her life hung by a thread. When she was better, she had no interest in anything. She would weep silently for hours; she would talk in a mournful tone that set the listener's nerves on edge. She drew her hair back into a tight knot, she went without makeup and her clothes hung shapeless from her thin body.

She was not acting. The death of her son had thrust her violently into an adulthood for which she had never prepared herself. All of the years of her marriage she had always been less than twenty in her mind. Now she felt every day of her thirty-seven years. Because to her, thirty-seven was terribly old, she turned into an old woman.

Margaret's collapse, and long illness, and slow disintegration had allowed John no moment of loneliness in which to give release to his own grief. When he came home from the office, after a harrowing day of holding himself in, he could not remove his forced bright look. He had to wear it through the long evenings of Margaret's expressed despair. When at last he let his mask slip off in his pillow, with Margaret lying awake and tearful beside him, he was not permitted the relief of a muffled groan.

One night in late fall, on his way to his suburban home, John drove past a kennel of wire-haired puppies. He had passed it innumerable times in the last years, but Margaret had been so much like a playful kitten, that he had never felt there was room for a frolicking puppy.

On a sudden impulse he turned into the driveway. In the world of adults, into which Margaret had made her belated and unhappy entrance, there was no one who could give her a reason for living. That world of death and tears and middle age offered her no inducement to laugh and be merry again. Margaret's maturity, which John had given up hoping for, had come to mock him for his folly in wanting to make her over.

When John walked into his living room, a three-month-old wire-haired puppy wriggled out of his grasp, tore a destructive path across the room, and leaped into Margaret's arms. He covered her startled face with kisses, then fastened his teeth in her sleeve and began to tug, growling idiotically, and slipping and sliding over her lap.

Margaret laughed. It was a crazy sound at first, because it was rusty. But then her laughter grew steadier and stronger, and was pealing silver bell. The puppy wagged his stub of tail joyously. He jumped from her lap and planted himself before her, looking up at her roguishly, imploring her to give chase.

Margaret rose. All of the tightness flowed out of her body. She was lithe and fluid again. Her eyes were sparkling with fun, her cheeks began to blaze with color. She snatched out her hairpins and shook her hair free of the restraint she had held it in. Her mouth puckered into a pout.

Margaret and the puppy romped together.

Quietly John left them and started up the stairs. Halfway up he grasped the banister and great sobs racked his body.

Margaret and the puppy did not hear him.

A Boy in the House

When Nora met Roy Ormsby, she thought he was ten years younger than he was. He had a frank, boyish quality that charmed her at once, and made him seem twenty-five instead of thirty-seven. She was twenty-nine. Some days later, when a friend informed her of his actual age, her feeling was one of intense relief. She examined this emotion with surprise, and blushed at the reason behind it. She was in love with Roy Ormsby. Something terrific had happened to her heart the first time she set eyes on him.

Quite by accident Nora ran into Roy one sunny Saturday. He held her outstretched hand a moment longer than necessary, and she felt excitement riding inside her. Perhaps he had liked her on first meeting, too. Anyway, it was plain he hadn't disliked her.

"Where are you off to?" he demanded.

"I'm waiting for a street car," she said. Then they both burst out laughing, much more heartily than her innocent witticism deserved.

"That one has whiskers," he said, still chuckling. "Why don't you admit you were waiting for me?"

She hated herself for blushing and being unable to think of a clever retort. "No, really," she said quickly. "I've a hundred and one things to do at home. That's where I'm going."

"That's what you think," he said agreeably. "Look, there's a park gate not a yard away. And beyond that gate there's not a care in the world. Come on and let me show you the spot where the wind blew off my toupee."

She laughed, and let herself be led through the gate with her hand again in his. Some magic was working inside her through the touch of his fingers. The world outside seemed far away. The thing she wanted most to do was to take off her shoes and pretend she was a little girl of ten.

"You see," he said triumphantly.

"What?" she said rather breathlessly, knowing that he had read her thoughts.

"You look like a happy little girl. I like the way the park makes you look," he said.

She wanted to say, "It isn't the park at all, it's you. You make me feel as young as you feel." She said instead, "I've got two rooms in a tall apartment house. When I can't stand them any longer, I look at the pictures in a garden magazine."

He stopped dead in his tracks and struck his forehead with mock solemnity. "You see before you a seer, seeing the house you've picked out. It's snug on a hill, white, with blue blinds. There's a flagstone walk and a lily pond."

Suddenly she couldn't be teased about it. She tried to laugh, but it was not very successful. She turned her face away and did not trust herself to speak.

"Is that the way you like a house to look?" There was no raillery in his voice. "Is it?" he persisted. She steadied her voice and said, lightly, "I'll let you draw the plans for my dream house."

"I've a better plan," he said, "And it isn't on paper. I'll show you that house, and I'm not a salesman. It's mine."

"I thought it was," she said simply. He thrust his hand through her arm and steered her toward the pond, where busy little boys were being admirals.

"Name the day when you can come, and I'll empty the ash-trays, and polish my shoes, and wash the dog."

That was his way of making love. She had thought the grand passion required soft lights. But nobody had to tell her she was being wooed. This was it. For in this short while she had learned enough about this man to know that if he had talked otherwise, neither of them could have borne it. Something had swept them both off their feet and only his light approach could control them. They stopped to smile at the little boys.

"Do you like kids?" Roy asked.

"I love them. Boys especially."

"I have a boy," Roy said. "Seventeen. His mother died when he was three. There's been just the two of us since."

Nora tried to conceal her surprise and shock. She said quickly, "You seem so young to be the father of a nearly grown boy."

"Skip's kept me young," he explained. "We've had a heck of a lot of fun together."

She was suddenly terribly jealous of his son. "Is that why you never remarried?"

"No," he said promptly and seriously. "I've never remarried be-cause I've never been in love. I'm not even sure I loved Skip's mother. I was only nineteen and she was the prettiest girl on the campus. We eloped one night. But I don't remember any bells ringing in my ears or any flags waving in my heart the way it was with me the day I met you."

She pressed his arm. "That's the way it was with me, too. That's the way it is when you're in love."

Two months later they were married, and Nora went to live in the white house with the blue blinds. Skippy approved of her. He was a senior in his last month in high school, certain to graduate with honors, and very serious about the war. He and Roy were armchair strategists nightly.

Nora liked Skippy best when she was alone with him. He was full of the joy of living, and his brand of humor was wonderful. But with his father he was different. He talked to him gravely about the war and life and even death. And sometimes Nora saw him look at Roy with an expression of such compassion that she would turn away quickly.

She could not understand it. Why should he look at Roy like that? Why was he different when Roy was around? Hadn't Roy said that Skippy's youth had kept him young? Well, Skippy was certainly acting like Old Man Moses nowadays. Was it because he didn't approve of his father's marriage, but wouldn't voice his disapproval because that wasn't the thing to do?

On the day that Roy and Skippy went for a long walk and Roy came back looking white about the mouth, Nora knew that Skippy had told him he didn't want a stepmother. Now Roy was going to be torn between his wife and his son. Nora steeled herself to face his decision.

Overnight, Skippy's attitude toward Roy changed. He was gay again with his father. Nora could guess what Skippy was doing. He was trying to take his father away from her.

On the eve of Skippy's graduation Nora decided to talk it out with Roy. For that was the night she came to the unhappy conclusion that Skippy had won.

Immediately and angrily she made up her mind to tell Roy to send the boy to some farm to work through the summer. And when Skippy got ready to choose his college, she would insist that Roy help him choose one that was far, far away. As it was, he hadn't said a word about higher education. Didn't want to leave home and Daddy.

Nora followed Roy to the front porch. He was leaning against the railing, pulling on his pipe. His face was controlled again.

"Marvelous night," she said lightly. "Let's go look at the lily pond."

They stood and looked at the flowers. She remembered how they had stood and looked at the little boys who could break hearts because their youth was so beautiful. "I want to talk about Skippy," she said desperately.

Her tone arrested him. "Do you? Did he tell you?" he said slowly.

"I've known for a long time," she said bleakly.

He sighed deeply and fully. "He didn't want you to know before tomorrow. He's a kid who loves laughter. He loved to make you laugh, and he didn't want to make you cry before he had to."

"What sweet consideration," she said bitterly.

He looked a little embarrassed. "Well, the kid took a fancy to you from the first, and I suppose he thinks you feel the same way. He told me about his desire to enlist because he had to have my consent. You may have noticed he's been standing on his head ever since to make me laugh again. That's why he's been so gay. He wants us to remember him that way. That's the way he wants to remember us."

Nora felt small and ashamed. Her eyes filled with tears. She sobbed against Roy's heart.

"Don't," he said gently. "You've known all along, and you haven't let down. Don't do it now. You see, he enlists tomorrow. Let's make tonight a lark."

He dried her tears, and they started back toward the house. They could see Skippy silhouetted against the porch light. She loved him so much that she wanted to weep again.

"Hey," she called, "just because you're a sweet boy graduate, you don't have to strike a pose so we can admire you."

He laughed, and so did Roy, and then so did Nora.

The Cottagers
and Mrs. Carmody

Mrs. Carmody got the cottages ready for weekenders. Someone would write her a letter, enclosing a list of provisions and a money order. Mrs. Carmody would sit down with a stub of pencil and a penny postcard and slowly, painfully inform the letter writer that message and contents had been received.

She rarely saw the weekenders. She had keys to all their houses. She would go in, air and dust, drag in firewood, check the piles of purchases on the kitchen table, and depart. When the cottagers had gone, leaving behind them a note of thanks, three dollars, and the leftovers, Mrs. Carmody returned to carry away a week's meals.

The bitter winter months, from December through February, were the period when Mrs. Carmody, sitting in her small, run-down house, talking monotonously to Pete, her old and adoring mongrel dog, was lifeless and lonely and often hungry for a tastier bit than oatmeal, the meatless stews, the bread and tea that her budget allowed. For most of the money that Mrs. Carmody made in the seasonal months went into her burial hoard. She had never had any insurance. She had been superstitious about it until Tim died. There was always a bit of money in the bank, enough to tide them through a brief illness. Insurance to both her and Tim, had seemed a macabre investment. The fact of death was something neither one of them would face. They were childless and could not bear the thought that one might die and leave the other.

Tim fell ill. It was a long dying, and Mrs. Carmody could not leave him and go to work. The money in the bank diminished, dwarfed, disappeared. And when Tim died, there was nothing with which to bury him.

Mrs. Carmody had never been beholden in her life. She was beholden now. Helplessly she had to stand by and see kindly neighbors contribute their hard-earned dimes and dollars to a coffin and a plot of ground. The only other choice was too heartbreaking, even for contemplation.

She was sixty, and she was old. The two years of nursing had taken their toll. There was no use her seeking steady employment. Her long confinement and anxiety by a sick bed had made her too nervous to work in one place all day.

Her work for the cottagers was ideal. She rarely had to see them, for they were people on rustic holiday, who wanted no waiting on. Spring and fall were the times of year when Mrs. Carmody, who had enjoyed good eating when Tim was alive and well, and had never quite lost her lusty appetite, was able to feel her flesh fill out with ends of lamb, chicken wings, slabs of pie, chunks of cake, and generous scoops of creamy potato and macaroni.

During the summer the pickings were less profitable, for the cottagers had come to stay, and often there were guests who kept the cupboard bare. But Mrs. Carmody's desire for good food was tempered by the summer heat, and she had no unwillingness to eat sparsely.

It was in winter that Mrs. Carmody sat close by her coal fire, describing to the half-asleep Pete all the delicious things she wished some good fairy would bring them to eat. She stirred her tea and ate her bread and tried to think of them as meat and macaroni. But despite her imagination, there was still an unsatisfied feeling in her stomach when she put her cup down and swept her lap free of crumbs.

By spring, Mrs. Carmody was so starved for one of those wonderful meals of leftover macaroni, full of cheese and milk and butter, and beef bones with generous shreds of beautiful meat, and crumbled cake covered with lovely goo, that she was as impatient as a child at Christmas in her nervous expectation, excited waiting for the first letter from the first cottager.

Mrs. Peters wrote first. Her list included a turkey, the finest that Mrs. Carmody could find. Her son had just been discharged from the Army. He had a hankering to see the old house in which he had spent the idyllic summers of his boyhood. He had an equal hankering for turkey. His return to America had been long months coming. He had hoped to be home for Thanksgiving. When his sailing orders were canceled, his disappointment was keen. He had made up his mind to have Thanksgiving dinner at home if he didn't set foot on American soil until summer.

Mrs. Carmody hadn't had turkey since Tim died. On feast days her friendly neighbors had invited her to join them. But she knows that these were courtesy invitations, freely extended but

sent out of sympathy for her aloneness. She did not wish to in-
trude upon their family reunions and recollections. The taste of
Mrs. Peters' turkey was as strong in her mind as if an ambrosial
bite of it were on her tongue.

It was a beautiful bird, big, buxom, and tender to her exploring
touch. She eyed it with more envy than she had ever eyed anything in the whole of her undemanding life. For Mrs. Carmody
knew her years on earth were numbered. And old Pete's, too. If
only once before they died, their kitchen could be filled with the
fragrance of a roasting turkey. If she could see a whole turkey, not
the wing of it, nor the end of it, nor the last part to jump over the
fence. If she could set it, browned to perfection, in the center of
her own table, and cut off a slice of the light and a slice of the
dark for Pete, and then eat her way through to the naked frame,
she would want nothing more this side of heaven.

Mrs. Carmody sighed and set the refrigerator humming. She
wasn't even sure there'd be any leftovers this weekend, including
a slice of this elegant bird. For young men were eaters, particularly young men who had been away to war and had their hearts
set on Thanksgiving dinner. They stuffed themselves sick and
wouldn't call quits until they had polished off the last bone.

Determinedly she turned her mind away from anticipation.
Still she spent a wretched weekend. She had remembered Mrs.
Peters' boy as a pleasant-faced youngster. Now she saw him as an
inhuman monster, entirely composed of interior and a wicked in-
tent to plague a poor old woman.

For plagued she was. Her conscience bothered her because of her
unkind thoughts. Her stomach refused to be solaced by her sorry
offerings. Her heart pumped painfully at every imagined meal hour
at the Peters' house. The interminable weekend dragged to its end.

Mrs. Carmody walked at a funeral pace into Mrs. Peters' kitchen. She was controlling her desire to race as fast as her shuffling gait could carry her. She mustn't be foolish. There might not even be the carcass. For Mrs. Peters was not the kind to leave bare bones as if she thought a lowly charlady could work some magic that would turn them into meat. No, there might be a bit of pie though she doubted this, too. There would probably be a dish of vegetables that the boy hadn't wanted, spinach or carrots, or similar pap.

Miserably, she crossed to the table. There were the note and the three bills. She picked up the note and scowled at it, not so much in anger as in her inability to see well without her reading glasses. The words blurred and she waited until they came into focus. Then slowly, haltingly she read aloud:

"'Dear Mrs. Carmody:
Thank you for everything. Hope to run down again soon. It was my son's idea to eat Thanksgiving dinner here. Then he decided he couldn't wait. So we had a huge turkey feast at home the day after I wrote to you. And he stuffed so, bless his heart, that he doesn't want to hear the word 'turkey' mentioned for another year. I didn't write you because I supposed you had already bought it, and I didn't want to upset you. We brought down a ham. Sorry, there is a shred, but the turkey is yours, and welcome.'"

Mrs. Carmody's old lined face was beautiful with its radiance. She turned toward the refrigerator like somebody walking in a happy dream.

And there it was. And there she was only a matter of inches away from it.

Skippy

Skippy was the least important occupant of the house. He was loved, but he was never consulted. It was taken for granted that the family's will was his will, and that he would follow blindly. He was their dog.

When the family decided to move, Skippy was not invited to voice his views. They decided quite suddenly, on a day when everything seemed to go wrong. Mrs. Adams watched the first prize go to Mrs. Cranston at the flower show. Mr. Adams came home from the publishing house with a book to read and report on and Mrs. Adams followed him up to their bedroom, where he had retired to escape the sounds of banging doors, telephones, and dinner preparations.

Buzz Adams stormed in cross as sticks because Sally, who lived next door, had given him back his class ring. Chottie Adams drifted in dreamily from her first meeting with a tall, dark, and handsome young man. When the Adamses sat down to dinner, they began a round of grievances.

"Mrs. Adams said, with her mouth beginning to waver again, "It isn't that Lola Cranston has a better growing hand than I have. It's because she has a bigger garden. She doesn't have to crowd things and let them run riot. I don't know what I wouldn't give to move to a house with extensive grounds."

Mr. Adams said vehemently, "I'd like to move, too. I'd like a house big enough to allow me the luxury of a room of my own."

"I wish we lived in a stately house," said Chottie wistfully.

"If I may put my two cents in," Buzz offered miserably. "I hate this whole neighborhood."

"That's it!" said Mr. Adams excitedly. "We will move tomorrow. I'll see the agent for the Thayer place. It's quite an estate, but I can swing it and the peace is worth the price."

Having arrived at the hasty decision to move within a matter of days, the Adamses settled down to their excellent dinner, which they all ate with relish for each thought that the major problem in his life had just been solved.

Except Skippy, who until this moment had had no problems.

Skippy lay with his head between his paws. Buzz relaxed his hand and let the piece of meat fall. It fell within an inch of Skippy's nose, a succulent sizable bit of beef. But Skippy did not stir. His nose did not even wrinkle. He was sorrowing. Buzz looked away from his beseeching eyes.

Skippy loved the house. He had lived in it practically all his life. Actually, you might almost say it was his. For the thing was, the Adamses had bought it because of him. He had been given to Buzz as a birthday surprise when he, Skippy was three months old. Until then, he had lived in a kennel which could not be considered home life. He and Buzz had recognized each other instantly as dog lover and boy worshiper. Two days later the apartment house

agent came over to register the complaint of the people downstairs, who could not accustom their ears to the overwhelming
sounds of a boy and his dog. The dog, the agent explained regret-
fully, must go.

They moved to a house in the suburbs as soon as a suitable one
could be found. It was a move the elder Adamses had been meaning to make ever since Chottie was born, but one thing and another kept them chained to the city. And fourteen years later a
little dog led them to the charming white house that might have
emerged from their dreams.

Skippy, racing wildly through the rooms with nobody rapping
on the radiator, romping madly on the front lawn with no police-
men commanding that he be put on a lead, and gnawing a bone in
the backyard quite out of the way of cook's complaints, knew very
well that this was his heaven on earth, this was home. In his most
horrendous nightmare he never dreamed of moving day.

Now after five years, as if they had slyly waited until he reached
the age when the most obliging dog balks at change and views the
moving of his basket from one corner to another as a complete up-
heaval of his lifetime habits, the family was preparing to depart.

In the cold light of the next morning, Mrs. Adams was not sure
either that the fields beyond were greener. Looking down on her
lovely garden with the next annual flower show a whole year away,
she felt a real pang at leaving it. Mr. Adams was thinking the same
thing. At the Thayer place he would have a library, which was a
fine thing, but then there would never be an excuse to pile his
books about. Mr. Adams loved books and he loved to see them in
whatever room he chose to sit in, just as some people like to see
flowers or clocks. Now he would have his own room where he
could lie abed and read without interruption.

Buzz was going to miss Sally. She had leaned across the fence that morning full of remorse of her fickle heart, and solemnly crossing it with the sacred promise never to stray again. "Oh, why," mourned Buzz, had he been such a dope as to dip his oar in?

Chottie was wondering the same thing. A letter from Bill had come that morning. He was out of the Army, free as a bird and flying to her side. He hoped she hadn't changed, except to have grown old enough to have a proposal. Bill was back!

The Adamses who had recklessly spoken before they thought, were now ashamed to recant and show the honest sentiment in their hearts.

Skippy was not ashamed to show sentiment. All that day he would not eat, or wag his tail, or bark, or frisk.

Skippy didn't lie by Buzz's feet. He wanted no scraps from this or any other table. He lay by the door where everybody could see him with his head between paws, and his eyes beseeching.

It was very hard to have an appetite in the face of his misery. Buzz put down his fork.

"Do you know what I think?" he said. "I don't think Skippy's sick at all. I think he's sad."

"Well, we're certainly not going to stay here to indulge a dog," said Mr. Adams, in the desperate hope that his wife, as usual, would take the opposite tack.

"Well, I for one," said Mrs. Adams defiantly, "wouldn't have a minute's happiness if I had to watch poor Skippy waste away to a shadow."

The Adamses stared at Skippy. Why, he was one of themselves. His loss was inconceivable.

"Oh, let's not move," Chottie wailed.

Instantly, Skippy was on his feet. He had an ally. Quickly he crossed to Chottie and licked her hand.

"Oh Dad, let's stay here," begged Buzz. And Skippy went to Buzz and put his head on Buzz's knee.

"Bless my soul," said Mr. Adams, observing this miracle, "that dog seems to understand." He wanted to try it himself. "Skippy, come here." Skippy came cautiously. They searched each other's eyes. Mr. Adams said slowly and distinctly, "We're not going to move. We're staying right here in this house."

The master of the house had spoken. For a moment Skippy looked as if he couldn't believe. Then he threw back his head and began to bark joyously.

"Oh," said Mrs. Adams, close to tears, "you shouldn't have fooled him."

"Who said I was?" asked Mr. Adams loftily, and cleared his throat.

A Matter of Money

Mrs. Howell had done her best for her children. She had been widowed when they were young. Through the years of their growing, she had made every penny count, so that neither Joel nor Peggy would ever have to go without the right food, the proper clothes, the clean attractive house, whose lack might make feel inferior to more fortunate children.

Mrs. Howell had never given much thought to money before her husband died. He had been a generous provider, too generous, it was seen when his modest will was read, and Mrs. Howell had had only to ask and any request was granted.

Then quite suddenly she was a widow with two children, ten and twelve, to send through school. Mrs. Howell settled down in a determined effort to make ends meet.

She had always indulged her children as much as she indulged herself. When she was out, they helped themselves to whatever money they found in her room. She had only asked that they tell her how much they had taken. She never asked them what use they had put it. Now she found that she must be as severe with them as she must be with herself. It was a harder task than she had thought, to be severe with her children, whom she loved dearly.

She had never lied to her children. Now she did. She no longer left money in view nor in an easily accessible place. She left her purse on a hook in her closet, hidden under an old coat.

When they were in their teens and having their lunch in high school, she went to work as a saleslady. Joel had already expressed his ambition to be a doctor. Peggy was entitled to a college education, too. The long hours on her feet, the fact of working for the first time in her life were her willing sacrifices for her children's future. What she did not realize was that their comprehension had increased, too. They were very conscious of her sacrifices and eager to be grown and working and able to make them up to her. Their common sense told them that she kept more money in the house that she ever admitted having.

Mrs. Howell did not know that. The morning she started out to work she locked her closet door and put the key in her bureau drawer. A good part of that day she worried about it. That night she hid her money under her mattress. And then the next night she scattered her money in separate places, in a book, in an old letter, under the rug, so that if one sum were taken, the rest would be left. And perhaps the most egregious thing was they were never large amounts, for weekly Mrs. Howell banked as much as she could. What remained was expense money.

Mrs. Howell loved her children to desperation. She did not know that she was treating them as if they were thieves. Nor did she know that she hid her money like a miser.

Joel received his medical degree, interned, and then volunteered for Army service. On her graduation from college, Peggy went to work as a laboratory technician at a very satisfactory salary.

Mrs. Howell suddenly found herself released from the long strain. Joel sent money home regularly. Peggy was more than generous. Their final years of college, Mrs. Howell had canceled her bank account. Now she was able to open a new one. She did not tell Pegg nor write Joel. She decided she would surprise them with her thrift when she had saved a thousand dollars. But when her savings reached that figure, she decided it would be better to wait until she had two. In her letters to Joel, she did not mention Peggy's money gifts. When a money order came from him, she put it away before reading his letter aloud.

These little subterfuges were unnecessary. Without being told, both Peggy and Joel knew that each was keeping his promise to make their mother's life easier as soon as they were in position to do so. They would not have been surprised to know that she was banking every cent.

The war ended and Joel returned with his bride, who had been a Red Cross worker in Paris. He opened his office in a factory town, where the ailments most common to the workers were those in which he was most interested. Regularly he wrote his mother, and almost always enclosed a check.

Peggy married a young singer, whose promising career was just beginning. Neither wanted to wait until Vic's success, of which they were happily confident, was assured. There were no available apartments. With Mrs. Howell's willing consent, Peggy and Vic took over the top floor of her house, turning a small back room into a neat kitchen. Peggy continued to give her mother a monthly sum, which was more than ample rent for her three rooms.

Vic received his first big chance, with steady pay, in a popular nightclub. Then the baby was on the way and Peggy left her job when the long hours at work became too arduous. One winter's day Vic fell on the icy street and broke his ankle. Neither he nor Peggy had saved enough to carry them more than a few weeks.

But the weeks added up. There was the day when Peggy had to tell her mother that she could not pay her rent. Mrs. Howell found that she had a strange sensation. She felt cheated. She quickly controlled her expression and assured Peggy that she must give the matter no more thought. A week later Peggy asked her for a fair-sized loan, with every expectation of receiving it. And Mrs. Howell felt a sense of panic. If Peggy was starting to borrow already, there was no telling when she would stop.

"I'm sorry, Peggy," she said. "I haven't a penny in the house. And you know that my bankbook was canceled a long time ago, and I haven't saved a cent since. And after I take care of my weekly expenses, the rest of my salary barely covers my carfare. I wish I could help, but I can't."

Peggy gasped and stared at her mother. Both knew that she knew Mrs. Howell was lying.

In his anxiety to return to work, Vic tried to walk and fell again.

The injury meant the prolongation of his confinement to a chair.

Thereafter Mrs. Howell avoided her daughter. One early evening she returned home to find that her rooms had obviously been searched. Peggy, in her complete unsuitability for stealing had done a poor job of covering her traces, though she had reaped a fair harvest.

Mrs. Howell's first alarmed thought was of an outside burglar.

She rushed to the window and stared up the street, hoping to see a passing policeman. Peggy was rounding the corner, walking slowly with the child so soon to be born and stopping every few steps to shift the many parcels in her arms.

Suddenly Mrs. Howell knew where her money had gone. Her legs were too weak to support her. She sank back in a chair. Anguish flooded her heart. Her own loss seemed immaterial now. The only thing that mattered was that Peggy had chipped the edge of her bright honor.

With clarity Mrs. Howell saw that she was responsible for Peggy's act. For years she had been underhanded with money. There was no wonder that a wide-eyed child had stored up this impression of deceit.

Mrs. Howell heard Peggy's step in the hall. She opened her door. Peggy paled, and Mrs. Howell pretended not to notice. "Oh, hello Peggy," she said quickly. "I just came in. Haven't even had time to take off my hat and coat. And I'm glad I didn't. For I've just remembered I've got to run out again." She opened her purse and pressed several bills into Peggy's hand. "With my love, darling. And may I have dinner with you when I come back?"

When Mrs. Howell returned from her walk, during which she had prayed harder than she had ever prayed in her life, she found that Peggy had replaced every dollar that she had taken earlier. Mrs. Howell retrieved this money and put it all together in one proper place. She had had an enchanted childhood and a wonderful marriage. But this was the happiest day of her life. She went upstairs and walked down the hall to the kitchen, where the good smells of Peggy's own paid for feast were emanating.

"Peggy," she said, "I've a surprise that I've been keeping for years. Now it's grown so big it won't keep any longer. I've several thousand dollars saved up, half of it money that you've given me. Tomorrow I'm transferring that half to you."

"Oh, Mother," said Peggy, her eyes full of tears and gratitude, "there's something I want to confess."

"Please don't, dear," Mrs. Howell said earnestly, "for I have just confessed to you, and there's no need for yours."

Wives and Women

After the last wedding guest had gone, Mr. Vincent, who with his wife had been bidding good-bye from the porch, turned back into the house. He felt a vast relief that everything was over. Ever since her birth, he had dreamed of a day when she, who had taken his wife away from him with the real demands of a child's growing, would return Beth back to him.

Now that day had come, was he over it? Beth had thought Anne at eighteen was too young to marry. He had been on the side of his daughter. He was forty-five. Beth was only forty-two. With their only daughter married and away, there would still be enough years remaining to recapture the blissful life that had been theirs before Anne's birth.

Mr. Vincent settled himself in a deep chair in the living room. He closed his eyes and smiled. When Beth came in he would offer her a place on his knee. They had not sat like that since the day that year old Anne had run in unexpectedly and burst out laughing because to her it looked funny to see her mother sitting on her father's lap. He pulled Beth down over her protests anyway. He remembered how she had murmured "parents should act like parents."

The little clock on the mantel chimed. Mr. Vincent stirred impatiently. He knew exactly what Beth was doing. She was staring pensively at the winding road down which young Philip had taken her daughter out of her life to a life of her own. He called with faint irritation, "Beth."

Her voice floated in, remote, sad, "What, Dad?" He stirred impatiently again. She called him Dad the way Anne did. He had never called her Mother. He had not wanted her to lose her identity. But she had aided and abetted Anne in trying to make him lose his. He listened to the echo of the word but would not answer.

"Dad," she called again. He unsealed his lips. Then, in an anxious voice, she said, "Carl, is that you calling?"

That was better. Her small anxiety had pushed her daughter a little way off her mind. "There's a chill in the air," he answered. "Better come in."

The door opened and closed. When she spoke, the subdued note had come back. "I still don't want to believe that only an hour ago Anne waved good-bye to her parents' home. She seemed such a child to be going away to a husband and home of her own."

"Nonsense," he chided kindly. "You were only nineteen when we eloped, and I distinctly remember that you were glad to leave home."

"That was because my home life wasn't as happy as Anne's. I didn't have a doting mother. She lived for my brother. I was determined that Anne should never feel my love was lacking, I think I can say she never did."

He didn't want to talk about her motherhood. She looked very lovely. She didn't look the mother of a married daughter. He held out his hand. His voice shook a little. "Beth."

She frowned a little. "Don't you agree?" The little wrinkle in her forehead was enchanting. "To anything," he said ardently.

Color flooded her face. She looked embarrassed. "Dad, how many toasts did you drink to your daughter?"

His voice and his face stiffened. "I'm sorry if I don't sound sober. But perhaps that's better than your thinking I sound like a fool in love."

Her flush deepened. She crossed the room to him. He could see the thin spot on the top of his head. She began to stroke it.

"Don't do that," he said irritably. She stepped away and moved to the fireplace. In the mirror above the mantel she could see their faces reflected. She saw his hand pat the concealing hairs over his bald spot.

"We're tired," she said. "It's been a long day. We're keyed-up. The smallest thing can make us cross or make us cry. We'll have an early supper and go early to bed."

He jumped to his feet, whirled away from the sight of her searching eyes, and said bitterly, "Did my bald spot remind you that I'm not young Philip's age? Is everyone old who's over twenty-one?"

She said gently, "Dad, don't be jealous of Philip. He was never the handsome lad that you were on your wedding day."

But her words did not comfort him. He turned back to her and said fiercely, "I'm not jealous of Philip. I'm jealous of Anne."

He hadn't meant to say that. He hadn't meant for her to know. "I'm sorry I said that, Beth." She turned around slowly. Little lines of tiredness had run into her face. "It's I who ought to apologize," she said.

He felt a muscle jerking in his own cheek. It seemed a million years since he had waked for Anne's wedding day. Suddenly he was infinitely weary. He could not try to interpret her cryptic remark.

"Sit down, Dad. You look so white."

Her command evoked no resentment in him. He sat down gratefully, and the deep chair eased him. He had a fleeting ironic thought that he wouldn't have wanted to hold Lana Turner.

Beth did not sit down. She stayed beside the mantel, her fingers twisting her strand of pearls. In the mirror he saw with a little surprise that her heavy dark hair was threaded with gray. But he could not quicken his surprise into a stronger emotion. He felt no sorrow, no regret. All that he was capable of feeling was this great weariness, which he knew was the foretaste of resignation.

"I've always known you were jealous of Anne," Beth said.

"It was very decent of you not to let me know that you knew."

"No," she said, "I wasn't as noble as that. I didn't want to bring it out in the open and face my failure as a wife."

He wanted to stop her. "We're both overtired, Beth. Let's not talk anymore."

She said passionately, "Hear me out, or I can't go on living with my conscience." Her voice was low, hurried, tragic. "I was never your wife after Anne was born. There was no moment when she was not first on my mind. I let her push you out of my heart."

"Don't torture yourself," he said quietly. And, curiously, her words did not torture him. For he had survived the anguish of the act itself. But she went on inexorably, "Some women are mothers, Some are wives. Few women are both. It was your bad luck to marry a woman whose child was her world."

He said kindly, even with humor, "I could never convince an impartial jury that a good mother is not a pearl beyond price."

Her eyes were hopeful, eager. "Then you forgive me, Dad?"

He looked at her with pity. He had lost her eighteen years ago. She had lost Anne today. She was more recently bereaved. She was more in need of comfort.

"There is nothing to forgive you, Mother."

The Letters

They had never been friends. Time had been too short and life too uncertain to waste either of them in exploring their pasts to see if they were suited to each other. In the feverish atmosphere of wartime haste they had plunged into marriage. The war had brought them both to the city, he to be shipped to a destination unknown, she to stay for the duration as secretary to the man whose special abilities had made him essential to the winning of victory, whose appointment had meant her uprooting, too.

Her courtship with Tim had not been carried on in privacy. There had been nowhere for either of them to go to be alone. And even after their marriage there was nowhere. He lived surrounded by soldiers where a sentry permitted no stranger to pass. She lived surrounded by girls in a rooming house with ironclad rules. There wasn't even a hotel that could give them a room on their wedding night. And then a few days later, Tim was gone.

The isolation she had felt in this strange city seemed even worse. Her nights were sleepless, her nerves were frayed. Her chief, who ever since their arrival, had been too busy to notice her, could no longer be unaware of her dark-circled eyes, her unquiet hands. Then he took notice of her wedding ring. He made gentle inquiries about her marriage. She told him the little there was to tell. Though he did not know it any more than she did, it was more loneliness than grief that was causing her pain. It was more loneliness than love that had prompted her marriage.

Her chief's name was Mark Granger. He had an aunt in the city. He'd been having guilty feelings about her. For she had been quite recently widowed. Because of the pressure of work, his contact with her had been mostly by telephone. He was always meaning to do something about her loneliness. He had half thought of moving in with her but he preferred the close proximity of his hotel to his office.

Then Jenny's lonely little face began to haunt his few brief moments of relaxation and he could not enjoy them. He began to dream about her and his dreams were troubled. After a while he knew that for his own peace of mind he would have to do something about her happiness.

He enlisted the aid of his aunt who said she would be delighted to have a young girl to fuss over. He enlisted Jenny's aid in her own behalf. He told her his aunt's need of young companionship to act as a tonic to her sorrow.

Jenny went to live with Mrs. Cutley because each had set out determinedly to be cheerful for the sake of the other; their naturally sunny natures gradually became a real part of them again. In not too long a time, there was no need for pretense.

Mark saw the changes in Jenny and was enormously pleased. Then Jenny began disturbing his dreams again. When he knew why, it was he who wore a haggard look. Jenny had thought of

Mark, first as her chief and then as her benefactor. She had never thought beyond that. Now as she saw the strain of what she concluded was over work, her heart was moved by a pity that frightened her with its intensity.

Tim was writing her as often as there was time in between the business of soldiering. His letters were beautiful, even extraordinary. In their short time together, she hadn't dreamed he was capable of such depth, such maturity. Her letters in reply were rather timid, for she did not have his mastery with words, nor, as she was beginning to know with a shamed, self-reproach, his ardor.

His letters piled up, each one a jewel in itself, each one a poet's testament. And then quite suddenly Jenny realized she was being unfair to Tim. She did not love him. She had never loved him. Now and bitterly she confessed it to herself. Now and remorsefully she must confess it to Tim. It was a monstrous thing to be the recipient of these outpourings and have no heart to hold them in.

She wrote Tim. He was unbelievably good about it. His reply, in fact, was as extraordinary in its way as his previous letters had been in their way. The very sound of the sentences had a different cadence. And through them all was an unmistakable undertone of relief, as if he were glad to be offered his freedom, as if he, too, had found out that she was not the wife for a man with a poet's emotions.

That was Tim's last letter except for the businesslike exchanges about their divorce. Then it was over. Then the war was over. She and Mark returned to their hometown. Mark asked her to marry him. Now it was two years since that exciting wedding day. And out of the blue had come Tim's telegram. It was important that he see her. He would arrive by plane the next day at noon.

The telegram had been sent to her mother's address, and Tim had addressed it to Mrs. Tim Holly. She sat at her mother's waiting in an agony of dread. Tim didn't know she had married again. He could have no reason for coming except to ask her if there was any hope for him. She supposed she knew why he had given her up so easily. She had been a fool not to guess before. He had been afraid of how he might come back to her and he thought she, too, was afraid. She was torn between shame that he could have thought her so light-minded and dismay that she must reopen what had undoubtedly been a deep wound.

A taxi drew up. Tim leaped out, whole, sound, handsome. He was ringing the bell, he was inside the house, and he was seated in the living room.

He had not tried to kiss her. She was grateful for that. He had shaken hands very easily and naturally. She had led the way to the living room and when they were both seated, she had told him she was married.

A look of acute dismay darkened his eyes. Her heart lurched. He was going to take it hard, and for a foolish moment, she had hoped he would take it gracefully.

"Then those letters," he said slowly, "I suppose you've destroyed them."

She wanted to say yes. To tell him she had not might make him feel she had never really stopped loving him. But the real reason was that it had struck her as an act of vandalism to tear up so much lyric beauty. At the back of her mind had been the intention to return them to him if their paths ever crossed. He would have to be the one to destroy them.

"No," she said finally. "I couldn't. They were too beautifully written. I wanted you to have them back."

He expelled a long breath of relief. "They're what I came for." Embarrassment flooded his face. "You see, I didn't write them myself. I tried to write you, but I couldn't think of anything to say. We knew so little about each other. And I'm not much on writing love stuff. So I copied what my buddy wrote for me. He was always writing anyway, poems, stories, things like that. And now he's writing a book, and there's a lot in those letters he thinks he can use, all that stuff about how a soldier thinks and feels. So I told him I'd ask you if you'd give them back."

"Of course," she said quickly, not taking time to examine her feelings to see if she felt any wounded pride. "As a matter of fact, they're here in the attic. I'll get them."

She rose. He rose, too. "Did you really think I wrote those letters?" he asked boyishly. He felt rather flattered.

"Why, no," she said suddenly. "I suppose I didn't. I mean, I knew they weren't written by the man I thought I had married."

He gave her a little rueful smile. "Do you suppose if I'd written my own letters we might have made a go of it?"

"Why, I don't know," she said truthfully, because she didn't.

"Gosh, neither do I," he said.

And for a moment they looked at each other curiously. Then their eyes fell, and she left the room.

Made for Each Other

The doorbell chimed. Mrs. Owens hurried down the hall. Her face had a harassed expression. She was at sixes and sevens trying to do several things at once with her usual domestic incompetence. She had got her husband off to work, her children off to school with breakfasts that were slightly burned. Lunches weren't quite in order. What mysterious thing happened to your daughter's blue socks on the day she wore her blue dress? Why did your husband want a clean shirt whenever there wasn't one in his drawer? How could your son cold-heartedly expect pants when he knew how badly you sewed?

Why did breakfast take so many dishes? Why did her fingers turn to thumbs in the kitchen? There were still the beds to do. And the lumps that no magic of hers could smooth out. Then the hopeless task of straightening up the living room. She could not think about dinner. She had run out of her few ideas about food.

Mrs. Owens sighed and opened the door.

"Good morning," said her caller brightly.

Mrs. Owens resisted the temptation to say, "Is it?" She smiled a wan smile and returned the greeting.

The woman who faced her was very well dressed. Mrs. Owens felt very disheveled beside her. The intelligent face showed strength and graciousness and her voice and demeanor suggested a background of gentility. She looked like the kind of person who would never live in chaos. Mrs. Owens decided against asking her to step inside while she stated her business.

"I'm Mrs. Marsden," the lady said.

'Oh," said Mrs. Owens politely but on a—inflection that would indicate to Mrs. Marsden that the name meant nothing to her.

"Are you Mrs. Owens?" Mrs. Marsden asked rather anxiously. "It's she I want to see. Have I the right address?"

"Why, yes. I'm Mrs. Owens," said the owner of the name in a tone of surprise. She was not so much surprised to be acknowledging this fact as she was to be confronted with it by a perfect stranger.

"Then may I come in?"

"Please do," said Mrs. Owens reluctantly.

She ushered her visitor into the living room. She tried to act nonchalant but it was not her nature. She said in a rush, "Please don't look around. I can't keep a house clean. The art of it eludes me. The wonderful person who's been with me for years had to leave suddenly to go west to live with her ailing mother. I've advertised for another housekeeper and I've taken leave from my office while I wait for an angel to answer my prayer." She remembered her manners. "Do sit down."

Mrs. Marsden sat down. She said quietly, "I'm not an angel, but I'm here."

Mrs. Owens stared, unable to reconcile this woman's appearance with her purpose. "You mean you've come about the job?" she asked incredulously.

The expectant look faded from Mrs. Marsden's eyes. "Do you think I'm too old?"

"It's not that," Mrs. Owens said quickly and sincerely. For Mrs. Marsden looked far more capable than Mrs. Owen felt. "I meant," she fumbled, "you just don't look like a housekeeper."

Mrs. Marsden tried to keep the indignation out of her voice. "My family always thought I was a very good one. I'm sure I was keeping house before you were born."

"Well," said Mrs. Owens, feeling squelched, "I suppose you were in the employ of a very rich family." For she would never have managed to dress so expensively on the kind of salary Mrs. Owens could pay. "I'm afraid you'd find us very different. Maybe my ad wasn't clear. I didn't mean the kind of housekeeper who just supervised the other servants."

It was Mrs. Marsden who looked defeated now. "We keep misunderstanding each other. I've never worked outside of my own home. I didn't stop to think that I hadn't any paid experience, and no references. I read your ad, and all I thought about was getting here ahead of anyone else."

She looked around the room, though she had been cautioned not to. It would be a nice room when knowing hands had charge of it. But what really took Mrs. Marsden's eye was the framed picture of a little boy and girl on the table beside her. Of course, they were in school at this hour, and she was sorry she would go away without ever seeing them. They made her remember her busy young motherhood. She smiled at their smiling faces.

Mrs. Owens was watching her. "They're my children," she explained. "I suppose," she said, rather resentfully, "you think I should stay home and take care of them. I tried it when they were quite small, and I wasn't successful at it. My husband and children find me much better company when I'm working at a job I enjoy than when I'm making a gloomy failure of being a housekeeper."

Mrs. Marsden said gravely, "Don't think I don't understand how you feel. I do. However, it seems to other people, one's happiest doing what one does best. When my husband died and my daughters married, I moved to a small hotel. I'd always had a big house that kept me busy all day long. Everyone, including my daughters, encouraged me to give it up and be waited on for the rest of my life. But I've been living in a hotel for a year now, and I can't even make up my own bed without offending the chambermaid." She said wryly, "If I went to live with either of my daughters, they'd let me make up my own bed, but that's about all. I brought them up to be perfect housekeepers. And I'd only be interfering if I tried to help."

"Help me, Mrs. Marsden," Mrs. Owens said fervently. "I think we were made for each other."

"Then may I consider myself hired?" Mrs. Marsden said happily.

"Please do," Mrs. Owens implored. "I know you've got to go home and pack. And I really don't expect you to take over for a day or two. But Mrs. Marsden, before you go, what would be nice for dinner?"

"Why, I'll make up a market list," Mrs. Marsden said efficiently. "And if you'll get the groceries for me, I'll borrow your apron and tidy up this room while you're gone, and I'll start the dinner before I leave. If you'd like to go back to work tomorrow, I'd be glad to come back to work tonight."

"Mrs. Marsden, you really are an angel," Mrs. Owens said with awe.

"Oh no," Mrs. Marsden said for the second time, but this time she did not say it quite so positively.

Homecoming

Ma Malloy couldn't help feeling excited and happy as she set the supper table. For the first time in years all of her children were home. They were upstairs now, getting settled in their old rooms, catching up on each other's news.

They had come without their families, so it was an easy thing to fall into the old ways, the old affections: to forget for a while that they had closer, stronger ties than those that once had bound them to a favorite brother or sister.

Why, there was a time when she couldn't tell the difference between Herbie and Harry, so alike they were in every way. Now, though they lived in the same city, they moved in separate spheres, with wives who were very conscious of the disparity in their incomes. The constraint they had come to feel in the presence of their wives made them avoid family gatherings whenever a plausible excuse made it possible.

Hearing them joyfully ragging each other, their delight in being together too strong to be subdued by any other emotion. Ma knew that the difference between them was only superficial, a shyness, a shame that each felt because he had more or less than his brother.

The others, too, Joan and Pam, Pete and Johnny had fallen under the spell of homecoming. Joan, the family beauty, and Pam, who had always called herself plain, were talking softly instead of shrilly, which meant they were relating on common ground instead of shooting from opposite poles.

Joan had wanted her name in lights and Pam had wanted six children. It was Pam, chic and clever, whose name appeared monthly on the editorial pages of a fashion magazine, while Joan, a suburban anonymity, felt cheated because all that her beauty got her was an early marriage and a houseful of children. But tonight, childless Pam was not jealous of Joan's completeness and Joan was not jealous of Pam's career.

Pete and Johnny, both in politics and stepping on each other's neck to reach the top of the heap, always spoiled their rare visits home by heated argument, with one or the other leaving summarily. Long ago, Pete, the elder, had been Johnny's protector, and Johnny had worshipped the ground Pete walked on. Tonight they had put politics aside in their need to share the same emotion, each searching the face of his brother for the old likeness of himself.

Ma set the steaming platters in the center of the table. The children would say she had spread a feast. But she had given little thought to this meal, just taken the first things that came to hand from the freezer to spare herself the grieving of being mocked by the overbountiful table if nobody came to sit down to it.

Just a month before, almost to the day, she and Pa had spent Christmas Eve staring at the foolish tree all bedecked and glowing for the sons and daughters whose telephone calls and telegrams had broken the heart of Christmas and made all the happy days of preparation seem like self-inflicted punishment.

None of the children had come, though, of course, none of them had known that all of them would find some valid excuse for staying away. They were good children, really. It was just that they were still too young to know that time had two faces, one for them, and one, less benign, for the old.

Pa had set such store by their coming. Though he went about his daily chores, not saying much, and saying that offhand, Ma knew Pa from all their married years, and she knew Pa's heart was full to bursting at the thought, at the hope of having all the children home for Christmas.

He had seen them so infrequently in these last years. She had visited them in their various homes a time or two, but Pa never had, he being bound to the farm as if with shackles and hating travel more than sickness. He used to say reasonably enough that his children knew the way back home better than he knew the way to wherever it was they hung their hats.

Tonight they had all come back, letting none of their private concerns dissuade them. Without laying blame this way or that, Ma couldn't help thinking that if they had made that same effort at Christmas, things might have been different, like going this road you meet a known friend, and going that road, you pass a dark stranger.

She went to the foot of the stairs. "Supper's on the table. Come get it while it's hot."

She knew their individual steps so well, the quick one, the slow one, the heavy one, and the light one. For a moment, the years rolled back for Ma. They rolled back as far as when it was the most natural thing in the world for her to stand at the foot of the stairs calling the children to supper. As always, Pa was waiting at the head of the table to ask God's blessing on their togetherness.

She shooed them into the dining room. "You go sit down while I get the coffee."

When she returned, Pete, her eldest, was hovering. "Ma," he said diffidently, "where do you want me to sit?"

"My goodness," she said, "next to the rolls, of course. You know you always sit next to the bread like you never had enough bread in your life."

He sat down in his old place and smiled at her. "You should have been resting."

She set the huge coffeepot down before Herbie, who had teased her for coffee ever since he was a toddler, and said briefly to Pete, "It's my day for baking. I wouldn't have known what to do with my hands."

Having made herself conscious of her hands, she began to fidget with her apron, while her eyes darted up and down the table to see that each plate was plentiful.

"Sit down, Ma," Pam said gently. "You've never learned to stay off your feet."

She sat down in Pa's place and heard the little movement of unease that went through her children as if for the first time they were afraid her courage might fail.

"I'll sit here a minute and ask the blessing. Then I'll go up and change."

"You eat first, Ma," Joan urged. "You've got to keep up your strength."

"I had a snack with Carrie Norton just before you came. I was snacking all day with this one and that who came in. It was nice to have them drop in. Made the kitchen so cozy. While you children eat, I'll get ready."

"We don't want you to go with us, Ma," Pete said firmly. "We'd rather you spared yourself tonight. It won't be easy for you tomorrow. We'll just stay a minute with Pa, and come right back."

They looked at her tenderly, protectively, as if they wished they could ease her inward grieving.

They still had most of their future before them. They didn't understand. She tried to explain, "When you're old as I am, you look at things different. You take your happiness wherever you find it. You can't afford to pick and choose the time and place. I grieved for your pa before you came, and I'll grieve again after you go. But now I can't take time to cry. I don't know when you'll come again. I want to make every minute count.

"I want to remember the joy of having children home. My mind don't want to dwell on how you came home to bury Pa. Forgive an old woman for her selfishness."

She bowed her head and asked God's blessings on their being together, as if Pa, approving, had put his own words in her mouth, as if Pa, behind her shut eyes, was back in his prime, with the children still in the spring of their growth, and her world still safe from the separation of time.

Ma opened her eyes. Pete had a sprinkle of gray in his hair and Pam had a tired sag to her shoulders. But Ma saw what she wanted to see, felt what she wanted to feel, and smiled at her children because it was like old times.

Summer Setting

When Beth asked Sara to take teenage Penny for August, Sara couldn't say no. Beth was her favorite sister. Besides, Beth had been ill, and a rest from Penny would speed her recuperation.

But Sara couldn't forgive her sister, Hallie, for making the same request of Jill. Except that was Hallie's way. She was not going to let Sara do more for one niece than she did for the other.

They were sweet kids, fourteen-year-old Penny and fifteen-year-old Jill. Any other summer she would have enjoyed devoting her time to them. But this year her vacation plans had included a more romantic role than indulgent aunt. She had set the stage for a proposal of marriage, and a couple of kids would only clutter up the scenery.

Until this spring Sara had never thought she would want to marry again. Her marriage to Ken had been so perfect and so brief. The war and Ken's joining up made each subsequent day a day to which they gave full meaning. Then Ken was sent overseas and the letters she wrote and received were testaments of love

and longing. When the telegram of regret came, Sara felt that perfection had ended its span on earth.

It was years before she realized that the reason no other man
measured up to her shining image of Ken was because other men
grew older. Other men had the problems of living to line their
faces and sober their laughter while Ken had escaped into time-
lessness with his youth and joy intact.

And facing the fact that Ken was young forever, and she was
fifteen years older, Sara gave up her dream of him, and waked
from her self-indulgent sleep to the world of her maturity, in
which she moved like one not really part of it.

There before her was Clay, as he had been for a long time.
Clay with that quizzical smile in his eyes, waiting for her to come
down from her ivory tower. Sara, seeing Clay really for the first
time, and liking, then loving what she saw, was impatient to prove
herself a woman, a woman ready to be a wife.

No occasion presented itself until summer. Clay's newspaper
sent him abroad on a three-month survey, with his return set for
late July, and his vacation to begin in August. Sara, who worked in
advertising, writing glamorous ads that she believed in completely,
who considered it a woman's bound duty to be beautiful, arranged
her own vacation for August.

She owned a storybook cottage on a lovely island. A fashionable
inn overlooked the bay. Before Clay left for Europe, Sara suggested
the inn for his holiday. In August there were always interesting
people at the inn. And whenever he wanted to escape their activi-
ties, he would find her cottage a quiet retreat, where the days
flowed one into one, calm and serene.

That was what she had promised Clay, the peace that he would
have with her. Now, three months later, here she was waiting at the

wharf for Penny and Jill, with Clay arriving by plane within the hour. She had expected Clay, but Penny and Jill were arriving a whole week sooner than planned. Some young friend of theirs was driving down with her family. She had begged her mother, and Penny and Jill had begged theirs, to let them drive down with her. Nobody had considered Sara's feelings in the matter.

The ferry came around the bend on schedule. At least Sara would not have to keep Clay waiting at the airport. But there would be no time to drop the kids off at the cottage. She would just have to take them with her and hope that Clay would forgive her for not coming alone.

There were embraces and introductions and the father of the flock, using legerdemain, extracted Penny's and Jill's luggage from the tottering mountain without breaking the head of any member of his family.

To Sara's horror a large dog was unloaded, too, and handed over to Jill, who carefully explained that Pete was a recent present, and didn't really know yet that he belonged to her. If she had left him at home, he might have thought he belonged to her mother and father. She had sneaked him out of the house—another act of legerdemain, Sara thought bitterly—and she must remember to telephone home that Pete wasn't lost.

Sara headed her car toward the airport, with the kids in the backseat, and Pete undecided. As the car got underway, he made a graceful leap from backseat to front, landing hard and lovingly against Sara. She steadied the wheel, cleared her throat of fright and ordered him back. Tail down he briefly obeyed, then hurled through the air again. This time it was Jill who entreated him to return. Reluctantly he did so, but only on the wing, for once more he sailed through space to take the seat of his preference.

Sara said shakily, "He seems to want to sit here. Let's let him."

Just as her nerves settled back in place a sudden burst of rock and roll tangled them up again. Pete, scared out of his wits, too, tried his best to climb her back.

"Girls," said Sara fiercely, "what's that?"

"It's my radio," Penny said in a hurt voice. "Mother gave me a battery radio, so I wouldn't play yours and waste your electricity."

"Well, you mustn't waste your battery either," Sara said with quick thinking. "You may not be able to get another one. The island stores are not stocked like the city stores."

"I brought some extras," said Penny cheerfully.

All Sara could answer was, "Oh."

As the plane taxied down the runway, they reached the airport. The plane doors opened and presently there was Clay. His searching eyes rested briefly on her and her entourage, wrote them off, scanned the other cars, came back to hers, widened with recognition, and she noted, surprise.

Smiling, he came to her. "It's wonderful to see you," he said, but she wasn't sure she believed him.

She introduced him to her nieces. "Will you get in back with them? I can't budge this beast. And, Penny, will you turn your radio off so Clay can tell us all about Europe?"

"Aunt Sara," wailed Penny, "this half hour is all Elvis Presley."

Clay said lustily, "I've expressed myself on that young man without ever hearing him. Now's my chance to arrive at an honest opinion."

"We're not far from the inn," Sara said in apology. "You can get settled, and I'll pick you up for dinner at eight?"

Now it was Jill who wailed, "Dinner at eight. We're starved, Aunt Sara. Why can he eat now and get settled later?"

"I'd like dinner now," Clay said quickly. "Island air sparks the appetite."

"Fine," said Sara weakly. It was much too early for a candlelit dinner. At this commonplace hour she could hardly dress or change at all if Clay was coming home with her.

They arrived at the cottage and Mollie, Sara's housekeeper, took the girls upstairs to their room, while the unfaithful Pete stayed behind with Sara and Clay. Leaving Clay to mix cocktails, Sara went ostensibly for ice, but privately to freshen her makeup.

She reckoned without Pete. Not wanting to let her out of his sight, he dashed past the unsuspecting Clay, who, busy with bottles, glasses, and pitcher, then got even busier with broken glass.

Sara, hearing the crash, rushed back into the room, while Pete flew to cover in the folds of a curtain.

"Oh, Pete," cried Sara. Pete, misunderstanding, rushed to join his protector, bringing the curtain with him. Entangled and terrified anew, he tore about the room, barking wildly.

Mollie raced downstairs certain the sounds below were those of a dog gone mad. She opened the back door, concealed herself behind it, and called, "Here, dog, here Dog."

Expecting deliverance, Pete galloped toward the voice, upsetting everything in his way, including a service table, on which Mollie had placed her filet mignon to thaw.

The curtain caught on the overturned table, and Pete was free. His fear dissolving, he took quick inventory, snatched up the filet mignon, and spirited through the open door.

Mollie slammed the door and rushed to the kitchen phone. Sara and Clay reached the doorway just as she began to dial.

"I'm calling the police," she said excitedly.

"The police?" echoed Sara.

"To shoot the dog," said Mollie impatiently.

Penny and Jill tumbled downstairs from their listening post with tears and entreaties to spare Pete's life.

Clay took command. "The dog isn't mad, Mollie. He was just frightened. Girls, stop crying. We'll all see the funny side on a full stomach. I suggest we have dinner."

The suggestion was so ill-timed that Penny and Jill stopped crying and began to giggle hysterically. Clay, with comprehension dawning, felt the laughter building inside him. He stole a glance at Sara. Their eyes met, and they burst into brighter laughter than either had ever heard from the other.

Mollie said indignantly, "You won't laugh if your flower beds look like my kitchen."

They crowded out the back door. Pete lay in a bed of beheaded snapdragons, gnawing on filet mignon.

"Oh, Pete," Jill shrieked.

He grabbed his prize and raced around the garden, with Penny and Jill and Mollie in pursuit, their feet tripping no lighter than his.

"I give up," said Sara. "I wanted everything to be right and everything's been wrong. Go back to New York, if you want to. There'll only be more of the same tomorrow."

Clay said gently, "I want to stay more than I wanted to come. I was afraid I was going to take part in a play in which you were the poised and lovely star, and I was the bungling amateur, missing my cues and entrances. But all of us seem to have two left feet. If there's going to be more of the same tomorrow, there's no use waiting for a better time and place. Sara, will you marry me?"

"What?" she said faintly.

"You see," said Clay triumphantly, "you missed your cue."

The Lean and the Plenty

Kate Callow had been Mother's youngest child, born into a large and extrovert family, where her soft, small voice never had a chance to be heard. On the rare occasion when someone stopped to listen, she was overcome by this unexpected feeling that everything flew out of her mind, tears of embarrassment flooded her eyes, and she knew she could say nothing at all.

In primary school, she did not emerge from her shell. Her classmates were too young and uncaring to sympathize with her shyness. They gleefully chanted that the cat had got her tongue, which tied it up more than ever. In grade school, Katie was still a stutterer. Her sisters and brothers were thoroughly ashamed of her. If they talked to her at all, it was only to scold her for being different. And she could not find the words to tell them that she longed to be the same. At home, her busy mother had no time to give thought to Katie's problems.

Instead, she found Katie's quietness a restful relief from the clamor in which she constantly moved.

She knew that boys of similar age expected girls to chirrup and chatter while they stood dumb and adoring. That she always came straight home from school and never had a date was a source of satisfaction instead of worry to her mother, who felt that none of her other children cared enough for their home to spend one evening enjoying it. As Katie grew out of her teens, she became an unobtrusive part of her parents' small circle of friends. Among them the widowed Mr. Keller. Mr. Keller had been a family friend during all the long years of his bachelorhood.

As a child, Katie had been at ease in his presence because Mr. Keller had never tried to make her talk. He was wary even of little girls because they grew up to be big girls with marriage intentions. Then, at forty-five, Mr. Keller fell headlong in love with a gay young girl who came to work in the office of his service station. Within two weeks, he proposed to Corinne and sweated out the days of waiting while her practical mother made up her mind for her. Mr. Keller never noticed that Corinne was too young to return his middle-aged love. He was a man bewitched and he lived in that state of bewitchment for the eight years of his marriage. When his twin sons were born, he endured their babyhood because he had to, but he never got used to having them in the house nor being called their father.

When Corinne died suddenly, as the result of neglected infection, all that gave Mr. Keller's life meaning died with her. He regarded his six-year-old sons with a kind of astonishment and tried a succession of housekeepers. These kindly women had a normal share of friendliness that they could not turn off and on to suit Mr. Keller's indifference. After a few weeks, they left because of loneliness.

That Mr. Keller married Katie Callow was the only thing he

could think of that was closest to living alone. That Katie accepted him was because she, too, had no other solution to her own problems of living. She was then six years out of high school and six years in and out of jobs. Mr. Keller's offer of marriage was like a lifesaver, which Katie clutched with both hands and pulled herself to the safety of a suburban house surrounded by tall shrubs. Mr. and Mrs. Keller settled down to their separate rooms and separate ways with Katie feeling only relief that she was unnoticed and ignored. But their father's attitude brushed off on the boys and Katie had no words with which to win them over.

When they were seventeen, they joined a branch of the services. Their father watched them go as if they had long ago worn out their welcome. Katie stood wordlessly before them knowing it was years too late to tell them how often her heart had embraced them. Now the silence surrounding her was complete. Mr. Keller left early and came home late, eating most of his meals in town and stopping at the living room door only long enough for a grudging good night. Loneliness Katie had always borne as the burden of the shy, but aloneness she had never really known until now. Though only the fewest possible words passed between herself and her stepsons, the sounds of their voices had kept the spark alive in her. In the shrouding aloneness, Katie sat unmoving for long hours, as if the spark was already extinguished. An act of fate fanned it alive.

Mr. Keller fell ill and the weight of his years put an end to his activity. With no sons to carry on for him, the only course was to sell his business. Though in time he left his bed, Mr. Keller refused to leave his room. He had no interest in anything outside it. Katie gave him a bell to ring but he never rang it. Katie was well over fifty when Mr. Keller, in a last spurt of stubbornness, died. The years of his retirement had exhausted his savings. There was little left for Katie except for the house. She saw nothing to do but sell it.

For the first time in years, Katie began to go out daily and spend more hours away from home than in it. Like all lonely people she went to the park and watched the life around her, trying to think through a life of her own that would have some reason for being. One day she noticed a newcomer to the park, a middle-aged woman who sat alone and looked as lonely as herself. Emboldened by sympathy, Katie smiled and nodded. The lady returned the greeting and observed that it was a nice day. Katie eagerly said yes, but could think of nothing to add to it. After a moment of expectancy, the lady lowered her eyes to her knitting.

The following afternoon, Katie found the lady seated on the bench she had come to think of as her own. She said "Good afternoon," and started past, not wishing to presume on their short acquaintance.

The lady rose at once and said, "I'm sorry, this is your bench, isn't it? I mean you always sit here. That's why I sat here. I want to be friends."

Katie knew what an effort it cost a shy person to make so revealing a statement. It persuaded her to make one of her own. "Please sit down again. I'm Katie Keller. I'm a widow. I live alone in a house that's too big for me. That's why I come to the park. I'm shy like you. I want friends, too."

The lady laughed. It was a great explosion of laughter, deep and joyous. She laughed as if these lusty sounds of life were part of her.

"I'm Martha Bigsby, I'm not shy. That's my trouble. I make friends too easy, like now. I'm making a friend of you. The next thing you know, I'll be bringing you home with me."

"Oh," said Katie, uncertainly.

"It's my married daughter's home," Martha explained. "She likes things quiet. I like things lively. I've only myself to blame. When my husband died, I sold my home and came here."

Katie said understandingly, "It isn't easy for a woman alone to make ends meet."

"I could have managed," said Martha, refusing to be forgiven. "But I let my daughter persuade me. I should have thought for myself."

Katie sighed in sympathy. Here they both were on a park bench because one had too many friends and one had none at all.

Martha continued, "So now I figure if I spend most of my time in the park, I'll be out when my friends call or come by. They're new friends. They'll soon stop trying to keep in touch and my daughter'll have her home like it was."

Katie said impulsively, "You can bring your friends over to my house."

Martha said blankly, "You're joking."

"No, I'm not," said Katie firmly. "I'm no talker and never will be. But I love to hear other people talk. I love to listen to laughter."

"Well say," said Martha laughing happily, "I believe you mean that." She added exploringly, "I believe you wouldn't bat an eye if I was to move in with you. I'd pay a fair share. Might be I'll find a friend of two who's dying to make a change from living with her married children. Anyway, we'll talk about that later.

"I tell you what, let's do right now," said Martha the organizer. "Let's go over to your place and call up the girls and ask them over. They're good for a lot of laughs. They'll love you for being a listener."

They hurried home together with Katie's role in life not really changed completely.

Babe

Mrs. Dieterling, at fifty, was still a great beauty who looked less than forty. No one who did not actually know, would have dreamed she was the mother of a married daughter of thirty. No one, still unaware of the facts, would have dreamed that Babe was a mother at all, let alone the mother of three. She could have passed for a teenager. It was as if time had forgotten both Babe and Mrs. Dieterling, or had given them some magic formula.

What was most remarkable, however, was Mrs. Dieterling's dedication to Babe. It would not have been so surprising if Babe had worshipped her lovely mother. But it was unusual that Mrs. Dieterling, adored for her beauty by so many, seemed not to have a spoiled bone in her body, and did everything but breathe for Babe.

Mrs. Dieterling had been widowed when Babe was five. Her husband had died just when she was beginning to wonder why she had married a man so much older. She might easily have re-married but she had been left a comfortable annuity and she could not decide on any one of her suitors.

Besides, there was Babe. Though Babe was a sunny child, who showed no disposition to dislike the men who called on her mother; nevertheless, Mrs. Dieterling maintained that children felt superceded by a stepfather and lost their sense of security.

"But you don't want to grow old alone," a meddlesome friend advised. "Babe won't stay a child forever. One day she'll have a life and a home of her own."

Mrs. Dieterling gave a bright little laugh to dispel this evil portent. Babe was five. To think of Babe growing up or herself growing old was an exercise of imagination that only a morbid mind would indulge in.

"When a woman has only one child," she patiently explained, "she keeps her a baby as long as she can."

Over the years, she tried, with undisputed success. Her meddlesome friend said that she was ruining Babe. Babe never made beds or helped with the housework.

"But what will she do when she marries?" the meddlesome friend inquired, when Babe was well in her teens, and no better equipped to be a wife.

"Marriage," said Mrs. Dieterling, as if the word were a new one. "Marriage has never entered Babe's mind."

She looked at her meddlesome friend with charity for her lack of understanding. "I've been Babe's whole world ever since she was five. We couldn't be closer. She'll think a long time before she leaves me, if she thinks about it at all."

Nothing then could have shocked Mrs. Dieterling more than Babe's elopement with Bill Taylor. Only that morning she had waved Babe good-bye, as she watched her board a bus for high school, where she would join the other members of her senior class who had won a week's tour of Washington as first prize in a

good citizenship contest. Mrs. Dieterling had bought Babe everything new for the trip, including handsome luggage. She had,
quite unwittingly, furnished her with a trousseau.

That night, Mrs. Dieterling was waked from an uneasy sleep
by the ringing of the telephone.

She knew at once that it was Babe, or worse, that it concerned
Babe, to whom something dire had happened her first time away
from home and Mother.

She picked up the telephone and it was Western Union calling. An impersonal voice read a telegram to her. "Just married to
Bill Taylor. Please wish us well. Will see you soon."

Mrs. Dieterling, walking agitatedly back and forth, had to think
hard to remember Bill Taylor. Then she remembered the little that
Babe had told her about him. He worked at one of the local televi-
sion stations in a minor job. Babe had been on a televised high
school panel in her second semester. Every week this Bill Taylor
had come to her school to help set up facilities for the broadcast.
Until her telegram, Babe has never referred to him as anything but
Mr. Taylor.

After her first few weeks on the panel, she had not referred to
him at all. How often had Mrs. Dieterling's friend, the meddlesome one, remarked that still waters run deep. And how often
Mrs. Dieterling had answered that if she meant Babe, Babe was
as easy to read as a book.

When the couple returned from their brief honeymoon, Mrs.
Dieterling was too happy to have Babe back to reproach them. Bill
had been sharing a flat with bachelor friends. Not too long out of
college, not too long employed, he had no money to embark on
marriage. Mrs. Dieterling still held high cards.

She played them well. She could have invited the newlyweds

to live with her, but she did not take this advantage of their improvidence. That very night Mrs. Dieterling moved to a small hotel and gave her house, as a wedding present, to the astonished pair, whose gratitude, not unnaturally, was boundless.

To her habitual inquisitor who wanted to know what she would do without a house to take care of, Mrs. Dieterling replied, somewhat testily, that the very point of her taking a room was to keep her time free for Babe, if she needed a helping hand.

Babe sent her a frantic call for help almost immediately. There was nothing she knew about keeping house or feeding a husband.

Mrs. Dieterling came without delay, deftly undoing Babe's apron, which was hers anyway, and tying it where it belonged.

"You're still a child," she said soothingly. "You can't be expected to learn a woman's work overnight. It's a lovely day. Go out and enjoy it. I'll have everything done by the time you get back."

Mrs. Dieterling was always gone by the time Bill got home. He saw her only on Sundays when she invited the couple to dinner at her hotel. She never asked them how they were getting along or if there was anything she could do. Bill was fairly sure he had the pick of mothers-in-law.

Despite Mrs. Dieterling's delicate hints that Babe had years to be a mother, a baby was on the way before Babe was nineteen. Mrs. Dieterling took Bill aside. He mustn't, she cautioned him, let Babe overdo or overtire. Her youth and inexperience could prove disastrous to both mother and child.

At his job the next day Bill could not settle down. He brooded all morning, hating the thought of Babe being alone, praying that everything was all right at home. Finally and desperately he telephoned Mrs. Dieterling, who was sitting complacently by the phone, waiting for his call. In an embarrassed rush he asked her if she would mind staying days with Babe while he was away at work. Detecting no trace of reluctance in her assent, he asked her if she would stay nights, too, until the baby came.

It was Mrs. Dieterling who brought young Bill home from the hospital. As the weeks added up, Babe, watching her mother take care of him, could never see more than her mother's back, which somehow, was always turned to her.

Bill, seeing Babe's inexpert handling of his son, confided to Mrs. Dieterling that he did not think Babe was ready to be left alone with the baby. Since Mrs. Dieterling did not think so either, she remained in charge. When the second baby, Laurie, was born, young Bill was still in the toddler stage. Since Babe hadn't learned to take care of one child, it went without saying that she couldn't take care of two. Susie's birth two years later made Mrs. Dieterling indispensable.

When Bill was going on ten, Babe was going on thirty. Mrs. Dieterling made a bright response whenever Bill mentioned his birthday, but she shied away from any mention of Babe's. This constant shying away slowly impinged on Babe's mind. She wondered about it, then she thought about it, with her thinking daily growing more serious, until she came to the startling realization that she was no longer a girl in her twenties.

She revealed this fact to her mother as an exciting discovery.

Mrs. Dieterling, reacting as if from a blow, said harshly, "If it weren't for Bill junior, you would be. You don't look a day over twenty, but your son will soon be ten. You can hide your age, but you can't hide your children."

"You couldn't hide me either," Babe said quietly, her celebration still in progress. "That's why you turned me into a doll. A doll stays a doll forever. We lived in a make-believe world, cut off from the real one where people grow old. But now I'm tired of let's pretend. I want to be my age."

"And what happens to me?" Mrs. Dieterling said bitterly.

"I need you more than I've ever needed you," Babe said earnestly. "I've as much to unlearn as I have to learn. You've as much to undo as you have to do. I'll suffer with growing pains. Your patience will grow thin. It won't be easy for either of us. We'll probably age in the process. But will you give it a try?"

There was a pause. Then Mrs. Dieterling had a most extraordinary sensation. She felt as if she were floating on air, weightless and serene.

"Yes," she said on a sigh of tranquility, "I'm willing."

The Richer, The Poorer

Over the years Lottie had urged Bess to prepare for her old age. Over the years, Bess had lived each day as if there were no other. Now they were both past sixty, a time for summing up. Lottie had a bank account that had never grown lean. Bess had clothes on her back, and the rest of her worldly possessions in a battered suitcase.

Lottie had hated being a child, sharing her parents' skimping and scraping. Bess had never seemed to notice. All she ever wanted was to go outside and play. She learned to skate on borrowed skates. She rode a borrowed bicycle. Lottie couldn't wait to grow up and buy herself the best of everything.

As soon as anyone would hire her, Lottie put herself to work. She minded babies; she ran errands for the old.

She never touched a penny of her money, though her child's mouth watered for ice cream and candy. But she could not bear to share with Bess, who never had anything to share with her. When her dimes began to add up to dollars, she lost her taste for sweets.

By the time she was twelve, she was cleaning after school in a small variety store. Saturdays she worked as long as she was wanted. She decided to keep her money for clothes. When she entered high school, she would have a wardrobe that neither Bess nor anyone else would be able to match.

But her freshman year found her unable to indulge so frivolous a whim, particularly when her admiring instructors advised her to think seriously of college. No one in her family had ever gone to college, and certainly Bess would never get there. She would show them all what she could do if she put her mind to it.

She began to bank her money and her bank became her most private and precious possession.

In her third year of high school, she found a job in a small but expanding restaurant, where she cashiered from the busy hour until closing. In her last year of high school, the business had increased so rapidly that Lottie was faced with the choice of staying in school or working full-time.

Bess had been in the school band, and had no other ambition except to play the horn. Lottie expected to be settled with a home and family while Bess was still waiting for Harry to earn enough to buy a marriage license.

That Bess married Harry straight out of high school was not surprising. That Lottie never married at all was not really surprising either. Two or three times she was halfway persuaded but to give up a job that paid well for a homemaking job that paid nothing was a risk she was incapable of taking.

Bess' married life was nothing for Lottie to envy. She and Harry lived like gypsies. Harry playing in second-rate bands all over the country, even getting himself and Bess stranded in Europe. They were often in rags and never in riches.

Bess grieved because she had no child, not having sense enough to know she was better off without one. Lottie was certainly better off without nieces and nephews to feel sorry for. Very likely Bess would have dumped them on her doorstep.

That Lottie had a doorstep they might have been left on was only because her boss, having bought a second house, offered Lottie his first house at a price so low and terms so reasonable that it would have been like losing money to refuse.

She shut off the rooms she didn't use, letting them go to rack and ruin. Since she ate her meals out, she had no food at home and did not encourage callers, who always expected a cup of tea.

Her way of life was mean and miserly, but she did not know it. She thought she lived frugally in her middle years so that she could live in comfort and ease when she most needed peace of mind.

The years after forty began to race. Suddenly Lottie was sixty and retired from her job by her boss' son who had no sentimental feeling about keeping her on until she was ready to quit.

She made several attempts to find other employment, but her dowdy appearance made her look old and inefficient. For the first time in her life, Lottie would gladly have worked for nothing to have someplace to go, something to do with her day.

Harry died abroad, in a third-rate hotel. With Bess weeping as hard as if he had left her a fortune. He had left her nothing but his horn. There wasn't even money for her passage home.

Lottie, trapped by the blood tie, knew she would not only have to send for her sister, but take her in when she returned. It didn't seem fair that Bess should reap the harvest of Lottie's lifetime of self-denial.

It took Lottie a week to get a bedroom ready, a week of hard work and hard cash. There was everything to do, everything to replace or paint. When she was through the room looked so fresh and new that Lottie felt she deserved it more than Bess.

She would let Bess have her room, but the mattress was so lumpy, the carpet so worn, the curtains so threadbare that Lottie's conscience pricked her. She supposed she would have to redo that room, too, and went about doing it with an eagerness that she mistook for haste.

When she was through upstairs, she was shocked to see how dismal downstairs looked by comparison. She tried to ignore it, but with nowhere to go to escape it, the contrast grew more intolerable.

She worked her way from kitchen to parlor, persuading herself she was only putting the rooms to right to give herself something to do. At night she slept like a child after a long and happy day of playing house. She was having more fun than she had ever had in her life. She was living each hour for itself.

There was only a day now before Bess would arrive. Passing her gleaming mirrors, at first with vague awareness, then with painful clarity, Lottie saw herself as others saw her and could not stand the sight.

She went on a spending spree from specialty shop to beauty salon, emerging transformed into a woman who believed in miracles. She was in the kitchen basting a turkey when Bess rang the bell. Her heart raced harder and she wondered if the heat from the oven was responsible.

She went to the door, and Bess stood before her. Stiffly she suffered Bess' embrace, her heart racing harder, her eyes suddenly smarting from the inrush of cold air.

"Oh, Lottie, it's good to see you," Bess said, but saying nothing about Lottie's splendid appearance. Upstairs Bess, putting down her shabby suitcase, said, "I'll sleep like a rock tonight," without a word of praise for her lovely room. At the lavish table, top-heavy with turkey, Bess said, "I'll take light and dark both," with no marveling at the size of the bird or that there was turkey for two elderly women, one of them too poor to buy her own bread.

With the glow of good food in her stomach, Bess began to spin stories. They were rich with places and people, most of them lowly, all of them magnificent. Her face reflected her telling the joys and sorrows of her remembering and above all, the love she lived by that enhanced the poorest places, the humblest person.

Then it was that Lottie knew why Bess had made no mention of the finery, or the shining room, or twelve-pound turkey. She had not even seen them. Tomorrow, she would see the room as it really looked and Lottie as she really looked and the warmed over turkey in the second day of glory. Tonight she saw only what she had come seeking, a place in her sister's home and heart.

She said, "That's enough about me. How have the years used you?"

"It was me who didn't use them," said Lottie wistfully. "I saved for them. I forgot the best of them would go without my ever spending a day or a dollar enjoying them. That's my life story in those few words, a life never lived. Now it's too near the end to try."

Bess said, "To know how much there is to know is the beginning of learning to live. Don't count the years that are left us. At our time of life, it's the days that count. You've too much catching up to do to waste a minute of a waking hour feeling sorry for yourself."

Lottie grinned, a real wide-open grin. "Well, to tell the truth, I felt sorry for you. Maybe if I had any sense, I'd feel sorry for myself after all. I know I'm too old to kick up my heels, but I'm going to let you show me how. If I land on my head, I guess it won't matter. I feel giddy already, and I like it."

Interlude

She didn't know why she was having twelve for lunch, except that she was indebted to twelve, and it just seemed easier to have them in one afternoon.

It wasn't that she didn't like to entertain. It was just that it was never easy to fit company into her daily routine of taking care of a small boy, who didn't know that she had any other reason for existence.

Children made such demands on adults. They thought everything was within your capacity because you were bigger than they were. They believed you could be in two places at once, that you were blessed with two pairs of hands, that you had a ready answer for no matter what was asked, plus time to spare for trivia.

If only she didn't let herself be persuaded that Jamie was old enough to have a puppy. But he had begged so hard and made so many promises, not that he hadn't kept them. He was like a hen with one chick. The puppy absorbed his day, and threatened to disrupt hers. Jamie discussed its care and feeding from sunup to sundown.

And it was just a mutt. Just a mutt that a wily neighbor had given to Jamie, knowing his mother would not have the heart to make him give it back. She gave him a female, of course, the runt of the father-unknown litter, her feet too big, her legs too short, her tail a comic curlicue, her whole ensemble adding up to nothing but a boy's first dog, that creative, invariably impossible to describe, with whom the boy learns devotion.

He named her Princess, finding no other name better suited to her beauty, intelligence, and charm. Like a mother with her first born, or that hen with her one baby chick, he could not imagine how he had lived in the world so long without her.

The screen door slammed. Joan sighed. She could hear Jamie coming on the run, as if the moments of his life were more important than those of other mortals.

"Mom," he began with his usual breathlessness.

She eyed him warily. She did not want to get involved with so much still to do.

"What is it, Jamie?" she said in a deliberately deflated voice to discourage a long story.

"It's Princess," he said excitedly. "She's too hot."

She put her hands against his flushed cheek. "You're too hot yourself. It's an August day, Jamie. It's not a day to race and run. Now go sit in the shade and cool off. If you want to go swimming this afternoon, you'll have to rest first."

"I'm not going swimming," he said. "I'm going to stay home with Princess."

She should have known it. He was going to be difficult because she was having company. Any other day you couldn't have kept him out of the water. He was jealous of this one afternoon she had reserved for herself in the long years that had come and gone. They're coming at one. They'll be gone by four. Three hours!

Her voice was slightly hysterical. "Is it too much to ask for three hours to be with people my own age, to enjoy them without interruption? Is it too much to ask of you, Jamie?"

He was staring at her, trying to sort her words into meaning, knowing only that he was not in her favor, and feeling frightened by her rejection.

He said, to make her love him again, "No, it's not too much to ask. You can ask me."

She felt ashamed. He was only seven. He was so innocent, so vulnerable. But just once this summer, just this once in a day that she would make up to him as soon as her guests were gone, could she not have a little while to laugh and talk with women like herself. Like herself, these women were taking these snatched hours to recapture a time gone, not regretted, but gone except for these illusory afternoons without children or husbands or pets claiming attention.

"You'll be surprised," she said gently, "how quickly time flies if you don't keep an eye on it. It'll be four before you know it." She gave a little start. "And it'll be one before I know it. Jamie scoot! That's my love. I'll save you something special from the party."

Her guests came, looking charming, acting carefree and gay. The afternoon passed beautifully. Her lunch was perfect. The right people were paired for cards. The prizes were just what the winners wanted. Promptly at four, they rose to leave. Everything went according to plan. Joan wished she could do it more often. But, anyway, it was a lovely oasis.

Twice she had glimpsed Jamie's anxious face at the window, but no one else had noticed. She had blocked his face with her back.

She was well aware her guests wanted no reminder; their children, too, were impatiently waiting for their mothers to stop this silly pretending that there were no chains that bound them.

The last car drove off and Jamie came, not running, but slowly, the door not banging, but sighing shut. His face was very white.

He said starkly, "Princess won't move. She's dead."

"Jamie, no! Are you sure? When? Why didn't you call me?"

Without reproach, he said dully, "You told me not to."

A child's logic, a child's unreasoning logic.

"But I didn't mean—Never mind. I'll go see. You've got to be wrong. It just isn't true." This last she said aloud, not to herself, but to whatever gods there were who worked miracles for mothers of small boys, so the sin of their omissions might not forever lie like lead in their remorseful hearts.

As she ran, her thoughts raced with her. Was she to blame? What was her misdeed? She had no power of clairvoyance. What should she have done when she glimpsed Jamie's face at the window? Brought an end to her party, sent her guests home unfed and unforgiving? They were the mothers of Jamie's friends. Had she been rude to them, they might have turned about and taken revenge where it would hurt her most, made a summer outcast of her son, calling their children away whenever he appeared, never letting them come to play.

How can you choose between a child's face at a window and a grown-up guest? How can you choose between a dying dog and an afternoon of cards? The choice is too bizarre. It is also unfair that a choice must be made. Mothers are people with the same disposition to error.

She was almost there. She saw the still form. She ran faster. She knelt down in her lovely dress, not caring. She felt a heartbeat. Princess was still alive. She was just too sick to move and too indifferent in her near dying to respond to a small boy, who did not know what to do for her.

But at Joan's touch, her tail gave a feeble flick of hope, her pain-washed eyes lost a little of their glare. Here was the one who could help her if anyone could. Here was the tall one, the mother one, who was all-powerful, all-wise.

Joan lifted Princess gently into her arms. "Run get the keys to the car, Jamie. You know where I keep them. We'll go straight to the vet's. He'll make her well—"

He gave her a look of adoration. "You made her not dead. You made her come alive. Oh, Mom, I knew you could if you tried."

He was gone for the keys before she could protest that she had no power to quicken the dead. He never would have believed her. He had seen with his own eyes a still form move for her that had not moved for him.

She walked toward the car. Jamie came running with the keys. He looked up at her and Princess was looking up at her, their world secure and safe again because she had put them first in hers.

The interlude of lunch and cards was over as it was for all the other mothers in their seaside town and in all the towns everywhere.

The Long Wait

Millie had finally outlived her family. At last she had her
house to herself. Long ago Papa had left it to her because she was
his spinster daughter. But except for a few weeks after Papa's
death, Millie hardly knew what it felt like to call her home her
own.

Those few short weeks of solitude were Millie's brightest
memory. All through Papa's sickness the doorbell rang, the telephone rang, or Papa was calling her to read to him, to rub his
back, to fetch him a glass of water. When it was over she was too
worn out to feel bereaved. All she asked was a little time of peace.

In the days following her doorbell rang and she did not answer
it. Her telephone rang, and she let it ring. She put her mail aside
unopened. Tomorrow she would make a fresh start, pick up the
pieces of routine living, but every tomorrow her resolution weak-
ened.

Millie was on leave without pay from her firm. When she
thought about returning to her desk with all those other desks

around her and the constant clatter of tongues and typewriters she could not think beyond her dread of being snowed under.

She was forty-five. She was single. Everyone else in the office was married, or engaged, or young enough to be hopeful. All of them talked down to her, or around her, as if she were not quite the same as they were, because she had no husband to prove it. To be part of them again and apart from them again took more mettle than Millie could muster.

There was only one alternative and Millie mulled over it in her mind. The house had no mortgage. There were no monthly payments to meet. She could sell Papa's car. He had never let her learn to drive it anyway. With her own fair-sized savings, and the little money that Papa had left her, she might be able to manage until she was old enough for a pension.

Millie began to live with excessive frugality. She had her telephone removed. She kept the house just warm enough to keep her teeth from chattering, and ate without ever appeasing her hunger.

She lived in this homemade Eden for a month of happy exile. Then one day her doorbell rang and kept on ringing loudly, insistently, as if it would never let up. The sudden, shrill assault on her ears was unendurable. She rushed to the door and flung it open, words she did not know she knew ready to leap from her tongue.

Surprise dropped her jaw before she could say them. Before her stood her oldest sister, Carrie, the one who had bossed her so when they were children, the widowed one with no husband or young ones to make her stay home.

"Why haven't you answered my letters? Why did you take out your phone? I even called your office, and they said they hadn't seen you. You might have been dead, and so might the rest of us for all it seemed to matter to you. What's got into you? You're thin as a rail and you look like a rag picker. You ought to thank your stars I came."

"Well, come on in," Millie said miserably.

Carrie stepped inside and stared around. She said with satisfaction: "The house looks a sight, like a hermit's hideaway. You're not the kind to live by yourself. It makes you live inside yourself. With all my children grown and gone, and my landlord planning to raise my rent, there's nothing to call me back home. You and this poor house need someone to take an interest."

Carrie sent instructions to one of her daughters who packed her mother's clothes and a few treasured keepsakes, and sold her furniture to the secondhand dealer who offered the best price.

These matters disposed of, her trunks unpacked, her treasures set in place, Carrie rolled up her sleeves to run Millie's life.

There was nothing for Millie to do but resign herself. The pattern was unchanged. She was the last born, late in Mama's life, and Mama had tried to keep her a baby, never letting go her hand. Her sisters had treated her like a plaything, making her conscious that she would never catch up with them, that they would always be older and wiser. Papa was fiercely protective, warding off barking dogs, cats with claws, and eventually boys. As his other daughters married, Papa gave them away without feeling forsaken. Millie was the child he chose to be the staff of his old age.

And now here was Carrie insisting that Millie didn't know her own mind, and marching her off to her office with the blunt explanation that there was nothing Millie could do at home Carrie couldn't do better.

Christmas came and Carrie told Millie to prepare for a big surprise. Sure enough on Christmas Eve in walked their sister Josie, come on Carrie's invitation to spend the holidays. Josie was so jolly, she was such good company that Carrie kept saying she hated to think of her ever going. Josie started saying she wished she didn't ever have to.

Carrie asked then why did she have to? Wasn't she in the way at her daughter's?

With no further persuasion Josie stayed on. And that left only their sister Lou outside the family fold. Letters flew between Carrie and Lou, Lou's letters growing more and more homesick for Carrie's cooking and Josie's laughter and Millie's quiet way.

Carrie put her thinking cap on. Lou's husband was planning to retire. They had only a home to tie them down that had always been too big for a couple without children.

Lou could talk Harry into selling it, and be ready to board the train the minute they found a buyer. A houseful of people could live more cheaply than two, and live a whole lot more happily.

Millie's life had come full circle. She slept on a cot in Carrie's room, just as she had done as a child. When all her sisters started talking at once her smaller voice was rarely heard. With Harry she was relegated to the piddling chores, Harry because no more was expected of a man, Millie because no more was expected of her.

The one thing that sustained Millie through the years ahead was the comforting knowledge that as the youngest, with luck, she would live the longest.

When that day of deliverance came, she was sixty-odd. But she wasted no time rewriting the years that were over and gone. There was not that much time to waste. In a fever of haste, she locked her doors and pulled her shades, her private world restored at last.

Millie drank deep of sweet independence and the after-taste was sour. The days began to drag, night brought no sleep, and silence drummed louder in her ears than all the lost laughter of her sisters. To live alone because you want to is quite different from living alone because you have to. To do as you please has lost most of its meaning when there is no one who cares what pleases you.

Millie put an ad in the morning paper, cleaned up the house almost as well as Carrie could have cleaned it, rolled up her shades, dressed in her best and waited.

That afternoon the doorbell rang, a sound as exciting as any she had ever heard. With racing heart, she opened the door. There stood a google-eyed family of six, a man, a wife, and four small children.

The woman said breathless: "Is it true? I couldn't believe it when I read your ad." She read it aloud, "'Woman old enough to be a grandmother wants ready-made family to live with her rent-free in return for their affection.'"

"Is it a gag?" the man asked suspiciously.

"Ads cost money," Millie said with a spirit. "I'm too old to waste it on silliness."

"We've got a dog," the woman added anxiously, "a very nice dog. We left him with our next-door neighbor until we get settled here. You see, we just came and we're bunking with my husband's brother, and, of course with all of us, and all of them, it's crowded. My husband's going into business with his brother. They've bought a garage. For you to let us live in your house rent-free until the business starts showing a profit is like having a fairy godmother."

"Grandmother," Millie said firmly. "And if you're going to live here, you'd better start calling it our house. Nobody ever called it my house anyway. My sisters thought what was mine was theirs, and it made us more of a family."

"Well, children," said the woman, "go and kiss your grandmother."

They all lived happily together for the rest of Millie's life. The children were always clamoring for stories, and Millie found her tongue. When she began to talk there was no end of stories to tell about Mama and Papa and Carrie and the rest. And in the telling Millie acquired a personality which gave her the identity that is come by no other way.

The Birthday Party

Aunt Em and the Binneys were summer neighbors. They had known each other before the Binneys bought the sprawling old house next door that had been untenanted for years. Their coming was providential. Aunt Em acquired neighbors when she most needed them, the summer after her husband's death, when she had to force herself to go down to her cottage alone, sure that this quiet retreat and the shuttered house next door would accentuate her loneliness.

Aunt Em found the Binneys already in residence, the lawn cut, new curtains sparkling, and the trim spruced up with paint. The lively sounds of their occupancy were clearly heard above the groans of the tired old taxi chugging its way up the incline. Aunt Em was childless and her relatives were scattered. Nothing could have pleased her more than to find a family waiting for her, as indeed the Binneys were, six small ones, two of parent size, putting their best foot forward in the hope that a neighbor who had no children would not be too dismayed by people who had a pocketful.

There was only a low ornamental fence between the two properties, which the young Binneys literally took in their stride. They thought children were the business of everybody. They asked Aunt Em for drinks of water. They brought her their cuts and bruises to be bandaged. They fell in her flower beds when they were wrestling.

Mrs. Binney was humbly grateful to Aunt Em for her endurance. She had stair steps for children, the youngest just two and the oldest not quite nine.

Kathy was the only girl. She was the one who was going on nine. She was also the one who gave Aunt Em—Mrs. Emmett—her affectionate title.

Kathy was soft-spoken and gentle. She was as completely fragile and feminine as her brothers, even the youngest, were stridently male.

Aunt Em's little sun parlor became her sanctuary. She chose a little corner where she kept her favorite possessions. On rainy afternoons she and Aunt Em had tea parties for Kathy's dolls.

One day she said shyly and proudly that tomorrow was her birthday. Aunt Em naturally asked her what she would like for a present.

"A tea party in our sun parlor," Kathy said fervently. "And only girls invited, no ole boys, not even brothers."

Aunt Em couldn't give consent until she had spoken to Kathy's mother, who certainly had a prior right to plan her only daughter's party. Mrs. Binney was delighted to hand over the reins.

Aunt Em gave Kathy the first birthday party that Kathy did not cry through. It was just a small dainty tea party, with Aunt Em's finest china and four prim little girls on their best behavior. None of Kathy's gifts was broken before the party was over. Nobody fought in the middle of the floor. Nobody stole a bite out of the birthday cake before it was brought to the table.

When it was over, with Kathy's face wreathed in smiles instead of streaked with tears, Kathy made Aunt Em promise that she could have her birthday party in the sun parlor every year forever, and never any boys, and only girls who didn't like boys either.

In the succeeding summers, Kathy's acquaintanceship widened. But the charm of her party was its setting in the small sun parlor. She made her prim selection of guests from the slowly decreasing number of girls who still didn't like boys.

The summer of Kathy's fourteenth birthday she did not seem quite the same to Aunt Em. Perhaps it was because she had grown so tall through the winter. The little girl look was gone. She still liked to sit in her corner of the sun parlor, but she sat there dreaming, answering without interest Aunt Em's questions about school.

Then it was the week of her birthday. Somehow Aunt Em knew that Kathy would not want a tea party. The very name suggested childish play. And when you are fourteen, you have put away childish things. Aunt Em wondered whether Kathy would like a buffet supper in the sun parlor, with the same kind of wonderful things to eat that grown-ups had at theirs.

"It's just a suggestion," Aunt Em said. "If you'd rather have another kind of party . . ." Her voice trailed off for Kathy's own suggestion.

"I was thinking of another kind of party," Kathy said in that new dreamy way.

Aunt Em felt a little disappointed, but she wanted Kathy to say what she wanted. Whatever she said, Aunt Em would be glad to do her bidding.

But Kathy didn't say. She rambled on vaguely, "Well, I asked my mother, and she said I could. I mean she said I cold have it over at my house. There'll be more kids. My mother said you wouldn't want the bother."

"It's never been a bother," Aunt Em protested. "It's always been a pleasure to give you a party. I'm sure we can stretch the sun parlor to hold as many girls as you like."

"Well, I already told the kids to come to my house," Kathy said. "So I guess it's too late to tell them not to."

The day before the party, Mrs. Binney, out of earshot of Kathy, called across to Aunt Em: "You'd think this was Kathy's first party. I've never seen her so excited. Let's hope it doesn't rain on the doings. I'll be glad when her birthday's over."

Aunt Em knew that little girls half-grown were no longer made of sugar. They didn't melt in the rain. She supposed the young ladies were concerned about their clothes. At fourteen, their sub-deb finery was given loving care.

But the girls didn't come in party dresses. They came in shorts, trailing them were boys in jeans. To Aunt Em, there seemed to be an unending stream of boys no different from Kathy's brothers except a little older. Yet Kathy flew to greet them as if they had come from another country.

The feature of the party was a barbecue in the backyard, frankfurters and toasted buns, most of which were at least half-burned except for those that got dropped in the dirt. There was a lot of horseplay and a good deal of showing off by the girls. Afterward they stampeded inside for the cutting of the cake and the opening of the presents, some of which, judging by Kathy's squeals and the whoops of laughter, were probably purchased by some unsupervised gift givers in the novelty shop that dealt in scary tricks.

When the last celebrators rode away on their bicycles, silence fell that hurt the ears. Aunt Em set about getting her dinner, feeling a little sad that it wasn't a buffet supper, feeling a little left out, knowing she could never take the place of anything as miraculous as a boy, but wishing Kathy had not forgotten her so completely.

A knock pounded. Aunt Em said, "Come," and in came Kathy, bearing a plate with birthday cake and dish with melted ice cream.

"Yours was the first piece of cake. It's the biggest and I made Mother save you some ice cream before she served the others."

"Why thank you for thinking you of me," Aunt Em said warmly. "Did you have a nice party?"

"Well, there were boys. That's why I had it over at my house. I never had boys at the other parties. I knew you didn't want boys in your sun parlor. . . . Boys who aren't brothers are nice," Kathy busily explained. "Like the boys at my party. They were not silly like my brothers. Of course," she conceded, "my brothers are still young."

"They'll get over that," Aunt Em assured her.

"But they won't get over being silly," Kathy said scornfully.

"They will for some girl on her fourteenth birthday," Aunt Em said.

Kathy looked for the joke but couldn't find it. "I don't know what you mean, Aunt Em."

"I mean boys always grow up on a girl's fourteenth birthday."

"That isn't funny either," Kathy said reproachfully. "You're teasing me."

"No," said Aunt Em, "I'm not teasing you."

Mrs. Creel

At a time of life when most women with adequate means were taking it easier, Mrs. Creel took into her home, and presumably her heart, six elderly women who had no near relatives to give them the care and comfort their remaining years deserved.

People who had said more than once in the past that Mrs. Creel had never had children because she thought children were more of a bother than a blessing, now saw her show tireless patience with the old, who spilled things, who broke things, who told tales on one another, who got in her way whenever she walked.

In thinking it over, and being fair, no one actually remembered Mrs. Creel ever saying outright that she didn't like children. But she had certainly recoiled from the jam-smeared, sticky-fingered children of her friends in the years when they were raising families.

Even when she was a child herself, the persistent recalled, she had rarely played with children her age. When she did, she ran home crying because they hadn't let her be first.

She was an only child, born to her parents in the middle years, and they never got over the miracle of it. Their friends' children were almost grown, and their own entrancing little girl was the baby of the circle. She went from lap to lap, from one compliment to another, from cradle to altar in an aura of admiration.

It was not surprising that she married a man old enough to be her father, nor that her parents approved her choice. Mr. Creel, a long-time friend, knew what was expected of him as a husband.

He put his young bride on a pedestal, and there he kept her very well. That they had no children relieved more than grieved him. His supply of love was on tap to Mrs. Creel, who managed to use every drop.

This review of Mrs. Creel's history was undertaken by those doubters who were still seeking some dark clue to the change in her character. But they had to come to the charitable conclusion that Mrs. Creel, who had taken so much and given so little, was reopening her past by this selfless dedication to six near-strangers who received so much more than their pittance paid for.

The old ladies called her "Mrs. Creel, dear love," and thought the sun rose and set in her. They spoke of her in superlatives to any ear that was trapped into listening—the doctor, the delivery boy, the handyman washing a window.

Only Sadie, the cleaning woman, who came daily, and stayed overnight if some minor emergency needed someone to spell Mrs. Creel through the crisis, was deaf to these worshipful sounds. She had shown the same indifference to Mrs. Creel's kind offer of a permanent room, preferring to arrive for work already worn out from a long, tiring ride on a crowded bus, which never seemed to save a seat for her and stopped blocks away from the shabby street where she rented a small, dreary room in a walk-up.

Behind her back the old ladies called her "sour Sadie." No one ever saw her smile or heard hear speak without a sigh.

She had had a hard life with a shiftless husband who was oftener out of work than at it. When he stumbled upon a janitor's job that included a flat rent-free, she saw to it that he kept it by doing his work herself. She never found time to change from her overalls to a dress or give her flat a proper cleaning, or take her children on an outing. When her children were grown up and gone, and her man was dead and gone, she had lived so long with resignation that she did not know she had been released.

Mrs. Creel could have picked a dozen other women instead of Sadie. But Mrs. Creel asked who else would have given her work. No one else would have had sour Sadie around if she had offered her services free. They were afraid her disposition would rub off on them.

It did not rub off on Mrs. Creel. If anything, she grew prettier and sunnier around Sadie. Perhaps it just seemed so because of the contrast. But whatever it was, the sight of sour Sadie made the old people more aware than ever that Mrs. Creel was the darling of the world.

When Sadie had been with Mrs. Creel a year, one of her daughters sent for her—the daughter who, like her mother, had married a man disinclined to work. They lived on a suburban farm that needed a hired man they couldn't afford. With a new baby only a few weeks away, and the old baby just beginning to walk, Sadie's daughter could use a pair of hands to do the rough chores her own hands were tied against doing.

Sadie told Mrs. Creel she was leaving without a quiver of regret, not because she looked forward to life on the farm, but because she looked forward to complaining about it.

Mrs. Creel asked Sadie whether there was anyone she knew who would like her job, sure that anyone in Sadie's sad circle would be so like her that the household would not have to adjust to a new personality.

A relative in a nearby town came readily to Sadie's mind, a cousin, Jennie Jilkes, whose married nieces and nephew were selling the family home from under her. None of them wanted it enough to be bothered with upkeep and taxes, and none of them wanted Aunt Jennie enough to be bothered with fitting her into their family.

Jennie, their father's sister, had been more of a mother to them than their natural mother, who renounced her responsibility when their baby brother was born. They had disappointed her by being born girls.

Jennie's sister-in-law was dry-eyed at the marriage of her daughters.

To her hurt surprise, her son missed his sisters and was restless with his elders. One day he announced that his office was sending him to a distant branch and did not add that he had asked for the transfer. With miles between him and his mother, he took a giant step into manhood, and married a girl who didn't believe in young couples seeing their in-laws too often.

His mother had never prepared herself to be supplanted, and saw a mocking I told you so in every casual glance. She kept to herself, talking only to Jennie and through a closed door, her devouring interest in the postman's ring.

Jennie's brother and sister-in-law lived long enough to have to live on their savings. There was nothing to leave but the house, which her brother left to his children, perhaps with the hope that they would maintain it for Jennie. But this wish was not father to their deeds.

At sixty Jennie did not know where to look for work. Who would hire a woman in the downhill years, with her only references a wretched life? Who would want her around, spreading gloom? Mrs. Creel alone had the charity to take the chance.

There came the day of Jennie's arrival. The old people knew what to expect, and were nonexpectant on the afternoon the doorbell rang, very loud, very long, as if the finger pressing it had so much energy behind it that a bell came hastily alive.

The old people began to chatter like birds. Whoever it was was bringing excitement.

Mrs. Creel went to the door and opened it to Jennie Jikes, whose drab old-fashioned clothes were forgotten the moment she smiled and stood in its radiance.

"I'm Jennie Jilkes," she said in a voice that promised laughter.

"Come in," Mrs. Creel said because she had to.

Jennie stepped inside and was surrounded by the old, warming themselves at her incandescence.

"You're not what I expected," was wrung out of Mrs. Creel.

Jennie said: "What did Sadie tell you?"

"Well, what she told me made me expect you'd be different."

"Oh," Jennie said, understanding, "Sadie makes everything a story. I don't mean she makes it up. I mean she tells it her way of seeing it. All I've got to show for my years is experience of living. But I learned to live with myself and that saved me a lot of misery. Sadie lives with the self she wishes she was and I guess there's nothing worse."

"But all of us want to be special," Mrs. Creel said with a kind of desperation. "If there's a front seat, you might as well sit in it."

"But then you can't see who's laughing behind your back."

The old ladies thought this was very funny. They cackled and cackled until Mrs. Creel felt a shiver go down her spine.

The Stairs

The grandmother stood on the front porch feeling summer's softness on her face. It was good to be back in her own cottage after so many months of being shut up in a city flat.

This was the morning the carpenter was coming to fix the porch steps. All of them were weak and some of them were wobbly. They were treacherous to the old. The grandmother's bones were growing too brittle to chance a fall.

A neighbor's dog trotted up the road to pay his respects, in the manner of country dogs, who make no unkind distinction between themselves and people.

"Good morning, Brownie," the grandmother said. "You couldn't ask for a better one. But I haven't time to entertain you. I'm expecting Mr. Hathaway. Look, there's his truck coming now. You come back later. I may have a bone."

The dog had listened intently, understanding all the important words like "come back" and "bone." He grinned, wagged his tail agreeably and ambled off, not flustering her by coming up for a

pat, knowing by animal instinct that she was too old to be confused by dogs and trucks dividing her attention.

Mr. Hathaway braked his little truck, scrambled down, and
smiled up at the grandmother. He was seasoned with living and
daily labor. A countryman who had had a long spell in the city,
with a sizable business, a wife who wore furs, and a house with all
the conveniences. When they were gone, the wife deceased, the
business sold because there was no one for whom to buy furs, and
the house sold, too, because it was too big for a widower, he came
back to where his roots were.

He had money in the bank, but he could not live out his days
on money alone. So he worked at his trade, working without a
helper because a younger man beside him made him do foolish,
reckless things like climbing a ladder too fast, making too long a
reach for a scaffold, carrying too many things at once time, just to
prove that he still had more go than a young whippersnapper.

"Mornin', Mrs. Edwards," he said. "I'm here."

"I see you are," she said brightly, with no attempt at sarcasm.
"Couldn't ask for a better day to start a job. But couldn't I get you
a cup of coffee before you start?"

It was a country courtesy. Everybody was on the same footing,
dog and man, servant and those he served. Besides, Mrs. Edwards
could trust Mr. Hathaway. He wouldn't add her cup of kindness
to his working hour.

"Well, thank you. I'd like that fine."

"You come sit while I get it. Walk with care. Those steps have
seen a lot of wear. So many children over so many summers have
bumped up and down them with their bicycles and tricycles. But
those days are gone now. I've already got a married granddaughter.
And the rest of my grands are up in their teens. Old enough to

find the country too quiet. They like to go where it's lively. They don't stay children forever. It isn't fair to wish they could." She gave herself a little shake. "Well, that's not getting the coffee. I'll be back soon."

She was back quite soon with coffee and buns on a tray. She settled the tray on the rail and dispensed her hospitality.

"My," said Mr. Hathaway, after a long, satisfying swallow, "there's nothing beats a good cup of coffee except the company of a good soul."

"Well," said Mrs. Edwards, "I always say if we haven't got time to take time with each other, we'll have plenty of time to be sorry."

Mr. Hathaway pondered this sage observation. "Say what you will, dog or cat, hunting or fishing, there's nothing the same as human talk."

Mrs. Edwards poured more coffee into his waiting cup and steered another sugared bun into his reaching hand. She sighed, not sadly, just routinely, as one who knew that the past was behind her.

"Every once in a while, I think I'll sell this house. It's got too many echoes of children's voices. None of my family have been here for over five years. Oh, I see them through the winter. But summer's when I have the most hankering. I guess that's because in summer there's more beauty in the country than you can bear alone."

Mr. Hathaway nodded agreement. "There's no place like here for soaking in love for everything the eye takes in. I wouldn't change my boyhood for anybody's. All those years I was away, I always knew I was coming back. I always knew that a countryman must walk a dirt road before he dies."

Mrs. Edwards said softly, "A child who sees the heart of sum-

mer in growing things and greening things has a store of memo-
ries to last him through the lean years of his life."

A station wagon drove up the road and parked behind Mr.
Hathaway's truck. A young blond mother poked her head out of
the driver's window. Three little girls leaned forward from the rear
seat to crowd their own fair heads around hers.

"God morning, Mrs. Edwards, Mr. Hathaway," the young
mother called, and the children chorused after her. She felt some
envy of the two old people. They were past life's harassments and
had only themselves to please. What bliss to look forward to,
thought the young mother, my children grown and my time my
own.

"Won't you come up and have some coffee, dear?" Mrs. Edwards asked. She had already poured the last of it into Mr. Hathaway's cup, but offered kindness anyway, and if it was accepted,
you pretended it wasn't putting you to any trouble. "Maybe the
children would like a cookie."

The little girls opened their eager mouths to answer but their
mother said firmly, "Thank you but we only stopped by to bring
you your mail."

"I'll come get it," said Mrs. Edwards. She explained to Mr.
Hathaway. "This dear child gets my mail every day. Time was I
used to enjoy the walk to the post office, but now the way there
and back gets longer every year."

"Let me," said Mr. Hathaway, rising. "I can save you these few
steps anyway." He got the letter and everybody said good-bye until everybody had given and received this gentle benediction. The
young mother drove away, with her children's hands fluttering out
of the window like banners waving in the breeze.

Mrs. Edwards thanked Mr. Hathaway, and made a great show

of gathering up cups and trays so that Mr. Hathaway would not take offense because she was going indoors to read her letter in private.

"Well, time to get started," Mr. Hathaway said, getting started. "Thank you for my repast."

Mrs. Edwards stood by the kitchen window and examined her letter. It was from her married granddaughter. The return address, the handwriting told her that much. But she couldn't imagine what Laurie had to say. Like all young people she never wrote unless there was a special reason.

But what could be special when it wasn't her birthday? Oh, dear, was it trouble? Was somebody sick? If she had any sense, she'd open the letter and see.

She opened the letter and read it, read it twice to be sure her old eyes were fooling her. Tears wet her lashes. The miracle of life had begun in her granddaughter. Laurie was going to have a child.

The news was too good to keep to herself. She went to the front door. Mr. Hathaway was measuring and putting marks on paper. She really shouldn't interrupt him.

"Mr. Hathaway, I really shouldn't interrupt you but I'll burst if I don't tell somebody. I'm going to be a great-grandmother. Come March. And my granddaughter and the baby will spend next summer here, and many more. That's what her letter said. She wants her baby to have the happy times she still remembers. So make those steps solid, Mr. Hathaway. It might be a boy."

Mr. Hathaway was something of a practical man. "And it might be another boy after that. This porch could stand a few new boards. You walking lady-like over it is one thing, boys stomping over it is another. You think about it. I'll quote a fair price."

"You do what has to be done. I'll find the money. Right now, I

feel like everything's possible. Next summer you may see me pushing a baby buggy to the post office. A baby keeps you stepping.
They don't give you time to feel old. My granddaughter only got
two hands. Mine will make the four she has to have."

The stoop in her shoulder seemed to vanish. She felt strong
and special and needed.

Bent Twig

Betty ran away and got married in her senior year in high school. Up to the day of her elopement she had been a bright and attentive student, among the top ten in her class. Any college would have accepted her. And her parents were unprepared for their crushing disappointment.

They had a long dream of Betty in cap and gown, receiving a college degree that would open the door of abundance that had always been closed to them. As the eldest children in large families, they had gone to work early, their educations unfinished, their talents unrealized, and their qualifications never adequate for any well-paid job.

When they met and married, they were past the years of expectancy. Betty's birth was their first real happiness. Their lives took on meaning and direction. They would give their child the chance their parents had been unable to give them, the chance to finish high school, the money to go to college. They would save that money nickel by nickel, if need be, and dime by dime. Betty's future would be insured against failure.

Over the years, it meant a great deal of sacrifice. Betty grew up in an atmosphere where a penny spent was a penny squandered. Her parents did not explain why this was so, at first because she was too young to understand, and then because their savings became a secret too precious to tell until the right time.

If Betty thought they were poorer than they were, that was as it should be. The less she asked for, the more they could save for her. They didn't know that she thought of herself as a burden, and wished she didn't have to be, and spent most of her time with her schoolbooks because they gave her too little allowance to do anything except get an occasional Coke at the drugstore where Jimmy Harris worked.

She married him to make her parents' lives a little easier with one mouth less to feed. Jimmy married her to impress his boss, old Mr. Maybrook, with his stability. A married man was a responsible man, capable of taking full responsibility for a drugstore. He deserved to inherit a business he worked harder at than the owner.

Old Mr. Maybrook had a niece somewhere, and her address was somewhere in his cluttered desk. But he had never bothered to write her, and finally she had stopped writing him. He didn't even know if she was living or dead, so there wasn't any sense in leaving her a drugstore. Besides, Mr. Maybrook was always saying he was just about ready to sell out when Jimmy came along and let him rest his feet.

Jimmy ran the place except for the prescriptions. Mr. Maybrook sat in back in carpet slippers, nodding most of the time and waking up to fill a prescription.

There weren't many to fill, since most people went to the bigger and busier drugstore on the next block. But the place did well enough for its size and stock. It was security for an old man who wanted very little, and for a young man, orphaned early, passed around among relatives, even a little was a lot.

Jimmy had a furnished room in a lodging house. With Betty he moved into a somewhat larger room with kitchen privileges.

Before his marriage, his meals had been snacks at the soda fountain. Though Betty did not say so, she was just as excited as Jimmy when they sat down to their first full meal.

When Betty felt that she could face her parents, she went to see them. Everybody explained, and everybody cried. At last, although the little ceremony was not as they had once planned it, Betty's parents presented her with her college fund, the bankbook kept secret so long, her name inscribed a few weeks after her birth.

She was overawed by the sum in four figures, and reluctant to accept it. But her parents pressed it on her as their wedding gift. They had never learned to spend money, only to save it. They had no need of it. They wanted Betty and her husband to have more in their marriage than they had had.

Betty want back to the furnished room with a head full of plans, hardly able to wait for Jimmy to come home. They could move to a real apartment house and have furniture of their own. They could make a down payment on a little house. They could buy a car instead of borrowing Mr. Maybrook's when he felt like lending it. They could go on a honeymoon, a real two-week honeymoon, all dressed up in all new clothes.

There were so many things to do with the money that Betty couldn't decide which of them they ought to do first. Maybe there were things she hadn't even thought of, maybe it was better to think a lot more. It had taken her parents so many years to save that money, they had done without so much to save it, that somehow it didn't seem fair to spend it the very minute she got it. And it wouldn't be fair to tell Jimmy if she wasn't ready to spend it. For a while at least she would let it be her secret.

She was very glad she did. Mr. Maybrook died suddenly, and nobody could find a will. But those who were looking found his niece's address. She arrived, as his nearest of kin, as his heir.

She was perfectly willing to sell Jimmy the drugstore at whatever figure he thought fair, even though she had an offer for the equipment and stock from the drugstore on the next block. But Jimmy could name no figure at all. And Betty could not bring herself to tell him about the nest egg. The other drugstore was too much competition. To buy a business that might fail would be like throwing her parents' money away.

Jimmy did whatever work he could find to do, mostly part-time. Occasionally they missed a meal, and once in a while their rent fell behind. But Betty kept her secret. If Jimmy knew about the nest egg, he might not try hard enough to find a steady job.

When Betty found out that she was going to have a baby, she was glad the money was still intact. Just knowing she had it, all of it, was as comforting as a warm hand. To spend it, any part of it, would be as foolish as pushing a warm hand away.

As if Betty had willed it by wishing, Jimmy started on a steady job the day he gave her his very last dollar, with no idea where to go to make another one.

It was winter, work was slow everywhere, nobody needed an extra, unskilled hand. But Jimmy kept on asking, kept on trying, walking up this street, and down that, his feet cold, his fingers numb, his stomach pleading. But he didn't stop and he might have stopped for second wind anyway, if he'd known about the nest egg. He didn't know and he kept on going until he got a job.

It was just a small job in a small garage. The man who had worked there before Jimmy had left because of the small pay. He was a mechanic, and so was the boss. There wasn't enough work for two mechanics, and the boss couldn't pay him the wages he wanted for work he wasn't doing.

If Jimmy was willing to start at low wages, he had all winter to learn about cars. He'd be learning a mechanic's trade, and getting paid for doing it. In spring business would begin to pick up, all summer it would be pretty good. There was talk of new houses going up in the neighborhood. Business might soon be good all year round. It might expand, and Jimmy's wages would expand, too.

Jimmy came home bubbling over with hopes. They grew and grew as he talked. In time he'd get to know the ropes as well as his boss. In time his boss might even make him a partner. In time he might save enough money to buy his partner out.

It didn't sound any more fantastic to Betty than it did to him. She believed him because she wanted to believe him. It kept her nest egg safe.

"You can do it," she said. "You can do it if you try. I'll help you. No matter how little you make, I'll save part of it. No matter how much you make, I'll save most of it."

He looked at her with admiration. "Where did you learn to be so wise about money?"

"I guess it's just in me," she said, with more wisdom than she knew.

A Tale of
Christmas and Love

She did not remember ever playing with dolls. But she did not remember much of anything before she was four. That being so, she would not have denied—if the facts were paraded before her—that in the year she was three, her mother had come toward her cradling a doll, and then attached it to her unready arms, wrapping her weak embrace around the china creature, and thereupon stepped back to admire the picture of miniature mother and make-believe child.

What, she asked, was Deedee going to name her new baby, helpfully reciting a list of lovely real life names for her to choose from. Deedee brushed them aside. "Her name is doll," she said in a voice that would have sounded dry had she been older. Maybe in time she gave the doll a more agreeable name and learned to treat it tenderly. Or maybe in time, a surer guess, she abandoned it, leaving her mother with no choice but to threaten to give the poor thing away to some more worthy child, and to have to follow through in the face of Deedee's instant acquiescence.

If her mother worried about Deedee's rejection of mothering, she tried to find an explanation in the fact that Deedee, the youngest of three daughters, was probably holding fast to her special place as the resident baby and was simply not ready to share it with a blond and blue-eyed doll. Deedee's family was colored—the description "black" not yet in compulsory use—and "colored" fitting them perfectly since they ran the whole spectrum of colors, every shade and every variation, with Deedee at the farthest end from the blond and blue-eyed doll.

Her mother's diagnosis of Deedee's condition was as wrong as most empirical judgments. At Christmastime in her fourth year, the year her remembering began, when asked what she wanted for Christmas, she said with inmmediate readiness, "A real baby."

Her mother could not have been more undone. "You don't even like dolls. What would you do with a baby? I'm still taking care of you. How can you take care of a baby?"

"You can teach me."

"You're not much more than a baby yourself."

"I'm going to be five." She held up five fingers to prove it.

Mother and daughter seesawed back and forth in a fruitless search for a resolution of the impasse. Until finally her mother told her she was sick of her foolishness and for her to go and play.

She was five, then six, then seven and through those years, particularly when Christmas was approaching their aging battle about babies would reactivate, the two facing each other in the most aggrieved way, presenting the same unacceptable pros and cons, and as usual, ending in a draw.

At eight, Deedee was old enough to know that she had been asking for a Christmas miracle, when there really weren't that many to go around. She said to her mother, "I want some books and some games for Christmas, and that's all." She gave her mother a lovely smile that said, "I really mean it."

Then the Christmas she was nine, her miracle happened. Her mother said "I have a surprise for you. You have two little cousins coming from Chicago to live with us. Chicago is too cold for them. We'll try to keep them warm and well. They're a brother and sister, and that's what they call each other, so we will, too. He's not quite three, she's not quite two. They're really only babies, and you can help me take care of them. They'll be here in time for Christmas.

There was such a swelling in Deedee's throat that she could not speak. Her mother gave her a lovely smile that said, "I know how you feel."

The parents of the children, too young themselves, had found it impossible to keep two children warm and fed. There was no welfare for the people then. They could only feed on poverty. Deedee's parents were well enough off to help when help was needed. An extended family was part of daily living. Sharing was a lifeline.

A Boston friend living in Chicago and coming home for Christmas brought the children to their new home on Christmas Eve. When Deedee and her sisters came in from play, coming in the back way as they always did to see what was happening in the kitchen, their mother said, "Sister and Brother are here. I've put them to bed upstairs. They had a long trip. Go see them before they fall asleep."

Her sister raced upstairs and Deedee couldn't follow. She had waited so long for this moment to happen and now it was more than she could bear. Her mother said gently, "Go see your babies. They're waiting."

She went upstairs, walking slowly because she could walk no faster. It seemed a journey that lasted forever. She reached the open door and stepped inside. She saw the little boy tucked in at the foot of the bed, half sitting up, while her sisters stood over him, telling each other how darling he was. Deedee loved him at once. He looked like a Christmas card angel, very blond and very fair, little trace of his black blood showing, and wiggling all over with friendliness.

She started toward him, and felt something pull her, though nothing and no one was touching her. The little boy was smiling straight at her, wanting her to come and hug him, and she took another step forward. Something pulled her again. Now she turned, feeling her smile erase itself from her face and some nameless ache rising inside her. A little brown girl, with an almost unearthly beauty, was tucked in at the head of the bed. She was not sitting up like her brother, who was full of euphoria at being in a warm house, in a warm bed, with good food warming his belly. She lay flat, she lay still. They stared at each other, silent, not smiling, their hearts interlocking. And Deedee heard her own heart say as clearly as if the words were said aloud, "I'm going to love you best of all."

It was over, but the spell was not broken. It had become part of her. She felt at ease. She joined her sisters and gave the little boy a big welcome hug and a big welcome kiss. They played with him until they were called to supper. They tiptoed past the little girl because she had fallen asleep.

Deedee filled a large part of the little boy's life. But the little girl was Deedee's life, and she was the little girl's existence. The affinity between the two could not be explained. It was as if they had both been born for this encounter, as if they had once been one flesh.

Then one day Deedee came home from school, and Sister was not at the door to greet her. She was upstairs in bed, as she was the next day, and the next day, and the day after that. And then one day she was not there at all. They had taken her to the hospital. A week passed, and another week passed. The grown-ups closed their faces, and nothing could be read in them.

There came a night when the telephone rang, and Deedee jerked awake, and then fell asleep again, surface sleep that was easily shattered. There were sounds in her room. She woke up. There was a bureau across the room with a mirror above it. Her mother and her Aunt Minnie were facing the mirror. Their faces were reflected, but they were not seeing what the mirror saw. They were standing there because it was the farthest away from Deedee's bed.

Her mother spoke: "I don't know what to do about Deedee. If I wake her up and tell her, she'll never forget it. If I don't wake her up, she may never forgive me."

Perhaps Deedee stirred, for suddenly her mother and aunt were really looking in the mirror, and they saw her lying in bed with her eyes wide open.

Her mother came quickly and stood over her, "Deedee," she said, "the hospital just called. Sister died. She doesn't have to suffer anymore. She's in heaven now. Now close your eyes and go back to sleep."

She closed her eyes and went back to sleep. When she awoke, it was morning. She felt excited. Something had happened in the night. What was it? Then she remembered. Sister had died. She jumped up and ran into her sister's room. "Genia, Helen, wake up, wake up. Sister died last night." She saw tears splash their faces. Then she was right. Something exciting really happened.

Her mother said she didn't have to go to school that day. She looked surprised. She wanted to go. She went to school and told everybody that her little cousin was dead. Somebody told her teacher. Her teacher said she could go home. She was surprised again.

The day of the funeral was a lovely day to go see Sister. Now they were all in the funeral parlor, where there were flowers and sad-faced friends. Deedee's mother pointed to a coffin and said, "Go look at Sister." Deedee went to the coffin and peered into it. She came back to her mother. "There's a little dead girl in there. Where's Sister? I came to see Sister."

Her mother said, "That was Sister you saw." That was the moment she came out of the shock that she had been in for three days. She had come to the funeral to take Sister home. It was not that she did not know about death. It was just that she did not know it could touch her. How could she know until it touched her? The smell of carnations was all around her. For years she could not bear the smell, for even more years, she could not touch one.

They were home now, she dry-eyed, icy. Brother had stayed home with an aunt. He ran to greet her. She turned away without touching him. She called her mother and took her aside. What she had to say she had to say outside of anyone else's hearing. She stared hard at her mother, and said the terrible thing, asked the haunting question.

"We're a colored family, aren't we? Why did God take our brown baby and let our white baby live?" Then she ran out of the room, knowing there was no answer to so cruel a question, knowing that only a mother would never reveal her wickedness. She had to strike out at someone, someone who would forgive her.

For days, for weeks she was mean to the little boy, dropping his bread on the floor to make him eat dirt, squeezing his hand so tightly when she held it that tears started in his eyes, doing every little hurtful thing she could get away with. And the little boy clung to her through it all, because he needed her now more than ever with Sister not there to play with, to sleep with, to talk to. Deedee had loved him once, and he did not know she had stopped.

It was summer, and the family came down from Boston to their summer cottage on the island. Deedee's little meanness continued, and Brother continued to trust her because love is forgiving.

One early evening, Deedee's sisters went to visit some friends their age, saying firmly she was too young to go but she was used to that, and watched them go. Then her mother said she was going to walk to a cottage down the road to sit awhile with an ailing friend. She put Brother to bed and told Deedee to go to him if he called.

Deedee went outside and sat on the porch, sitting as still as a mouse, so that Brother would think she had gone out, too, and feel scared being by himself. After a while she could hear him talking and she wouldn't comfort him by saying, "Go back to sleep, I'm right here."

He went on talking, and she wasn't answering, and he didn't sound scared.

It made her feel funny. Now it was she who began to feel scared. Who was he talking to? What was happening? She had to get up and see.

She went to the little bedroom at the back of the house. He scarcely noticed her coming. He was talking away, and he didn't stop. "What are you talking about?" she said crossly. "You go straight to sleep or you'll catch it."

"I'm talking to Sister," he said.

"Where is she?" Deedee asked softly.

"Right here," he said in surprise at the question.

"Do you see her?"

"Don't you?"

"No," said Deedee. "She doesn't want to see me. Will you tell her I'm sorry?"

"Deedee's sorry."

The tears that she had never shed began to fall. "Oh, Brother," she said, "I love you, let me love you."

She lay down beside him, and his hand crept into hers, the dark hand, the fair hand, entwined together.

That was the way her mother found them, asleep together. And the mother smelled a faint scent of carnations.

Then it was home again. The summer ended. They were home again, and it was Christmas again. And there they were around the tree, all of the faces filled with Christmas joy.

Deedee went over to Brother. She bent down to him. "Is she here?" He understood.

"Yes. Can you see her?"

"No."

And the ghost was laid.

Chronology

1907 Born in Boston, June 2, to Isaac Christopher and Rachel Benson West. Her father, a former slave, owned a restaurant and a wholesale fruit company. He was called the Banana King.

West was tutored privately and graduated from Girls Latin School in Boston.

1926 "The Typewriter" appears in *Opportunity* magazine in July. "Hannah Byde" appears in *Messenger* in July.

1928 "An Unimportant Man" appears in *Saturday Evening Quill,* a local literary newsletter, in June.
West appears as an actor in the Theatre Guild's production of *Porgy* (1928–29).

1929 "Prologue to a Life" appears in *Saturday Evening Quill* in April.

1932 West travels to the Soviet Union to appear in a failed production about Negroes in America.

1934–37 West launches *Challenge,* a literary magazine later renamed *New Challenge.*

1934 "Cook" appears in *Challenge* under the name Jane Isaac. "The Black Dress" appears in *Opportunity* in May.

1936 "The Five Dollar Bill" appears in *Challenge* under the pen name Mary Christopher.

1938   Dorothy West joins a New Deal work relief program, the New
York Writer's Project for the Work Progress Administration, an
arm of the Federal Writer's Project commonly known as the WPA.

September 6	David Lawrence
September 9	Gardenia Banta
September 14	Mrs. Tommie Clicko
September 21	Mayme Reese
October 20	Mrs. Ella Johnson
October 26	Anecdotes (interview with Mrs. Ella Johnson)
October 7–14	Games, Songs, Rhymes of Children
November 2	Mrs. Emma Ayer
November 9	Mrs. Martha L.
November 18	"Ghosts"
November 28	"Pluto"
December 1	"Amateur Night in Harlem: 'That's Why Darkies Were Born'"
December 8	"My Baby . . ."
December 21	"Temple of Grace"
Unknown	"Berry Picking"

1939   January 1   "Cocktail Party"

1941   June 25   "The Penny"
September 8   "Papa's Place"
November 3   "Bessie"

1942   April 21   "Mother Love"
May 9   "The Puppy"

1944   August 9   "Fluff and Mr. Ripley"
August 24   "A Boy in the House"

1946   April 15   "The Cottagers and Mrs. Carmody"
April 29   "Skippy"
May 15   "A Matter of Money"

1947 March 7   "Wives and Women"
      August 13   "The Letters"

1948 *The Living Is Easy*, a novel, is published by Houghton and Mifflin.

1949 August 25   "Made for Each Other"

1957 March 6   "The Lean and the Plenty"
      April 17   "Homecoming"
      May 21   "Summer Setting"
      July 11   "Babe"
      August 23   "The Maple Tree"
      December 28   "The Blue Room"

1958 May 14   "The Richer, The Poorer"
      August 2   "The Summer of Wonderful Silence"
      June 5   "Interlude"

1959 November 2   "The Long Wait"

1960 April 29   "The Birthday Party"
      June 6   "Mrs. Creel"

1961 February 10   "The Fun Ball"
      December 11   "The Stairs"

1962 March 17   "The Bent Twig"
      July 5   "The Dinner Party"

1963 July 23   "Nothing Lasts Forever"

1964 August 24   "The Bird Like No Other"

1967 "The Richer, The Poorer" appears in *The Best Short Stories by Negro Writers: An Anthology from 1899 to the Present.*

1970 "Jack in the Pot" appears in *Harlem: Voices from the Soul of Black America*. The story originally appeared in the *New York Daily News* in the 1940s.

1983   "The Living Is Easy" is republished by the Feminist Press.

1995   "The Wedding" is published by Doubleday.

1995   *The Richer, The Poorer: Stories, Sketches, and Reminiscences* is published by Doubleday.

Selected Bibliography

Andrews, William L. *Classic Fiction of the Harlem Renaissance*. New York: Oxford University Press, 1994.

Baker, Houston A., Jr. *Afro-American Poetics: Revisions of Harlem and the Black Aesthetic*. Madison, WI: University of Wisconsin Press, 1988.

Dalsgard, Katrine. "Alive and Well and Living on Martha's Vineyard: An Interview with Dorothy West, October 29, 1988." *Langston Hughes Review* (Fall 1983).

Ferguson, SallyAnn H. "Dorothy West and Helene Johnson in *Infants of the Spring*." *Langston Hughes Review* 2.2 (Fall 1983): 22–24.

Jones, Sharon L. "Rereading the Harlem Renaissance: The 'Folk,' 'Bourgeois,' and 'Proletarian' Aesthetics in the Fiction of Jessie Fauset, Zora Neale Hurston, and Dorothy West." (March 1997).

McDowell, Deborah E. "Conversations with Dorothy West." In *The Harlem Renaissance Re-examined*. Edited by Victor A. Kramer, 265–82. New York: AMS, 1987.

Roses, Lorraine E. "Interviews with Black Women Writers: Dorothy West at Oak Bluffs, Massachusetts, July, 1984." *SAGE* 2.1 (Spring 1985): 47–49.

Rueschmann, Eva. "Sister Bonds: Intersections of Family and Race in Jessie Redmon Fauset's Plum Bun and Dorothy West's The Living Is Easy." In *The Significance of Sibling Relationships in Literature*. Edited by JoAnna Stephens-Mink, 120–31. Bowling Green, OH: Popular, 1992.

Wade-Gayles, Gloria. "The Truths of Our Mothers' Lives: Alice Walker, Dorothy West, Paule Marshall." In *Mothering the Mind: Twelve Studies of Writers and Their Silent Partners*. Edited by Ruth Perry and Martine W. Brownley, 142–63. New York: Holmes & Meier, 1984.

ONE

Early Fiction

The WPA Years

"My Baby" (written December 8, 1938) was published in *Connecticut Review* (Hartford: Connecticut State University, 2000) and was republished in *The Best American Short Stories 2001*, edited by Katrina Kenison and Barbara Kingsolver. (Boston: Houghton Mifflin, 2001). Used by permission of the Estate of Dorothy West and the Dorothy West Scholarship Fund of Martha's Vineyard Regional High School.

"Ghosts" (written November 18, 1938) was published in *A Renaissance in Harlem: Lost Essays of the WPA, by Ralph Ellison, Dorothy West, and Other Voices of a Generation,* edited by Lionel Bascom. (New York: HarperCollins, 2001). Used by permission of the Estate of Dorothy West and the Dorothy West Scholarship Fund of Martha's Vineyard Regional High School.

"Pluto" (written November 28, 1938) was published in *A Renaissance in Harlem: Lost Essays of the WPA, by Ralph Ellison, Dorothy West, and Other Voices of a Generation,* edited by Lionel Bascom. (New York: HarperCollins, 2001). Used by permission of the Estate of Dorothy West and the Dorothy West Scholarship Fund of Martha's Vineyard Regional High School.

"Amateur Night in Harlem: 'That's Why Darkies Were Born'" (written December 1, 1938) was published in *A Renaissance in Harlem: Lost Essays of the WPA, by Ralph Ellison, Dorothy West, and Other Voices of a Generation,* edited by Lionel Bascom. (New York: HarperCollins, 2001). Used by permission of the Estate of Dorothy West and the Dorothy West Scholarship Fund of Martha's Vineyard Regional High School.

"Temple of Grace" (written December 21, 1938) was published in *A Renaissance in Harlem: Lost Essays of the WPA, by Ralph Ellison, Dorothy West, and Other Voices of a Generation,* edited by Lionel Bascom. (New York: HarperCollins, 2001). Used by permission of the Estate of Dorothy West and the Dorothy West Scholarship Fund of Martha's Vineyard Regional High School.

"Cocktail Party" (written January 10, 1939) was published in *A Renaissance in Harlem: Lost Essays of the WPA, by Ralph Ellison, Dorothy West, and Other*

THREE

Pulp Fiction

1995 by Dorothy West. Used by permission of Doubleday, a division of Random House, Inc.

"Interlude" was published in *New York Daily News* (June 5, 1959). Used by permission of the Estate of Dorothy West and the Dorothy West Scholarship Fund of Martha's Vineyard Regional High School.

"The Long Wait" was published in *New York Daily News* (November 2, 1959). Used by permission of the Estate of Dorothy West and the Dorothy West Scholarship Fund of Martha's Vineyard Regional High School.

"The Birthday Party" was published in *New York Daily News* (April 29, 1960). Used by permission of the Estate of Dorothy West and the Dorothy West Scholarship Fund of Martha's Vineyard Regional High School.

"Mrs. Creel" was published in *New York Daily News* (June 6, 1960). Used by permission of the Estate of Dorothy West and the Dorothy West Scholarship Fund of Martha's Vineyard Regional High School.

"The Stairs" was published in *New York Daily News* (December 11, 1961). Used by permission of the Estate of Dorothy West and the Dorothy West Scholarship Fund of Martha's Vineyard Regional High School.

"Bent Twig" was published in *New York Daily News* (March 17, 1962). Used by permission of the Estate of Dorothy West and the Dorothy West Scholarship Fund of Martha's Vineyard Regional High School.

"A Tale of Christmas and Love" was published in *Vineyard Gazette* (December 21, 1979). Used by permission of the Estate of Dorothy West and the Dorothy West Scholarship Fund of Martha's Vineyard Regional High School.